Praise for Michel Butor

"A gifted disciple of French antinovelist Alain Robbe-Grillet, Butor is notable because he uses a different technique with every book and turns out intense and interesting fiction just the same."
—*Time*

"Emulating the great innovators of modern fiction—Dostoyevsky, Proust, Joyce, and Faulkner—Butor has sought new forms through which to express the problems of his time."
—Leon Roudiez, *New York Times*

"Michel Butor is a major young French novelist who has written several intricate and beautiful books which are just now getting proper attention in this country."
—*Virginia Quarterly Review*

"*Mobile* is not only a memorable experience, accomplishing that rich task of all true art—providing the reader with new eyes—but it also is a work which fellow writers and artists can profit from because it supplies that best of all ingredients: stimulation."
—*New York Herald Tribune*

"There is both humour and sadness in this arid catalogue of facts, because Michel Butor, defying the austere principles on which his novel is based, has a tender and beguiling imagination—he catches the tone of voice, the unspoken fear and pleasure, precisely by choosing affective language for his dialogue. . . . One finds oneself mentally stimulated and purged by the involvement of Butor's demands, and this, after all, is surely one of the signs of a good novelist's technique."
—*Times Literary Supplement*

Other Books by Michel Butor in English Translation

A Change of Heart

Degrees

Description of San Marco

Frontiers

Improvisations on Butor

Inventory

Letters from the Antipodes

Niagara

Passing Time

Portrait of the Artist as a Young Ape

The Spirit of Mediterranean Places

Mobile

Introduction by John D'Agata
Translation by Richard Howard

Michel Butor

Dalkey Archive Press

Originally published in French under the same title by Editions Gallimard, 1962
Originally published in English by Simon and Schuster, 1963

Copyright © 1962 by Michel Butor
English translation copyright © 1963 by Richard Howard
Introduction copyright © 2004 by John D'Agata

First Dalkey Archive edition, 2004
All rights reserved

Library of Congress Cataloging-in-Publication Data

Butor, Michel, 1926-
    [Mobile. English]
    Mobile / Michel Butor ; introduction by John D'Agata ; translation from the French by Richard Howard.— 1st Dalkey Archive ed.
        p. cm.
    "Originally published in New York by Simon and Schuster, 1963"—T.p. verso.
    ISBN 1-56478-343-X (alk. paper)
       1. United States—Fiction. I. Howard, Richard, 1929- II. Title.

PQ2603.U73M613 2004
    848'.914—dc22

2003070087

Partially funded by a grant from the Illinois Arts Council, a state agency.

Dalkey Archive Press books are published by the Center for Book Culture, a nonprofit organization located at Milner Library, Illinois State University.

www.centerforbookculture.org

Printed on permanent/durable acid-free paper and bound in the United States of America.

Introduction

I

In 1944, when General Eisenhower was in Europe, he saw how efficiently the continent's roads allowed Germany to move troops across neighboring states, and thought, one decade later, that America should build the same.

The National Development Highway Fund of 1954 was the first bill President Eisenhower sent to Congress to fund his roads—$175 million for the network of 47,000 miles of highway he envisioned. Initially pitched as an economic development fund, the project was justified to the American people as aid to the many new communities growing up outside of cities. "An investment in the growth of our nation," President Eisenhower called it.

Two years later, however, the project's budget was entirely gone, and only 3,000 miles of the 47,000 total had been laid. In 1956, *Time* magazine called the project "the biggest boondoggle of the decade," the *Saturday Evening Post* called it "the most expensive couple thousand miles of nothing going nowhere," and the White House press secretary announced in September that year that the White House was "now considering a new strategy for the roads." By November, Eisenhower had a new bill he was sending to Congress called the "National Defense Highway Act," a $25 billion expenditure for what was described this time as a network of "wartime civilian evacuation routes."

"We are not saving ourselves alone," Eisenhower famously said at the time, "we are investing in the survival of our great-great-grandchildren."

By an overwhelming majority, the National Defense Highway Act passed that year in Congress.

Then, in 1969, a similar bill entitled the "National Defense Highway Systems Act" passed.

In 1980, the "Provision of Defense Roads Bill."

And in '88, the so-called "Healthy Highways, Healthy Homefront" bill.

By the time the Dwight D. Eisenhower National System of Interstate and Defense Highways was dedicated in 1994, it was twenty-four years and eight months over schedule, it was $328 billion over budget, it was 112,000 miles longer than anyone originally intended it be, and it was still only 96% complete.

The American Society of Civil Engineers called this highway system "the largest public works project in the history of human civilization," 43% of which remains to this day under control of the United States Department of Defense. According to Edward Kearney in *Defense Highway Policies: America's Roads in the Cold War Era*, however, that 43% is not part of a network of "wartime civilian evacuation routes" but instead part of what the Department of Defense calls its "National Strategic Highway Corridor Network," a 68,000-mile-long system of "fort to port facilities" that can "mobilize in two days 100,000 ground troops anywhere in North America," serve as "emergency wartime landing strips," and even, if the nation should find itself domestically attacked, provide "easily mutable blockading material."

"What are *you* going to do," asked the Department of Defense in a 1956 pamphlet before Congress passed the new highway act, "when the bombs first reach your town?"

The department's pamphlet offered several suggestions to the mother on the cover of the pamphlet whose child frowned in her arms. She could relinquish her freedom at the closest Communist Party headquarters, it said. She could stay in her house with her husband and child and hope that the bomb's radius would not engulf them. Or she could drive out of town as fast as she could, away from the blasts of the bombs.

"But," asked the pamphlet, "how far would you get on an unpaved road with only two lanes for traffic?"

In a 1955 Gallop poll, 79% of Americans believed that the Soviet Union "unequivocally" wanted to "destroy the world."

Sixty-eight percent of those respondents owned a car.

At the time, the United States was producing an average of 1,200 nuclear warheads each year, a rate that would yield, by the end of their stockpiling in the year 2000, over 72,000 warheads in all.

Yet the first substantial peace talks between the United States and the Soviet Union would not occur for another thirteen years.

Before the Department of Defense had begun distributing its pamphlet with the mother and frowning child, the most that the Federal Civil Defense Administration had recommended citizens do in the event of a nuclear war was "duck and cover." This was during the same period in which the New York City Civil Defense Bomb Shelter Committee proposed developing a system of fallout centers in the basements of the city's apartments, each equipped with a "fire extinguisher, first-aid kit, hand-held radio, pail of water." And it was within that same time period that the National Cotton Manufacturers Association released a study in which the safest clothing material one could wear in the event of a nuclear war was proven to be, it so happened, cotton—because synthetic fibers, "like rayon," the association's study read, will "melt easily to the skin" and "impede one's ability to run."

In other words, President Eisenhower's proposal to evacuate American citizens away from the paths of Soviet missiles along new superhighways was the only working option apparent at the time.

"Tell your friends," the Department of Defense's pamphlet read, "that you support the National Defense Highway Act!"

But, as Edward Kearney notes, this was a national highway system whose purpose "was never intended to serve as a network for the evacuation of American communities," but was designed instead to "mobilize military personnel in the opposite direction . . . into communities . . . essentially blockading any civilian evacuees." Indeed, America's highway system became so quickly integral to the nation's domestic military infrastructure that by 1959, when novelist Michel Butor first visited America to write about its highways, the Department of Defense had confirmed that at least 185 specific locations in America were targeted by Soviet missiles—126 of which were highways.

II

When *Mobile* first appeared in 1962 it was widely viewed in France as scandalous. It was "*laid*" and it was "*stupide*" and it was "*gaffes de Butor.*" It was a book, said the critics, that did not look like a book, and therefore, they reasoned, was not. It was doing what Artaud had recently done, and it was doing what Mallarmé before him had done, and it was doing what Butor, given the sensibility he'd established in thirteen previous books, was logically expected to try to do next. Yet the book nevertheless was "*mouillé*," and the book nevertheless was "*illisible*," and the book was just plain "*mauvais*." When *Mobile* appeared in England in 1963 it was called by one critic a "bloody mess," and when it appeared the same year in the United States it was called "impenetrable... doggerel."

Today, the book is considered by some to be Butor's masterpiece, although it took twenty-three years for the first critic to say so. What is most remarkable about the book upon rereading it today, however, is how spectacularly unshocking it actually is. In *Mobile* one finds Kathy Acker's experiments with appropriation. In *Mobile* are John Cage's obsessions with typography. In *Mobile* there is even Joan Didion's proclivity for the indicting juxtaposition.

If today there is anything about the book that might indeed still surprise us, however, it is the odd discovery that the book is comprised richly of clichés.

America is a nation of big-sky country.

America is a nation of endless possibility.

In America, the southern states are secretly still racist.

And in America those who are persecuted are therefore prophetic souls.

But, as one American poet was writing at the time of Butor's visit, a cliché only remains useless in a language if writers fail to use it enough. For, as John Ashbery later argued, clichés are sacred forms of language because they are developed by an entire community rather than by an individual.

"Every bit of this land is sacred," Butor quotes one nineteenth-century Native American as saying. "At night, when all sound has died away in the streets of your villages, and when you think they are empty, they will swarm with the host of those who once lived there, faithful to that sublime site.... The white man will never be alone again."

The white man indeed was never alone again in America, but if not because he was conscious of the "emptiness" on which he lived now, then because he was unconscious of how quickly it soon would fill.

Three years after the first piece of new highway opened in America, seventeen Howard Johnson's restaurants stood along its sides. Within ten years of that new highway's opening, four hundred Howard Johnson's restaurants were built.

"One of the points that struck me most during my first stay in the United States was the phenomenon of reduplication," Butor wrote in *Improvisations on Butor,* a 1993 collection of essays on his own work. "If you take one of the big highways that extends away from the east toward the west, you cross first, for example, the state of New York, and there you find the city of Springfield and that of Manchester. If you continue, you enter Pennsylvania, and you find again a Springfield and a Manchester. Then you cross Ohio, where you find once again Manchester and Springfield. You arrive next in Indiana and, oh surprise!, there are Springfield and Manchester.... These names return perpetually."

Formally, Butor organizes *Mobile* around the repetitions that he sees inherent in his subject—imaginatively visiting smaller towns, for example, whose names most states are likely to have in common—yet because he structures these components of his narrative alphabetically—state by state, from Alabama to Alaska to Arizona to Arkansas—these repetitions become more than duplications. Indeed, because of this repetition, the name of a founding father or a famous tree or a popular diner evoked in one state will return inevitably as a township or a river or a street name in another.

New York, for example, becomes implicated in the apparent racism of Louisiana, if only because of the states' formal, rather than geographical, proximity to one another.

Similarly, a historical discussion of the Salem witch trials in

Massachusetts is subsequently felt each time we enter a new Salem in Oregon or a new Salem in New York or a new Salem in New Mexico or a new one in Missouri.

And even when Butor's juxtapositions seem slightly strained, as when the observation of a "for whites only" sign is dissolved and then sprinkled into other contexts as "whites only" and "for whites" and then finally "only," the vulnerability of Butor's form—restricted by the arbitrariness of his alphabetical template—bolsters the book's profound ambitions.

For Butor's rigorous formal experiment in *Mobile* can be said to be both an exhilarating illustration of faith and a beautifully desperate struggle with chance.

As he himself has written elsewhere, "The problem of the United States is the problem of what happens to European civilization when it arrives in a landscape that permits it to develop on a larger scale." If *Mobile,* therefore, could be said to behave in any regard as an essay, as "étude" as its subtitle suggests it might, it does so in the book's own enactment of this idea: in its insistence on chauffeuring us from state to state, not by the expository nature of its argument, but by the harmonic currents of its prose, by syntax and reference and varying degrees of associative leaps, bearing us as readers not across America, nor even across Butor's America, but into a place in which formal invention can show us just how much the world has changed since the last time we bothered to look. In his historical allusions, figurative displacements, and geographical puns, Butor allows the clichés of a nation to freight new meanings along the way, both revelatory and mysterious, like great ribbons across the land.

> *The Europeans have stripped the plains of buffalo and Indians—*

he writes. And

> *the Europeans drew long perpendicular lines on the plains—*

he writes. And

> *the Europeans have covered the plains with a thin film, like a layer of paint, in which the reservations now make snags.*

And, he writes,

> *the exiled Europeans have begun to await their harvest.*

III

Even as early as 1959, when Michel Butor was driving across the new highways of America, John F. Kennedy was repeating a single fact on his presidential campaign trail. In the event of a nuclear war with the Soviet Union, he said, over seventy million Americans would be killed within the first ten minutes.

Within the first six hours, he said, 100 million would be killed.

And one year after the blasts had dragged their radiation clouds away, over 160 million would be dead.

Kennedy got these figures not from the United States Department of Defense, not from the United States Senate in which he served, and not from the connections his father had in the F.B.I., but instead, as one biographer has explained, from the United States Department of Transportation, which had already estimated, by 1959, that 90% of the American population lived within five miles of the new Interstate Highway System. One hundred sixty million Americans, in other words, were living within five miles of one of the Soviet Union's 126 American nuclear targets. According to a Gallop poll that year, about 160 million Americans had also urged their friends to urge their own friends to support the National Defense Highway Act, as they also did for the National Defense Highway Systems Act, and then the Provision of Defense Roads Bill, and finally the Healthy Highways, Healthy Homefront bill.

Perhaps, however, as Michel Butor later wrote during a subsequent visit to America, such support did not necessarily betray the stupidity of 160 million American citizens, nor did it suggest that those 160 million had secretly wanted to die. It told Michel Butor instead that "the great majority of American citizens understands that it is upon its highways that America can sing."

For perhaps, in 1956, those 160 million Americans had realized that in the event of a nuclear strike by the Soviet Union on one of its 185 American targets—126 of which were highways—the initial blast from such a strike would occur in one-millionth of one second. That it would expand into a fireball ten miles in diameter. That it would travel at a speed of 758 miles per hour. And that its temperature, according to a study by the Department of Defense in 1953 entitled *The Effects of Nuclear War*, would be five times hotter than the sun.

Perhaps 160 million Americans had not actually calculated the effects these weapons would therefore have on them and their towns and the land on which they lived in 1956, but perhaps they assumed instead that if the temperature of the sun is, as *The Effects of Nuclear War* estimates it is, about 25,199,500° Fahrenheit, and if five times that amount is 125,997,700° Fahrenheit, and if the temperature at which the average human body combusts is 1,652° Fahrenheit, and if such a blast of heat would reach their bodies, five miles away from the site of detonation, in four and one-half millionths of one second after the blast, and if the heat it produced would then combust their bodies in four and one-quarter millionths of that first second, and if pain impulses in the human body are said to travel, head to toe, at an average of 382 feet per second, then it was more than likely that in the event of a nuclear strike by the Soviet Union on one of its 185 American targets—126 of which were highways—the minds of those 160 million Americans would literally not know that they were being destroyed until sixteen-hundredths of one second after they had been.

Perhaps, as Michel Butor has written in his study for a representation of the United States,

. . . we've been waiting for you, America!

How long until you stop?

O land of speed . . .

O America without the bank . . .

O intersection . . .

How long we've been waiting for your return!

John D'Agata
2004

TO THE MEMORY OF JACKSON POLLOCK

                              pitch dark in
CORDOVA, ALABAMA, the Deep South,

pitch dark in
CORDOVA, ALASKA, the Far North, closest to the dreadful, the abominable, the unimaginable country where it is already Monday when it is still Sunday here, the fascinating, sinister country with its unexpected satellite shots, the country of bad dreams that pursue you all night and insinuate, among your daylight thoughts, despite all your efforts, so many tiny ruinous whisperings like a leak in the ceiling of an old room, the monstrous country of bears,—pitch dark in

DOUGLAS, near Glacier Bay National Monument (any natural or archaeological curiosity considered worthy of being preserved from the indiscretion of settlers or tourists is called a national monument),

pitch dark in
DOUGLAS, Mountain Time, ARIZONA, the Far West,—the Navajo
Indian Reservation. (Most of the approximately five hundred
thousand Indians of the United States live on reservations scattered
throughout the country, to which they have gradually been confined
during the occupation of the land by the white invader. It would not be
kind to compare them to concentration camps. It would even be rather
unfair: some of these reservations are tourist attractions.)

*"Despite the bigness of the Southwest, little things—sights, sounds, and
smells—often create the most lasting impressions. Here are some:*
– strings of scarlet chili drying against adobe walls,
– golden aspens mantling a mountain's shoulders,
– lithe relaxation of Navajos outside a trading post,
– awkward speed of a fleeing roadrunner,
– massive thunderhead dragging its braids of rain,
– immobility of tumbleweeds banked against a fence,
– line of resigned autos waiting out a flash flood,
– single-file string of steers approaching a waterhole,
– echoes and silences in a great cliff-dwelling ruin,
– bawling of restless cattle at a roundup,
– heady aroma of campfire coffee,
– carefree boys 'in the raw' splashing in a stock tank,
– squeal of a fighting, bucking horse at a rodeo,
– wail of a coyote—and yapping of others—at night,
– drum throbs and shrill chant of an Indian dance,

– *musty odor of creosote bush after rain,*
– *bray of a distant wild burro just after sunrise,*
– *harsh smell of singed flesh at a branding corral,*
– *sudden pelting rush of a summer thunderstorm,*
– *unbelievable immensity of the Grand Canyon,*
– *juiciness of thick steak broiled over mesquite coals,*
– *stars that you can reach from your sleeping bag,*
– *splash and tug of a mountain trout hitting your fly,*
– *tang of enchiladas smothered in chili sauce,"* (from The American Southwest *by Dodge and Zim, "with more than 400 subjects in full color.*
– *Natural Wonders,*
– *Indian Villages,*
– *Historic Sites,*
– *Scenic Routes,*
– *Guide Maps,*
– *Public Parks,*
– *Minerals,*
– *Animals,*
– *Birds,*
– *Trees,*
– *Flowers").*

Petrified Forest National Monument,—pitch dark in

FLORENCE, on the Gila River, near Casa Grande National Monument,

               already not so dark in
FLORENCE, Central Time.

Blue night.

The Ozark Mountains,—across the southwest state line,

               FLORENCE.

GEORGETOWN, White County.

The mountains at night.

A Buick on the highway (speed limit 60 miles).

               GEORGETOWN, county seat of Williamson County,—continuing west,

               GEORGETOWN, New Mexico,—the Zuñi Indian Reservation.

LA GRANGE, Lee County, ARKANSAS.

The alarm clock goes off.

B. P., British Petroleum.

LA GRANGE, county seat of Fayette County, TEXAS.

The sea at night.

MARSHALL, in the Land of Opportunity.

He was dreaming.

Ouachita Lake.

MARSHALL, county seat of Harrison County.

In the first of his magnificent large plates devoted to the birds of America, John James Audubon (1780–1851), one of America's greatest naturalists, painted the male wild turkey.

ELDORADO.

EL DORADO, ARKANSAS, the Wonder State.

He was dreaming he was tall.

The Roman Catholic church,—over the western state line,

ELDORADO, OKLAHOMA,—the Osage Indian Reservation.

Two yellow-billed cuckoos, on a branch of blemished leaves, the one on the left exposing its white belly, the one on the right grasping the body of a large butterfly.

MARSHALL.

GREENWOOD, Sebastian County. State Flower: apple blossom.

She was dreaming she was beautiful . . .

Mystic Cavern,—across the Father of Waters,

> GREENWOOD, MISSISSIPPI, the Deep South.

BENTON, with its bauxite mines, county seat of Saline County.

That she won a beauty prize . . .

Big Hurricane Cavern,—across the Father of Waters, but farther north,

> BENTON, TENNESSEE, the South.

The prothonotary warbler, clinging to a cave vine, head and breast bright yellow, black and white fan-shaped tail,—across the southern state line,

> BENTON, LOUISIANA, the Deep South.

The parula warbler, perched on a large salmon iris known as the Louisiana flag,—across the northern state line,

> BENTON.

Two pairs of mourning doves billing on a bush with large white flowers.

> MARSHALL, Saline County seat,
> MISSOURI, Middle West.

The night sky paling.

> LA GRANGE, Lewis County seat.

The morning star.

> CORNING.—Continuing north,
>
> CORNING, IOWA,—the Tama Indian Reservation. At the vernal equinox, when it is dawn in

CORNING,

pitch dark in
CORNING, Pacific Time.

The sea at night.
The desert at night.

In the mountains, the Colorado columbine, with its blue, white-centered blossoms.

LA GRANGE, on the Tuolumne River that flows into the San Joaquin River, Stanislaus County.

The ships waiting to sail for Japan.
The ships waiting to sail for Formosa.

A dusty Ford, overloaded with trunks, parked beside the highway, "get gas at the next B.P.,"—in the mountains, the harebell; on the plains, the evening primrose.

MARSHALL, on Tomales Bay, Marin County, CALIFORNIA, the most heavily populated state after New York, on the border of the Mexican state of Baja California,—the Manzanita Indian Reservation.

I was dreaming of San Francisco.

Esso,—in the mountains the yarrow which the Indians used in their medicines; on the plains the gaillardia, known as firewheel or Indian blanket; in the desert, the hairy whitish poppy.

BENTON, between Inyo and Toiyabe National Forests, near Black Lake in the Sierra Nevada, in enormous and almost empty Mono County, the sequoia state,—the Inaja Indian Reservation.

The plane I took to San Francisco stopped in Los Angeles three times: Long Beach, International Airport, Burbank. Beneath me passed the acres and acres of tiny, dimly lit perpendicular streets . . .

In the northern forests, the Pacific trilliums, white petals and green leaves in threes, and the twin flower with its pink bells in pairs.

GREENWOOD, El Dorado County.

I reached San Francisco at night. There were not many lights on the bay. But in the morning . . .
I am dreaming of San Francisco.

The Washington palm, whose hairy fronds, as they dry, cover the trunk with a sheath of rough ochre fur.—When it is five A.M. in

CONCORD, near the mouth of the Sacramento River in San Pablo Bay, which opens onto San Francisco Bay,

WELCOME TO NORTH CAROLINA

        it has already been daylight for a long time in CONCORD, Eastern Time, where you can order apricot ice cream in the Howard Johnson Restaurant.

The sea,
        the waves,
the salt,
        the sand,
the foam,
        the seaweed.

The Cherokee Indians invited the missionaries to settle among them and to open schools in order to teach them their secrets; but the missionaries, supposing that the Indian language could not be written and refusing to modify the methods they had brought from England, obtained negligible results . . .

Negro man.

Angola Swamp, "Hello, Al!"—Across the southwest state line,

        CONCORD, GEORGIA, Atlantic Coast (for whites only) (in the Southern states, a section of the streetcars and buses may not be occupied by colored people).

The sea,
        the tide,
the swell,

> *the breeze,*
> *the islands,*
> *the lagoons.*
> *Inkberry,*
> *rose laurel,*
> *dahoon holly.*

The Ocmulgee mounds reveal traces of six successive civilizations, the oldest dating back to about 8000 B.C., the most recent dying out in the eighteenth century . . .

Negro woman.

"Hello, Mrs. Greenwood!"—The enormous Okefenokee Swamp,—continuing south,

> CONCORD, FLORIDA (. . . whites only),—
> the Seminole Indian Reservation.

> *Tornadoes,*
> *tidal waves,*
> *roofs torn off.*

> *Florida jays,*
> *Key West quail doves,*
> *fork-tailed flycatchers,*
> *Maynard's cuckoos*
> *gray kingbirds.*

> *The sea,*
> *fighting conchs,*
> *hawk-wing conchs,*
> *incongruous arks,*
> *turkey wing shells,*
> *queen conchs.*
> *banana palms,*
> *Valencia oranges,*
> *Jaffa oranges,*
> *bronze-leaves,*
> *caterpillar plants,*
> *aloes.*

The first explorers discovered numerous Indian tribes in southern Florida. The Calusas, for instance, numbering over three thousand in 1650, hunted, fished, gathered shellfish. Excellent sailors, they traveled at least as far as Cuba. In 1800, under the Spanish domination restored after a brief English interlude, they numbered only several hundred. In 1835, under United States rule, the last survivors were deported to Oklahoma, then known as Indian Territory, with the majority of the Seminoles. Some fled to Cuba.

Negroes.

The gigantic Everglades.

GREENVILLE, on the Tar River, county seat of Pike County, NORTH CAROLINA (. . . only),—the Cherokee Indian Reservation.

The sea,
        jingle shells,
sunrise tellins,
        sunbeam Venus clams,
chitons,
        calico scallops.
Black women.

A Cherokee Indian named Sequoyah, mistrusting the teachings of the missionaries, refused to attend their schools, but studied their books closely and decided to invent a system of writing. Great opposition in the missions and among the other Cherokees. A new, powerful witchcraft, which it was wiser to nip in the bud . . .

On the highway, a battered gray Oldsmobile going much faster than the 60-mile speed limit, "get gas at the next Caltex,"—Dismal Swamp and Holly Shelter Swamp.

        GREENVILLE.

        GREENVILLE.

CLINTON, county seat of Sampson County.

Negro men.

The sea,

> *Atlantic clams,*
> *butterfly clams,*
> > *bleeding teeth,*
> *tulip shells,*
> > *spiny lobsters.*

Encouraged by the missionaries, the Cherokee Indians burned Sequoyah's house and the papers that were inside. . . .

Flying Service,—Green Swamp, Lake Waccamaw, Croatan National Forest,—across the Great Smoky Mountains,

> CLINTON, on the Clinch River that flows into the Tennessee, a tributary of the Father of Waters, TENNESSEE, the South (. . . only). Continuing west,

> > CLINTON, ARKANSAS (. . . only).—west,

> > > CLINTON, on the Washita River that flows into the Red River, forming the Texas state line, a tributary of the Father of Waters, OKLAHOMA, the Middle West (. . . only),—the Osage Indian Reservation.

The Carolina parakeet, a species extinct since 1904,—across the northern state line,

> MARION, on the edge of Jefferson National Forest, VIRGINIA, Atlantic Coast.—When it is nine o'clock in

MARION, on the edge of Pisgah National Forest,

WELCOME TO SOUTH CAROLINA

              nine o'clock in
MARION, over the southern state line.

The sea,
              blue crabs,
stone crabs,
              hermit crabs,
horseshoe crabs,
              sea urchins.

The old houses of Charleston.

He's black.

The swamps of the Pee Dee River.

CLINTON, on the edge of Sumter National Forest, Laurens County.

The sea,
              bluegills,
pompanos,
              nurse sharks,
dolphins,
              sailfish.
Very black.

The old houses of Beaufort.

On the highway, an indigo Studebaker driven by a white man (speed limit 55 miles), "get gas at the next Esso,"—Black Swamp and Jones Swamp.

GREENVILLE, where you can order almond ice cream in the Howard Johnson Restaurant, county seat of Greenville County, SOUTH CAROLINA, one of the original thirteen states (for whites only).

A beautiful black.

The sea,
       tide pools,
channels,
       rocks,
the blue of the sea,
       the white of the foam.

The old houses of Columbia.

Mobil,—the swamps of Francis Marion National Forest, of the Black River, Moselle Swamp.

GEORGETOWN, at the mouth of the Pee Dee River, near the gardens of Belle Isle, county seat of Georgetown County in the state of the yellow jasmine (men, women, colored people) (in the Southern states, there are not only two doors for rest rooms in public places: men and women, but three; four in the more elegant places: men, women, colored men, colored women).

Isn't he? An ebony statue . . .

The old houses of Georgetown.

The sea,
       the rolling sound,
the movement,
       the flow.

ebb,
> *tidal wave.*

Snuggedy Swamp and Calfpen Swamp, "Hello, Bill!"—Across the Savannah River,

> GEORGETOWN, on the Chattahoochee River forming the Alabama state line and joining the Flint River to form the Apalachicola River, GEORGIA, Atlantic Coast (. . . whites only).—Continuing south,

> GEORGETOWN, on Lake George, on the edge of Ocala National Forest, FLORIDA, the Gulf of Mexico (. . . only),—the Brighton Indian Reservation.—When it is ten o'clock in

FLORENCE, near the swamps of the Pee Dee River, county seat of Florence County, which also contains

LAKE CITY,

WELCOME TO COLORADO

        still eight o'clock in
LAKE CITY, Mountain Time, between Lake San Cristobal and Devils Lake, between Gunnison and Uncompahgre National Forests.

Blue.

Basalt,
        pumice stone,
                obsidian,
                        granite.

The oldest known civilization in the American Southwest, known as the Sandia Culture, dates back some twenty-five thousand years. The Folsom Culture is situated somewhere between 23,000 and 8000 B.C. *San Jon Culture; Yuma Culture. Then the Cochise Culture, between 10,000 and 500* B.C. *Here the growing of maize is first recorded* . . .

Red Cloud Peak, "Hello, Ben!"—Across the western state line,

    LAKE CITY.

    Blue.

    She's scarcely black at all.

"Hello, Mrs. Florence!"—El Dorado Lake.

DERBY, near the Rocky Mountain Arsenal, Adams County.

I flew by jet from San Francisco to Chicago; the Rocky Mountains were below us, deep blue.

The word Anasazi means "the ancient ones" in the Navajo language. Archaeologists call the earliest Anasazis "Basketmakers." They kept dogs, lived in caves in which they dug pits to store their maize . . .

Rocks,
        peaks,
                boulders,
                        ridges.

On the highway a blue Plymouth driven by a white man (speed limit 60 miles), "get gas at the next Flying Service."—Democrat Peak and Mountain of the Holy Cross.

    DERBY, on the Arkansas River, tributary of the Father of Waters, KANSAS, Middle West (for whites only), —the Pottawatomie Indian Reservation.

    Just looking at her, you'd never say she was black.

    The gigantic green and brown chessboard of the fields.

    An old green overloaded Oldsmobile driven by a white woman going much faster than the 70-mile speed limit, "how much longer?"—Webster and Kirwin Dam Lakes.

John James Audubon made three portraits of the bald eagle, the nearly extinct national bird, now protected by Federal law.

    FLORENCE.

FLORENCE, near San Isabel National Forest, Fremont County, COLO-RADO, the West,—the Southern Ute Indian Reservation.

Approximately 400 A.D., *the Basketmakers began using the bow and arrow; pottery gradually replaced basketware. They cultivated gourds, maize and beans; they raised turkeys. It was at this period that they began building the splendid villages the Spaniards called "pueblos." Architecture developed from 750 to 1100* A.D.: *rectangular houses of several stories with vertical stone walls, inner courtyards and round chapels or "kivas" . . .*

Blue.

Creeks,
        stones,
                cliffs,
                       gorges.

In Denver, Colorado, Germans read the weekly "Colorado Herald."

Shell,—Mount Deception, Storm King Mountain,—past the only point in the United States common to four states,

        FLORENCE, ARIZONA,—the border of the Mexican state
                of Sonora,—the Hopi Indian Reservation.

GEORGETOWN, on the edge of Arapahoe National Forest, county seat
        of Clear Creek County, lark bunting state,—Ute Mountain Indian Reservation.

The classical period of the Pueblo Culture began around 1100 A.D. *Splendid constructions under the cliffs, magnificent pottery, cotton fabric, parietal painting, turquoise jewelry, irrigation . . . At the end of the thirteenth century, a terrible drought forced the Anasazis to abandon their territory in the present state of Colorado and to travel south into what was to become Arizona and New Mexico, where their reservations are today . . .*

Clouds.

In Denver, Colorado, Italians read the monthly "Il Risveglio."

Sharp,
        cold,
                vertical,
                       wind.

Mount Etna and Horseshoe Mountain,—across the southern state line,

>GEORGETOWN, in Gila National Forest, NEW MEXICO, state bordering on the Mexican states of Sonora and Chihuahua, the largest state after Alaska, Texas, California and Montana,—Rio Grande pueblos.

WINDSOR, Weld County.

One day in December, 1888, two cowboys, Wetherhill and Mason, while looking for lost cattle, came upon the enormous ruins of Mesa Verde, abandoned for centuries by the Anasazi Indians. The Ute Indians avoided them in terror, regarding them as the city of the dead . . .

In Denver, Colorado, Japanese read the daily "Colorado Times."

Blue.

Pale,
   stiff,
      rough,
         glittering.

Montezuma Peak.—When it is nine o'clock in

BRISTOL, near the upper Arkansas River,

WELCOME TO CONNECTICUT

       already eleven o'clock in
BRISTOL, Eastern Time, with its clock museum, and the Howard John-
     son Restaurant, where you can order pineapple ice cream,
in Hartford County, as are

WINDSOR and

BERLIN, CONNECTICUT, New England.

The outskirts of New York City.

The sea,
       beach cabanas,
lounge chairs,
       suntan lotions,
dark glasses,
       pedal pushers.

Candlewood Lake, "Hello, Bob!"—Across the eastern state line,

    BRISTOL, RHODE ISLAND.

The Canada warbler, baptized by Audubon the Bonaparte flycatcher, on a magnolia branch,—across the western state line,

> WINDSOR, NEW YORK, the most heavily populated state, bordering on the Canadian provinces of Quebec and Ontario,—the Cattaraugus Indian Reservation.

The blue of the sky.

> BERLIN, near its pond.

The white-throated sparrow and female on a branch of flowering dogwood,—across the northern state line,

> WINDSOR and

> BERLIN, MASSACHUSETTS, the smallest state after Rhode Island, Delaware, Connecticut, Hawaii and New Jersey,—continuing north,

> WINDSOR, on the Connecticut River, the New Hampshire border, VERMONT, the least densely populated state after Alaska, Nevada, Wyoming and Delaware.

> *In the village of Shelburne, Vermont, a number of old, condemned houses have been rebuilt, thus comprising a curious museum. Perhaps their most remarkable feature is a collection of patchwork quilts. This "Mobile" is composed somewhat like a quilt.*

> Lake Champlain, on the New York state line.

The magnolia warbler on a white oak branch.

> BERLIN.

A passing cloud,—continuing north, but farther east,

> BERLIN, NEW HAMPSHIRE,—the border of the Canadian province of Quebec.—When it is noon in

DERBY, on the Housatonic River,

WELCOME TO NORTH DAKOTA

     still eleven o'clock in
BERLIN, Central Time.

Blue.

Duck hawks,
   blue-headed vireos,
     red-shouldered hawks,
       hermit thrushes,
    chestnut-sided warblers,
  swamp sparrows,
redwings.

In winter,
   the icy wind,
     lifting the snow
       off the frozen ground.

Black Butte, highest point in the state.

BUFFALO, NORTH DAKOTA,—the border of the Canadian provinces of Manitoba and Saskatchewan,—the Turtle Mountain Indian Reservation.

Gray.

In summer,
> *the scorching wind,*
>> *lifting spirals of dust*
>>> *off the dry ground.*

Cliff swallows,
> blue-breasted warblers,
>> house wrens,
>>> Harlan's Hawks,
>> evening grosbeaks,
> downy woodpeckers,

bluebirds.

An old red Chevrolet, its radio blaring the "North Dakota Hymn," parked beside the highway, "get gas at the next Mobil Station,"—Camel Butte and Calf Butte,—"Hello, Charles!"—Across the Red River of the North,

> BUFFALO, on Buffalo Lake, MINNESOTA,—the border of the Canadian provinces of Manitoba and Ontario,—the Lake Nett Indian Reservation.

The white-crowned sparrow on a summer grapevine with dark-blue fruit, the female hidden by a large yellowing leaf,—over the western state line,

> BUFFALO, MONTANA,—the border of the Canadian provinces of Saskatchewan, Alberta and British Columbia,—the Tongue River Indian Reservation.—When it is noon in

WEBSTER,

WELCOME TO SOUTH DAKOTA

        noon in
WEBSTER, Central Time, across the southern state line.

Blue.

Wood peewees,
        rose-breasted grosbeaks,
                prairie pipits,
                        field sparrows,
                ovenbirds,
        yellow palm warblers,
nighthawks.

In winter,
        frozen lakes,
                icy wind,
                        cold sun.

On Mount Rushmore, the enormous, clumsily carved faces of Washington, Jefferson, Lincoln and Theodore Roosevelt.

Eagle's Nest Butte, "Hello, Dave!"—Across the Bix Sioux River, which flows into the Missouri River, a tributary of the Father of Waters,

        WEBSTER, IOWA, the Middle West,—the Tama Indian
        Reservation.

The Europeans sliced up the Great Plains.

"Hello, Mrs. Webster!"—Storm Lake.

A grasshopper sparrow, perched on a rock near a pond, in the middle of a clump of phlox subulata with red-striped pink blossoms.

>BUFFALO, on the Illinois state line constituted by the Father of Waters.—Only eleven o'clock in

BUFFALO, SOUTH DAKOTA, Mountain Time,—Cheyenne River Indian Reservation.

Gray.

In summer,
>*cracked mud bottoms of the dry lakes,*
>>*the sun through a haze,*
>>>*roasting heat.*

Pine siskins,
>*golden-crowned kinglets,*
>>*tree sparrows,*
>>>*snow buntings,*
>>*yellow-bellied sapsuckers,*
>*alder ptarmigans,*

Lincoln sparrows.

On the highway an orange Cadillac driven by a pink-faced white man (speed limit 70 miles), "get gas at the next Sunoco Station,"—Arrowhead Butte and Antelope Butte.—When it is noon in

NEWARK, Central Time,

WELCOME TO DELAWARE

                one o'clock in
NEWARK, Eastern Time, seat of the state university, DELAWARE, Atlantic Coast, smallest after Rhode Island.

The sea,
            jellyfish,
sand,
            sky,
cockles,
            mussels.

The Du Pont de Nemours state.

Big Stone Beach, "Hello, Dick!"—Across the northern state line,

        MILTON, on the Susquehanna River, PENNSYLVANIA, the most heavily populated state after New York and California,—the Cornplanter Indian Reservation.— When it is two o'clock in

MILTON,

WELCOME TO FLORIDA

          two o'clock in
MILTON, on Pensacola Bay that opens onto the Gulf of Mexico.

Tornadoes,
electricity cut,
automobiles overturned.

White ibis,
         oyster catchers,
                 long-billed curlews,
                            sooty terns,
                 Florida gallinules,
        brown pelicans,
double-crested cormorants.

The sea,
         ivory-bush corals,
brain corals,
         sea fans.

Lemons,
         limes,
                 navel oranges,
                           grapefruit,
traveler's-trees,
         lady's tongues,
                 orchid trees,
royal poincianas,
         sea grapes,
Antilles mahogany.

The most powerful tribes of northern Florida were the Apalachees and the Timucuas; the latter, numbering thirteen thousand in 1650, were annihilated in less than a century by war and disease. A few survivors may have been deported to Oklahoma, then known as Indian Territory, with a group of Seminoles. Others emigrated to Cuba in 1763 . . .

But she's black . . .

Lake Okeechobee, the largest contained within the boundaries of a single state.

MADISON, FLORIDA (for whites only),—the Seminole Indian Reservation.

Tornadoes,
lashing branches,
bridges washed out.

Frigate birds,
       sandpipers,
              royal terns,
                     Cabot terns,
            great white herons,
      little blue herons,
greater yellowlegs.

The sea,
       Florida ceriths,
alphabet cones,
      pear whelks,
queen triggerfish,
       butterfly fish.
Bigarades,
      tangerines,
            grapefruit,
                 pomelos,
tamarinds,
      red mangroves,
            strangler figs,
coco plums,
      poisonwoods,

gumbo limbos.

A gleaming black shoulder, an arm, a wrist . . .

The Choctaw Indians flourished along the Gulf of Mexico; a century ago there were about twenty thousand of them. Forced to emigrate, some vanished into the wastes of Oklahoma, others fled farther west; several hundred remain in Louisiana and Mississippi . . .

On the highway, a battered orange Buick, driven by a very fat old white man with a deep-pink face, going much faster than the 65-mile speed limit, "get gas at the next Texaco station,"—Lake George, Orange Lake with its floating islands, "Hello, Ed!"—Across the northwest state line,

> MADISON, near the Redstone Arsenal, Alabama, the Deep South (. . . whites only).

> *Beware of this continent!*
> *Beware of poison ivy!*
> *Poison ivy is a vine with three-pointed leaves that are reddish at the tips when they are young. Their contact produces a rash and itching which may be accompanied by high fever lasting for weeks and recurring periodically. This infection is contagious; even ashes may provoke it . . .*

> *Under the trouser leg he raises to scratch himself, a shiny black knee . . .*

> *In Birmingham, Alabama, alcohol is served in tiny one-ounce bottles, whose seal must be broken in the consumer's presence.*

> "Hello, Mrs. Milton!"—Guntersville Dam Lake, formed by the waters of the Tennessee River, a tributary of the Father of Waters.

The zenaida dove, brown-breasted, with royal-blue markings on the head, not found in Florida since the time of John James Audubon.

> GREENSBORO.—When it is three o'clock in

GREENSBORO,

WELCOME TO GEORGIA

          three o'clock in
GREENSBORO, across the northern state line.

The sea,
          sea stars,
sea anemones,
          shrimps,
prawns,
          oysters.
Bougainvillaea,
          crepe myrtle,
                    poinsettias,
                            hibiscus.

The first inhabitants of Ocmulgee are known as the Wandering Hunters. It is believed that they remained there about five thousand years. Then came the Shellfish Eaters, who disappeared about 100 B.C., *succeeded by the First Farmers, who remained about nine hundred years. They cultivated beans and squash; they made pottery. In their turn they were driven out by the Master Farmers, who also cultivated tobacco and maize, constructed clay pyramids on which they placed their temples, and sculptured admirable figures . . .*

The grainy black skin of her neck . . .

The bald cypress that in winter loses its thin, flat leaves; its conical trunk sticks up out of the swamps, surrounded by a court of "knees"—woody round or pointed protuberances that rise from the sunken roots, "Hello, Frank!"—Across the northern state line,

> GREENSBORO, where you can order banana ice cream in the Howard Johnson Restaurant.

The sea,
       the green,
drops,
       swell,
currents,
       ships.

The Cherokee Indian Sequoyah left with a certain number of friends in search of a place where the White Men would leave him in peace. He crossed the Father of Waters and settled in Arkansas . . .

The black nipple, but a different black, on the black breast.

"Hello, Mrs. Madison!"—Mount Mitchell, highest point in the state.

MADISON, county seat of Morgan County.

The sea,
       nets,
oars,
       traps,
floats,
       baskets.

Gardenias,
       swamp azaleas,
             star jasmine,
                    camellias.

The black of her belly, through the opening of her unbuttoned blouse.

Then the First Farmers returned to Ocmulgee, and are henceforth known as the Reconquerors by archaeologists. They lived in small villages in the swamps, surrounded by palings. They made pottery and also built clay pyramids . . .

A yellow Buick overturned beside the highway, "get gas at the next station,"—the laurel oak, the myrtle oak.

> MADISON, Rockingham County, NORTH CAROLINA, the South (for whites only),—the Cherokee Indian Reservation.

The sea,
        seamarks,
skates,
        mullet,
swimmers,
        bathing beauties.

The blackness inside her womb . . .

In 1821, the Cherokee Sequoyah returned to his tribe, bearing a message from the Arkansas Indians. He had invented an alphabet for his language. . . .

A shiny green Cadillac driven by a very fat old white man with a red face and a black shirt (60 m.p.h.), "How much longer is it? An hour?"—Black Mountain and Sassafras Mountain,—continuing north,

> MADISON, VIRGINIA, Atlantic Coast.

Thomas Jefferson, born April 2, 1743, Old Style, author of the Declaration of Independence:

". . . We hold these truths to be self-evident: that all men are created equal . . . ,"

of the Act for establishing Religious Freedom passed in the Assembly of Virginia, and founder of the University of Virginia, in Charlottesville, whose plans he drew up himself, certainly one of the most remarkable minds of his nation and his age, wrote in reply to the inquiries of the Marquis de Barbé-Marbois, then Secretary of the French Legation in Philadelphia, the

"Notes on the State of Virginia; written in the year 1781, somewhat corrected and enlarged in the winter of 1782, for the use of a Foreigner of distinction, in answer to certain queries proposed by him respecting its
— boundaries,
— rivers,
— sea ports,
— mountains,
— cascades and caverns,
— productions mineral,
— vegetable,
— and animal,
— climate,
— population,
— military force,
— marine force,
— aborigines,
— counties and towns,
— constitution,
— laws,
— colleges, buildings and roads,
— proceedings as to Tories,
— religion,
— manners,
— manufactures,
— subjects of commerce,
— weights, measures and money,
— public revenue and expenses,
— histories, memorials, and state papers,"

from which I quote the following passage:

"... It will probably be asked, Why not retain and incorporate the blacks into the State, and thus save the expense of supplying by importation of white settlers, the vacancies they will leave? Deep-rooted prejudices entertained by the whites; ten thousand recollections, by the blacks, of the injuries they have sustained; new provocations; the real distinctions which nature has made; and many other circumstances, will divide us into parties, and produce convulsions, which will probably never end but in the extermination of the one or the other race . . ."

Cedar Island,—to the north,

    MADISON, WEST VIRGINIA, beginning of the
Middle West.

A house on fire!

Seneca Caverns.

Three male ground doves, one female and her young, underwings reddish, on a wild-orange branch, the fruit still green.

  OXFORD, county seat of Granville County.

Under her skirt, that black thigh . . .

The sea,
    divers,
kelp,
    pebbles,
  sand.

Gradually, the Cherokee Indian Sequoyah succeeded in convincing the members of his tribe, and soon all of them could read. The astonished Europeans bestowed a medal upon him . . .

Sunoco,—Jefferson, Rendezvous and Snake Mountains.

CLEVELAND, county seat of White County, GEORGIA
(. . . whites only).

The sea,
          cavallas,
tarpons,
          barracudas,
yellowtails,
          plaice.
A Negro woman's kinky hair . . .

Flame azaleas,
          Indian azaleas,
                    kurume azaleas,
                              Cherokee roses.

In 1690, the Europeans established a supply post in the environs of Ocmulgee, and the Indians living there at the time, Creeks and Cherokees, abandoned their agriculture to become hunters and sell to the traders the skins which they bartered for rifles, knives, bells and rum. In 1715, the Emperor Brim of the Creek Nation decided to drive out the invaders. He was conquered in 1717, and the Ocmulgee mounds were abandoned . . .

Texaco,—"turn left,"—on trees, the green fly orchid; in bogs, the pink lady's slipper; in the underbrush, the yellow fringed orchids.

CLEVELAND.

CLEVELAND.—Driving back to Georgia,

CLEVELAND, SOUTH CAROLINA (. . . only).

The sea,

>> *inlets,*
> *creeks,*
>> *straits,*
> *estuaries,*
>> *lagoons.*

> *The treasures buried by the pirates.*

> *Where did she get those long black braids from? Half Indian?*

> The Spanish oak.

The Swainson's warbler on a spray of azalea with orange blossoms, surrounded by two butterflies.

> SPRINGFIELD.

SPRINGFIELD, on the Ebenezer branch of the Savannah River, county seat of Effingham County,—across the northwest state line,

>> SPRINGFIELD, TENNESSEE, the Tobacco State (. . . only).

> *In Nashville, Tennessee, the full-size reproduction of the Parthenon, with the casts of the Elgin Marbles inside.*

> *That tempest of black hair . . .*

> Norris Dam Lake,—continuing north,

>>> SPRINGFIELD, KENTUCKY, the Whiskey State (. . . only),—north,

>>>> SPRINGFIELD, where you can order coffee ice cream in the Howard Johnson Restaurant, OHIO, a farm state.

The clapper rail, neck outstretched, and its mate, in the reeds of their swampland.

                CLEVELAND.

A drop of rain,—across the Chattahoochee River, which joins the Flint River to form the Apalachicola River,

                        OXFORD, at the edge of the Talladega National Forest, ALABAMA, cotton belt (. . . only).

The sky clears,—continuing west,

                        OXFORD, which Faulkner calls Jefferson, seat of the state university, county seat of Lafayette County, which Faulkner calls Yoknapatawpha County, MISSISSIPPI, the fringe of the rice belt (. . . only). —When it is four o'clock in

OXFORD

        (still eleven o'clock in
HAWAII, the fiftieth state, the Pacific islands),

WELCOME TO IDAHO

       two P.M. in
OXFORD, at the foot of its peak, Mountain Time, Franklin County, which also contains

CLEVELAND.

Blue.
    Hematite,
magnetite, chalcopyrite,
    galena.

Borah Peak, highest point in the state, "Hello, Fred!"

      CLEVELAND, UTAH, Far West,—the Koosharem Indian Reservation.

Deserts.
    Calcite,
turquoise, gypsum,
    pyrites.

According to the revelations of Joseph Smith, the Mormons would one day rediscover the lost tribes of Israel hidden in some region of the extreme north among the glaciers. Now the Mormons of Salt Lake City believed they had identified the latter with the Indians who followed the teachings of Wodziwob, prophet of the spirit dance. They sent emissaries to the Bannock group in Oregon, to invite them to join their Mormon brothers and receive baptism. Then, they said, all disease would vanish, an eternal youth would be established among men, each would have his proper role and function; this would be the Kingdom of the Lord . . .

In Salt Lake City, Japanese read the "Utah Nippo," published every three weeks.

"Hello, Mrs. Springfield!"—Zion National Park.

STERLING, on the huge lake formed by American Falls Dam, Bingham County.

Sphalerite,
pyrolusite, scheelite,
wolframite.

Wind.

On the highway, a white Dodge driven by an old, very thin white man in an indigo shirt with light-blue polka dots (speed limit 60 miles), "get gas,"—Bald Mountain, Bachelor Mountain.

STERLING.

WARREN, near the River of No Return, Idaho County, IDAHO,—
 the border of the Canadian province of British Columbia,
—the Nez Percé Indian Reservation.

Snows.

Smithsonite,
argentite, freibergite,
rose quartz.

B. P.,—Heart, Signal and Big Hole Mountains.

 WARREN, near Custer National Forest, MONTANA,—border, British Columbia, Alberta and Saskatchewan,
—Blackfeet Indian Reservation.

Ice.

Horned larks,
    American bitterns,
        pine grosbeaks,
    Bohemian waxwings,
common linnets.

Baldy Mountain.

Two pairs of wood ducks on the branch of a buttonwood tree, the males crested with bright-blue wing feathers, one of the females nesting in the trunk.

FAIRFIELD, near Greenfields Lake.

The blue of the sky.

FAIRFIELD, NORTH DAKOTA, Middle West, —border, Saskatchewan and Manitoba,—Fort Totten Indian Reservation.

FAIRFIELD, near Magic Reservoir, in the syringa state,—Coeur d'Alene Indian Reservation.

Chalcedony,
jasper, carnelian,
    morganite.

Echoes.

Agates,—Snow and Elk Peaks,—through Sears, Roebuck & Co., a huge mail-order store serving every part of the United States, you can obtain "three superb wall decorations in dramatic natural color . . . idyllic American landscapes transform your wall into a window open onto the world. Marvels of space . . . Enliven the office, the den, the living room, bedroom or playroom. Covers more than twenty square feet. A special process permits the faithful reproduction of the most delicate color photographs. Paste your decoration directly onto the wall (see page to the left for pasting directions), or on beaverboard or cardboard, frame it and hang it as a picture. Easy to clean; a damp cloth is all you need. Choose from:

A) Jackson Lake and the Grand Teton Range. An awesome panorama! Notice the refined, delicate coloring of the mountains framed by the majestic trees in the foreground. A refreshing scene.
B) Cape Sebastian. The rocky coast of Oregon. For those who like to feel the call of adventure . . .
C) Cypress Gardens. 'I remember that,' you'll often hear apropos of this gem taken in Florida's famous park. Its myriad colors make it one of our most popular decorations."

>FAIRFIELD, WASHINGTON, Pacific Coast,—the border of British Columbia,—Port Madison Indian Reservation.

PRESTON, between Caribou and Cache National Forests, IDA., the ski state,—the Kootenai Indian Reservation.

Rainbow.

>*Beryl,*
emerald, aquamarine,
>>*garnet.*

The Presbyterian church,—amethysts, sapphires,—Rainbow Peak.

>PRESTON, NEVADA, Far West,—the Pyramid Lake Indian Reservation.—When it is two P.M. in

WINCHESTER, Pacific Time, Lewis County . . .

>*Obsidian,*
pumice stone, andesite,
>>*basalt.*

Sea of clouds.

The opals.

>WINCHESTER, WYOMING, the least heavily populated state after Alaska and Nevada,—Wind River Indian Reservation.

The golden eagle, soaring over a landscape of snowy mountains, with the trunk of a dead pine forming a bridge over a gorge, a sky of threatening clouds brighter toward the top, holding in its talons a white rabbit, one of its claws thrust into the bleeding eye.

WINCHESTER.

American pipits,
  flickers,
    ospreys,
  belted kingfishers,
ruby-throated flycatchers.

The sea,
  northern sea lions,
harbor seals,
  harbor porpoises,
fur seals,
  sea otters.

The Indian Smohalla, born at the confluence of the Snake and Columbia Rivers around 1815, had been brought up among Catholic missionaries. In 1860, after a duel of honor with a medicine man of a neighboring tribe, beaten senseless, wounded, he was carried by the river and rescued by a white man far from his native region. Slowly, in exile, he regained his strength. But instead of returning directly to his nation, he traveled through Arizona, California and even Mexico, beginning to tell that he had died and visited the world of spirits, and that he had thus been able to learn that the Great Spirit or Heavenly Chief bitterly deplored the apostasy of the Indians who were abandoning their own culture and religion to follow the example of the Europeans . . .

Aneroid Mountain.

John James Audubon painted the yellow warbler three times: on a branch of cassia occidentalis, commonly called Spanish coffee; on a spray of yellow bignonia, called vamping trumpet flower; on a wisteria branch.

WARREN, OREGON, Pacific Coast,—the Klamath Indian Reservation.

orange-crowned warblers,
  ring-necked ducks,
    tufted puffins,
  Wilson's phalaropes,
horned puffins.

The Indian Smohalla said that the Supreme Being was the creator of the earth, of men, of animals, of all things. The first men were the Indians. Then came the French and the priests. Much later, the Americans and the British, "King George's men," and lastly the Negroes. The land therefore belonged without any kind of restriction to the Indian nations. "You ask me to work the soil; I would have to cut off my mother's breast. When I die, she will no longer take me in. . . . To cut the grass to make hay. How would I dare cut my mother's hair?" And to the white men who seized his land: "I want my people to remain here with me. The dead will return, their spirits will be reincarnated. We must stay, for here was the abode of our fathers; we must prepare to meet them again in the breast of our mother the earth."

The sea,
  oysters,
razor clams,
  mussels,
littleneck clams,
  Washington clams.

A white Oldsmobile driven by a young, tanned white man in a pineapple-colored shirt with coffee polka dots (55 miles), "How much longer? Two hours?"—Dead Indian and China Hat Mountains.

The sparkling snow.

SPRINGFIELD. . . . and three o'clock in

SPRINGFIELD, Mountain Time, on the desert plain of the Snake River, near the lava fields,

WELCOME TO ILLINOIS

                 already four in
SPRINGFIELD, Central Time, where you can order black-currant ice cream in the Howard Johnson Restaurant.

The Chicago World's Fair in 1893.
"The New York World," April 9, 1893:
"Ward McAllister has given careful attention to the question of how New York society will be treated in Chicago during the World's Fair. He is disposed to think that fashionable persons in this city need not fear anything but the best treatments at the hands of Chicagoans . . ."
                Quoted by John Szarkowski: "The Idea of Louis Sullivan."

The trains coming from New York.
The trains leaving for San Francisco.

Allerton Hotel, 843 rooms,
        Hotels Ambassador East and Ambassador West,
                Hotel Atlantic, 400 rooms.

Round Lake, "Hello, George!"

        SPRINGFIELD.

John Rave, a Winnebago Indian from Wisconsin, preached the cult of peyotl in his state, and in Nebraska, North Dakota and Minnesota. As a child, he had participated in the medicine-dance rituals, attempting, upon puberty, to achieve the visions that were supposed to reveal the secrets of his ancestors' religion, but without success . . .

"Hello, Mrs. Warren!"—Anvil Lake.

MONTICELLO, county seat of Piatt County.

"The New York World," April 9, 1893:
"Ward McAllister said yesterday: There are really a great many fine people in Chicago. New York Society has hardly a proper conception of what Chicago is. A number of our young men are already beginning to make investigations as to the wealth and beauty of the Chicago women with the result that they are now more anxious to go to the Fair than ever . . ."

Belden Stratford Hotel, 900 rooms,
  Hotel Belmont, 700 rooms,
    Bismarck Hotel, 600 rooms.
The trains coming from Los Angeles.
The trains leaving for Boston.

Beside the highway, a white Plymouth overturned,—Horseshoe Lake, Little Grassy Lake.

MONTICELLO, Green County.

The Winnebago Indian John Rave went to bed at night, as was the custom, with two comrades; he had fasted in hopes that the divinity would consent to manifest itself. But the fear of the dark having been stronger than faith, instead of remaining in contemplation and prayer, they had begun fooling and joking in order to master their anxiety. . . .

A huge gray Plymouth driven by an old yellowish white woman in a currant-colored dress with cerise polka dots and a hat with chocolate flowers (65 miles), "How much longer? Three hours?"—Balsam Lake, Bear Lake.

MONTICELLO.

In Minneapolis, Norwegians read the weekly "Minneapolis Posten."

Alpine Lake.

ALBION, county seat of Edwards County, ILLINOIS, a farm state.

"The New York World," April 9, 1893:
". . . The fact that a man has been brought up in the West does not mean that he is not capable of becoming a society man. I could name over many men and women who have been forced to spend a large part of their early life in the West, but who have nevertheless established themselves in a good position in Eastern Society . . ."

The trains coming from Minneapolis.
Blackstone Hotel, 400 rooms,
    Congress Hotel, 1,100 rooms,
        Conrad Hilton Hotel, 3,000 rooms.
The trains leaving for New Orleans.

Caltex,—"We must have taken the wrong road,"—Crab Orchard, Murphysboro and Moses Lakes.

    ALBION, in Dane County, as is

    CAMBRIDGE, WISCONSIN, cheese state,—the Menominee Indian Reservation.

Restless, the Winnebago Indian John Rave began traveling from tribe to tribe, and even sought escape abroad by hiring himself out to a circus. Disappointed, exhausted by fits of vomiting, he returned to his country and began to drink. "Before my conversion to the religion of peyotl, I nursed perverse thoughts, I plotted to kill my brother and my sister . . ."

Caltex,—through Montgomery Ward, another huge mail-order store, you can obtain a clarinet imported from France, "the country where the finest clarinets are made, properly tested, inspected and adjusted to United States standards by experts. . . . Accessories include a small imitation-leather plush-lined case,
– a lyre-back music stand,
– grease,
– two reeds,
– a wool bag,
– and a swab."

CAMBRIDGE, county seat of Isanti County, MINNESOTA, the North Star State, —the White Earth Indian Reservation.

In Saint Paul, Germans read the weekly "Der Wanderer."

A huge shiny yellow Lincoln, driven by an old, fat white woman in a mango-colored dress and a hat with pistachio flowers (60 miles),—Bald Eagle and Perch Lakes.

CAMBRIDGE, Lincoln's state.

"The New York World," April 9, 1893:
". . . I see that the newly elected Mayor of Chicago has announced that visitors to the Fair need not fear a lack of hospitality. It may be a little rough, he said, but it will be genuine. In reply to this I may say that it is not Quantity but quality that the society people here want. Hospitality that includes the whole human race is not desirable . . ."

Del Prado Hotel, 400 rooms.
The trains coming from Seattle.
  Drake Hotel, 675 rooms.
The trains leaving for Kansas City.
  Eastgate Hotel, 300 rooms.

The Galena River, tributary of the Father of Waters,—Grass and Fox Lakes,—through Sears, Roebuck & Co., an original pet, for instance an eighteen-month-old Mexican burro, "the simplest shelter is all that is needed. Shipped express from Freeport, Ill., with health certificates. Pay three times the normal shipping price. Order saddle and bridle separately."

CLINTON, Rock County.

"In 1893 or 1894," writes the Winnebago Indian John Rave, "I happened to be among the peyotl eaters of Oklahoma. We ate peyotl in the dead of night. All of us participated, myself included. It was pitch black, and I was panic-stricken, for I felt as though something living had entered my heart. 'Why do such a thing?' I asked myself. Suddenly I felt sick. Surely this was going to be the end of me! The best thing

would be to vomit. I tried, without success. 'How terrible I feel! I never should have done such a thing . . . I'm going to die!' At this moment the day broke and we began to laugh. But up till then, I assure you, it was no laughing matter . . ."

Bearskin and Big Arbor Vitae Lakes.

CLINTON, Big Stone County.

In Saint Paul, Germans read the "Volkszeitung Tribune," published every three weeks.

Esso,—Bear Head and Bear Island Lakes, Big Marine Lake.

PRINCETON, county seat of Bureau County, ILL., the Prairie State.

Edgewater Beach Hotel, 1,000 rooms.
                              Taxi!
"The New York World," April 9, 1893:
". . . I should suggest that the Chicago society import a number of fine French chefs. I should also advise that they do not frappé their wine too much . . ."
                              Porter!
The trains coming from Saint Paul.
            Gramercy Hotel, 350 rooms.
The trains leaving for Memphis.
            Hotel Knickerbocker, 450 rooms.

The Episcopalian church.—Apple and Plum Rivers, tributaries of the Father of Waters,—Wonder Lake,—or a monkey, page 1552 of the general catalogue, "plays with dogs, cats or children. Needs a cage to sleep in (see birdcages). Interesting and amusing. Pay twice the normal shipping charges outside Greater Chicago. Your choice of species, not sex. Choose from:
– spider monkey, acrobatic, easy to train, likes to hang by its tail,
– ring-tailed monkey, the species generally used by organ-grinders,
– squirrel monkey, small and affectionate.
Note: all our animals are shipped humanely, supplied with food and water to last the trip. No shipments outside the American continent. The authenticity and health of our specimens are guaranteed."

PRINCETON, on the Fox River that flows into Lake Winnebago.

PRINCETON.

AUBURN, Logan County. State Bird: cardinal.

Lake Shore Drive Hotel, 400 rooms.
The trains leaving for Philadelphia.
Porter!
"The Chicago Journal," April 12, 1893:
"The Mayor will not frappé his wine too much. He will frappé it just enough so the guests can blow the foam off the tops of their glasses without a vulgar exhibition of lung and lip power. His ham sandwiches, sinkers and Irish Quail, better known in the Bridgeport vernacular as pigs' feet, will be triumphs of the gastronomic art . . ."
La Salle Hotel, 1,000 rooms.
The trains coming from Saint Louis.
Morrison Hotel, 1,400 rooms.

Apple Creek that flows into the Illinois, tributary of the Father of Waters, —the Baptist church,—Rock River, another tributary of the Father of Waters,—or an alligator, "harmless when young. Eats meat, fish, leftovers. Requires a small pen with a basin of water. No shipments after November 15. Normal shipping price from Monroe, Louisiana."

AUBURN.

The Europeans have stripped the plains of buffalo and Indians.

Storm Lake.

AUBURN.

In Lincoln, Germans read the weekly "Die Welt Post."

Pony Lake.

> AUBURN, WYOMING, the Far West, the Wind River Indian Reservation.

John James Audubon painted the hooded warbler twice, calling it by different names, first alone on a stem of pheasant's-eye, then with its mate on a plant with blue flowers and large seed-pods.

> PRINCETON, Scott County.

The Europeans drew long perpendicular lines on the plains.

A huge pineapple-color Mercury overturned beside the highway—Spirit Lake, Virgin Lake.

The sky is overcast.

> CLINTON, Clinton County, IOWA, wheat belt,—the Tama Indian Reservation.

The Europeans have begun planting their wheat and their corn.

Flying Service,—Lost Island, Goose and Swan Lakes—or a drum major's baton, "Ward's batons have perfect weight, balance, beauty that pleases experts and beginners . . . Batons should be about twice the length from thumb crotch to inside of elbow. Order nearest size. All have shock-absorber ball of white rubber. 'Baton Twirling Book,' fundamentals, tricks, 250 illustrations."

A cloud passes over the sun.

> CLINTON, in huge and almost empty Sheridan County.

In Omaha, Czechs read the "Hospodar," published every three weeks.

A shiny pineapple-colored Kaiser, driven by a light Negro woman in a cerise dress with tan polka dots (65 miles),—Alkali Lake, Pelican Lake.

The wind is rising.

CAMBRIDGE, on the southern branch of the Skunk River, tributary of the Father of Waters. State Flower: wild rose.

The Europeans have covered the plains with a thin film like a layer of paint, in which the reservations make snags.

The Upper Iowa River, tributary of the Father of Waters,—Silver Lake, Five Island Lake,—or the astonishing autoharp, "easy and fun for everyone. Plays the accompaniment or even the melody; sounds like a banjo, harp or guitar. All you do is press the button corresponding to the harmony you want and let the plectrum slide over the strings. No need for musical training. Maple table, solid frame. Clef-back music stand, two plectrums, book of tunes and directions."

A cloud of dust.

CAMBRIDGE, Furnas County, NEBRASKA, a Great Plains state.

In Omaha, Danes read the bimonthly "Den Danske Pioneer."

Mobil,—Skull, Horseshoe and Spring Valley Lakes.

A rift in the clouds.

ALBION, on the great Iowa River, tributary of the Father of Waters, IOWA, corn belt.

And since with Iowa the free states would have had the majority in Washington, in order to keep the balance, it was decided in 1845 to make Florida a state too.

The Lutheran church,—the Yellow and Turkey Rivers, tributaries of the Father of Waters,—Black Hawk Lake,—or a stereophonic guitar with two loudspeakers, one that can be plugged in for the high notes, the other for the low notes.

A glitter of sunshine on the prairie.

ALBION, county seat of Boone County.

In Omaha, Germans read the weekly "Volkszeitung Tribune."

Diamond and Joy Lakes.

SAINT CHARLES, in Kane County.

AURORA, ILL., a hot summer state.

Palmer House, 2,200 rooms.
The trains coming from Lincoln.
Hotel Parsons, 300 rooms.
"The New York World," April 15, 1893:
"In another interview yesterday, Mr. McAllister has endeavored to make himself more clear: The leaders of society in the Windy City, I am told, are successful pork-packers, soapmakers, Chicago gas trust manipulators and dry-goods princes. These gentlemen are undoubtedly great in their way, but perhaps in some cases unfamiliar with the niceties of life and the difficult points of etiquette . . ."
Taxi!
The trains leaving for Omaha.
Saint Clair Hotel, 500 rooms.

Thirsty? Drink Coca-Cola!—the Sangamon River that flows into the Illinois,—or guinea pigs, "sold in pairs. Eat grass or vegetables. Artificially colored. Pay one and one half times the shipping costs express from Greenville, Ohio."

SAINT CHARLES, Madison County.

And, in terror, the exiled Europeans have begun to wait for their harvest.

The Maquoketa River, tributary of the Father of Waters.

A patch of sunshine slides from one field to the next.

FAIRFIELD.

The rift in the clouds closes over.

FAIRFIELD.

FAIRFIELD, county seat of Wayne County, the oak tree state.

Seneca Hotel, 600 rooms.
The trains coming from Des Moines.
   Sheraton Hotel, 500 rooms,
The trains leaving for Saint Louis.
      Porter!
"The New York World," April 15, 1893:
". . . It takes nearly a lifetime to educate a man how to live. Therefore Chicagoans can't expect to obtain social knowledge without experience and contact with those who have made such things the study of their lives. In these modern days society cannot get along without French Chefs. The man who has been accustomed to delicate fillets of beef,· terrapin, pate de foie gras, truffled turkey and things of that sort would not care to sit down to boiled leg of mutton with turnips . . ."
      Hotel Sherman, 1,501 rooms.

The Little Wabash River that flows into the big Wabash, a tributary of the Ohio River, itself a tributary of the Father of Waters,—Be Sociable! Have a Pepsi!—the Spoon River that flows into the Illinois, another tributary of the Father of Waters.

FAIRFIELD.

In Saint Louis, Germans read the weekly "Deutsche Wochenschrift,"
   Hungarians the bimonthly "Saint Louis Es Videke,"
      Italians the weekly "Il Pensiero."
The Negro waiter in the diner.

> The Des Moines River, the Iowa border, tributary of the Father of Waters.

A family of pileated woodpeckers, the male, its blue claws showing, pecking at a dead branch almost stripped of its bark and covered with gray lichen, spiraled by a tendril of raccoon grapes with clusters of blue fruit; the female, perched higher, holding a caterpillar in her beak; two young males quarreling on a second branch, opening their black wings and showing the inner white patches.

> SAINT CHARLES, on the Missouri, county seat of Saint Charles County.

> *The Negro porter of the sleeping car.*
> *Porter!*
> *In Kansas City, Polish services in Saint Stanislaus' Church, Serbian in Saint George's Church.*

> A chocolate Plymouth driven by a very light Negro in a cerise shirt with maroon polka dots, whose radio is blaring "Saint Louis Blues" (65 miles),—The Fox and Wyaconda Rivers, tributaries of the Father of Waters.

The gray of the sky.

> AURORA, Lawrence County, MISSOURI (for whites only).

> *In Kansas City, Spanish services at Our Lady of Guadalupe, Greek services at the Greek Church.*
> *The Negro porters on the railway platform.*

> Shell,—The Fabius, North and Salt Rivers, tributaries of the Father of Waters,—or an "Airline" radiophonic alarm clock, "Makes getting up almost fun," "the radio-clock that takes the disagreeable shock out of your alarm, treats you with kid gloves during those difficult first few minutes. It soothes you with soft music, and if you still aren't in the mood all you have to do is touch the snooz-alarm to get a few more precious minutes of sleep,—then it wakes you again,—and can do the same thing over five times if you want it to. At

night, it gently lulls you to sleep, then the snooz button, set for sixty minutes, automatically turns off . . . Yes! It will even turn on the percolator or toaster and light your bed-lamp; all you need to do is plug it into the socket. And so beautiful! so smart! so functional! Brown or white plastic case with gold trim."

The wind is stronger.

>AURORA.

>*The clouds of dust over the checkerboard of the fields.*

>*The Negro taxi driver.*

>The Kansas River that flows into the Missouri, tributary of the Father of Waters.

It stirs the pages of newspapers.

>AURORA, COLORADO, the Far West.—The Ute Indian Reservation.

Brown thrashers had built their nest in a black-jack oak. A blacksnake is trying to eat their eggs. The pair is shown in two positions at once, apparently the beginning and the end of the battle. The female resists at first, pecking the enemy with her beak, then we see her smothered to death.

>PRINCETON, hawthorn state (men, women, colored people).

>*The uniformed Negro porter in front of the hotel.*
>>*Whistle.*
>*A fire in Saint Louis.*
>>*A murder in Kansas City.*

The Tarkio River that flows into the Missouri,—the Copper and Meramec Rivers, tributaries of the Father of Waters,— or the 1960 model, page 625, "with a telechron movement with luminous hands, gold dial, white front, charcoal-gray sides. The snooz-alarm lets you go back to sleep for seven minutes before waking you again, up to five times. Snooz button set at sixty minutes. Excellent reception. Also in coral and light blue."

It rustles wrapping paper.

> PRINCETON, Franklin County, KANSAS (. . . whites only),—the Iowa, Sac and Fox Indian Reservation.
>
> *A dead-drunk Negro.*
>
> *The noisy swell in the fields of dry corn.*
>
> A pistachio Chevrolet driven by a brown-skinned white woman in an orange dress (70 miles),—the Marais des Cygnes River that, in Missouri, turns into the Osage River, which flows into the Missouri, a tributary of the Father of Waters.

The washing snaps.

> MONTICELLO, on the northern branch of the Fabius River, MO., a plains state ("This establishment is restricted") (in other words, the management has the right to refuse entrance, for instance for reasons of race or color).
>
> *A suicide in Kansas City.*
>   *Holdup in Saint Louis.*
> *That's a bar for Negroes.*
>
> The Seventh-Day Adventist church,—the Nodaway and Platte Rivers that flow into the Missouri,—the Apple River, tributary of the Father of Waters,—or another, cheaper model, "Ward's high quality. Wakes you to the sounds of sweet music. Fast colors. Comes in white, gray or turquoise."

The television aerials quiver.

LEBANON, county seat of Laclede County. State Bird: bluebird.

That's a church for Negroes.
The organ, no, the harmonium.
The tiger in the Saint Louis Zoo,
the lion in the Kansas City Zoo.

Mark Twain National Forest,—The Church of the Assemblies of God,—the Grand River that flows into the Missouri, —or "our cheapest model. Recommended for local reception only."

The first drops of the squall.

LEBANON.

Streaming across the panes.

SPRINGFIELD, county seat of Greene County.

The zebra in the Kansas City Zoo,
the gorilla in the Saint Louis Zoo.
That's a Negro school.

Clark National Forest.

Flooding the roads.

CLINTON.

CLINTON, county seat of De Witt County.

Hotel Sherry, 304 rooms,
The trains coming from Louisville.
Hotel Shoreland, 1,100 rooms.
The trains leaving for Detroit.
Stock Yard Inn, 170 rooms.
"The New York World," April 23, 1893:
Further remarks by Mr. Ward McAllister:
"I have never called Chicago a pork-packing town nor a vulgar town.

In regard to Chicagoans coming here to get points like gaping natives, which Mrs. Sherwood says they do not, I may say that it is never too late to learn . . ."
"The Chicago Times," April 18, 1893:
One of a list of questions to be asked of those seeking high social position: "Do you consider Ward McAllister a great man, a simple poseur or an ordinary everyday matter-of-fact damn fool?"
The World's Fair.

The Embarrass River that flows into the Wabash that flows into the Ohio, tributary of the Father of Waters.

      CLINTON.

      This is a Negro neighborhood.

      Mammoth Cave National Park: Indians have lived in it; mummies, tools and moccasins have been found there. A hundred and fifty miles of galleries have already been explored . . .

The Tennessee River, which flows into the Ohio.

      CLINTON.

      In the Nashville Pantheon, the Negroes looking at these white statues.

The Wolf River, tributary of the Father of Waters.

      CLINTON, ALABAMA, the Deep
      South (. . . only).

The Tennessee warbler, gray head, greenish back, a white line over the eye, on a prunus branch.

      SPRINGFIELD, county seat of Washington County.

      Mammoth Cave: the water rich in calcium and other minerals drips from the sides and the ceilings, forming stalactites and stalagmites, draperies, petrified fountains, ghosts.

Needles, pendentives, gypsum flowers. Iron and manganese have added their reds, yellows and purples.

The Negro preacher has just arrived.

A muddy tomato-colored Chevrolet parked beside the highway,—the Cumberland and Tradewater Rivers that flow into the Ohio.

Streaming over the cars.

SPRINGFIELD, TENNESSEE (. . . only).

In the Nashville Pantheon, the Negroes looking at these white horses.

A tomato-colored Buick driven by a fat young Japanese in a green shirt (65 miles),—the Hatchie and Obion Rivers, tributaries of the Father of Waters.

The raindrops falling on the river water.

AUBURN, Logan County, KENTUCKY (. . . only).

Probably a new Negro sect.

In Mammoth Cave, guided visits for seven miles:
— King Solomon's Temple,
— the Hall of Draperies,

Texaco,—the Green, Kentucky and Licking Rivers that flow into the Ohio,—or plastic tiles for your bathroom:
"five new pastel shades:
    — pink mist,
    — turquoise,

SAINT CHARLES, Hopkins County.

        — orange sherbet,

Mammoth Cave:

        – mother of pearl,

– *Crystal Lake,*

        – apricot,

twelve marbleized shades:
        – rose ice,

– *the Saltpeter Mines of the War of 1812,*

        – mist green,

– *the Bridal Altar,*

        – desert sand,

– *Jenny Lind's Armchair,*

        – flame,

– *the Onyx Colonnade*

        – Dresden blue,

– *the Star Chamber,*

        – driftwood gray,

– *the Bottomless Pit,*

        – burgundy,

– *the Fat Man's Misery,*

        – charcoal,

> *— the Ruins of Karnak,*
>
> — heather,
>
> *— Frozen Niagara . . .*
>
> — caramel,
> — lemon peel,
>
> *It's a Negro baptism, another new black baby.*
>
> — turquoise,
> Plain black or white."

Clearing.

The Grayson River and the Big Sandy River, the West Virginia border, that flows into the Ohio, the Ohio border.

A rift in the clouds.

LEBANON.

The last drops.

LEBANON.—When it is five o'clock in

LEBANON,

WELCOME TO INDIANA

                    five o'clock in
LEBANON, across the eastern state line.

Smile!

The big Pigeon Creek that flows into the Ohio, the Kentucky border,
"Hello, Harry!"

          LEBANON.

Around the beginning of the Christian era, the Adena Indians appeared in the Ohio valley and left in the state that now bears the name of this river over five thousand mounds, fortifications, and ruins of villages. They made ornaments of hammered copper, carved stone pipes and cut hands and other figures out of mica.

"Hello, Mrs. Auburn!"—The Miami River that flows into the Ohio, the Kentucky border.

          LEBANON.

Treaty of William Penn, founder of Pennsylvania, with the Delaware Indians in 1682:
"The Great God who is the power and wisdom that made you and me, incline your hearts to Righteousness, Love and Peace. This I send to assure you of my Love, and to desire your Love to my friends . . ."

"Information to Those Who Would Remove to America":
"Many Persons in Europe, having directly or by Letters, express'd to the Writer of This, who is well-acquainted with North America, their Desire of transporting and establishing themselves in that Country; but who appear to have formed, thro' Ignorance, mistaken Ideas and Expectations of what is to be obtained there; he thinks it may be useful, and prevent inconvenient, expensive, and fruitless Removals and Voyages of improper Persons, if he gives some clearer and truer Notions of that part of the World, than appear to have hitherto prevailed . . ."
Benjamin Franklin.

Raccoon Creek that flows into the Ohio.

LEBANON.

Orchard orioles,
red-shouldered hawks,

redwings,

cliff swallows,
downy woodpeckers.

The sea,
waves,
sand,
waves,
slipways,
waves.

The Pequest River, tributary of the Delaware, the Pennsylvania border, —telephone ringing.

AURORA, on the Ohio, Dearborn County.

Smile!

"Hello, I want Lebanon, Illinois,"—on the highway a tomato-colored Chevrolet (speed limit 65 miles), "get gas,"—Little Pigeon Creek and the Anderson River that flow into the Ohio.

> AURORA, Portage County.
>
> *The Adena Indians were followed by the Hopewell Indians, who constructed huge funeral mounds and considerable fortifications.*
>
> A shiny tomato-colored Chrysler driven by an old white man (60 miles), "two more hours,"—the Little Miami River and Owl Creek that flow into the Ohio.

CAMBRIDGE CITY, Wayne County, INDIANA, a livestock state.

Keep smiling!

Sunoco, "we took the wrong road, we have to go back,"—the Little Blue River and the Big Blue River and Deer Creek that flow into the Ohio.

> CAMBRIDGE, county seat of Guernsey County, OHIO, the most densely populated state after New York, California, Pennsylvania and Illinois.
>
> *After the Hopewell civilization, some four centuries before the Europeans arrived, the Woodland civilization.*
>
> B. P.,—Raccoon Creek and the Muskingum and Scioto Rivers that flow into the Ohio,—through Montgomery Ward, you can obtain a solitaire diamond with the new "Glo" setting that makes the diamond look bigger than it is: "Look at the difference our new setting makes! How much bigger the diamond looks! Four little reflector diamonds, slipped under the central stone, increase its sparkling beauty, its brilliance, —make it look almost twice as big as it really is."

HANOVER, in the zinnia state.

Keep smiling!

Perch Lake,—Silver Creek and Laughery Creek that flow into the Ohio, —through Sears, Roebuck & Co., the "Automobile Repair Manual," 1,120 pages, "covers 1,967 models, from 1952 to 1959; 2,850 explanatory illustrations to make things ultra-simple; 225,000 repair problems, with 219 rapid reference tables, covering more than 30,000 essential specifications and dimensions. . . . All pointers on maintenance, repair and emergency service for these 24 makes:
– Buick,

>HANOVER, scarlet-carnation state.

– Cadillac,

> *Indians of an unknown period and civilization constructed large mounds in the shape of eagles, quadrupeds or serpents; the greatest of the latter measures 411 yards, has a spiral tail, twists its body into seven deep curves and holds a kind of huge egg in its open mouth.*

– Chevrolet,

> The Maumee River that flows into Lake Erie,—Polson Creek that flows into the Ohio,—or an engagement ring, page 440 in the catalogue, "eleven sparkling diamonds, totaling almost a carat, in the new 'Glo' setting described above. Four chatoyants around them. Adjustable wedding band with six large brilliants. Standard quality."

– Chrysler,

> HANOVER, York County, PENNSYLVANIA, —the Cornplanter Indian Reservation.

– Clipper,

> ". . . *He finds it is imagined by Numbers, that the Inhabitants of North America are rich, capable of rewarding, and dispos'd to reward, all sorts of Ingenuity; that they are at the same time ignorant of all the Sciences, and, consequently, that Strangers, possessing Talents in the Belles-Lettres, fine arts, &c., must be highly esteemed, and so well paid, as to become easily rich themselves; that there are also abundance of profit-*

          able Offices to be disposed of, which the Natives
          are not qualified to fill . . ."
                  Benjamin Franklin.

– Continental,

          ". . . and when the Great God brings me among
          you, I intend to order all things in such manner
          that we may all live in Love and Peace one with
          another, which I hope the Great God will incline
          both me and you to do. . . ."
          Treaty of William Penn with the Delaware
                      Indians.

– De Soto,

          A chocolate Frazer driven by an old Negro (50
          miles),—the Beaver and Allegheny Rivers that
          flow into the Ohio.

– Dodge,

                HANOVER, NEW JERSEY, smallest
                    state after Rhode Island,
               Delaware, Connecticut and Hawaii.

– Edsel,

               The sea,

– Ford,

         sand,

– Hudson,

               trunks,

– Imperial,

         sand,

– Jeep,

               shorts,

– Lincoln,

         sand.

– Mercury,

               Bluebirds,

– Nash,

         Carolina kinglets,

– Oldsmobile,

      swallow-tailed flycatchers,

– Packard,

         rose-breasted grosbeaks,

– Plymouth,

– Pontiac,
wood peewees.

A chocolate Kaiser driven by a young Negro (50 miles),—the Musconetcong and Assunpink Rivers, tributaries of the Delaware,—telephone ringing.

A black-throated blue warbler on a spray of Canadian columbine; on another plate, two females on a viburnum.

WASHINGTON COURT HOUSE, county seat of Fayette County, OHIO, a livestock state.

– Rambler,

In 1772, David Zeisberger and other Moravian Brothers built villages for the Delaware Indians whom they had converted. In 1782, in order to avoid any conflict with the Europeans in Pennsylvania, the missionaries decided it was best to make them leave their Gnadenhütten (Cabins of Grace) and to withdraw to the "City of Captives," today Upper Sandusky, Ohio. But since these missionaries had ordered them to return to sow their former fields of corn, the Indians were discovered by the Pennsylvania militiamen under the orders of Colonel David Williamson, who disarmed them, bound them, and exterminated them with axes and cudgels, for they wished to save their ammunition; 35 men, 37 women and 34 children were massacred in this way. They sang until their death the hymns the missionaries had taught them.

– Studebaker,

"Hello, I want Cambridge, Ohio,"—the Christian Science church,—the Portage and Sandusky Rivers that flow into Lake Erie,—the Rattlesnake River that flows into the Scioto River,—or a pearl pendant, "skillfully cultivated, scientifically produced in a living oyster raised for at least three years in the warm waters of Japan. The romance, the charm, the flattery of cultured pearls is eternal,—they never lose their beauty."

A slanting sunbeam on the wet leaves.

WASHINGTON, where you can order cherry ice cream in the Howard Johnson Restaurant.

— Thunderbird,

Treaty of William Penn with the Delaware Indians:
". . . I seek nothing but the honor of His name, and that we who are His workmanship, may do that which is well pleasing to Him. The man which delivers this unto you is my special friend, sober, wise and loving, you may believe him. . . ."

— Willys."

" . . . and that, having few Persons of Family among them, Strangers of Birth must be greatly respected, and of course easily obtain the best of those Offices, which will make all their Fortunes; that the Governments too, to encourage Emigrations from Europe, not only pay the Expence of personal Transportation, but give Lands gratis to Strangers, with Negroes to work for them, Utensils of Husbandry, and Stocks of Cattle. These are all wild Imaginations; and those who go to America with Expectations founded upon them will surely find themselves disappointed . . ."
                              Benjamin Franklin.

Caltex,—the Monongahela River (which, after its junction at Pittsburgh with the Allegheny River, becomes the Ohio River) and its tributaries: Youghiogheny River and Tenmile Creek.

A slanting sunbeam on a spattered puddle.

WASHINGTON, Warren County.

meadowlarks,
field sparrows,
oven birds,
the sea,

skin,
                thighs,
elbows,
                toes,
backs,
                the outskirts of New York City,
fish crows,
                pine siskins.

Esso,—Rancocas, Salem and Oldmans Creeks, tributaries of the Delaware, —telephone ringing.

MILFORD, Kosciusko County, IND., a hard winter state.

Keep smiling!

"Hello, I want Cambridge, Indiana,"—the church of the Latter-Day Saints, called the "Mormons,"—Cedar and Dalecarlia Lakes,—or the "Truck Repair Manual," new 1959 edition, page 1030 in the catalogue. "Over 30,000 facts about virtually all models of gasoline trucks from 1952 to 1959. Over 2,000 illustrations, 200 practical tables. Clear 'step-by-step' instructions tell you all you need to know to make easy repairs. Chapters on the maintenance of diesels:
– Autocar,
– Brockway,
– Chevrolet,

MILFORD, Clermont County.

– Diamond T,
– Divco,
– Dodge,

Tecumseh, chief of the Pawnee Indians, a tribe of the Algonquin group, who had succeeded in forming a coalition against the United States: "The Great Spirit has given this great island to the Redskins; the Great Spirit has settled the White Men beyond the ocean. Today, the White Men, not content with their own lands, have come among us and have driven us from the coastal regions to the great lakes; but from

here we will retreat no farther . . ." *1810. Tecumseh died in battle in 1813.*
– Ford,
– GMC,
– Cummins,
more details about gasoline or diesel engines used in building work: cranes, bulldozers, etc."

    The Vermilion River that flows into Lake Erie.

The sky is clearing.

    MILFORD, on the Delaware, the New Jersey border.

The shadows grow longer.

    MILFORD, on the Delaware, the Pennsylvania border.

The copper sun.

    CLINTON.

The glowing panes.

    CLINTON, KENTUCKY, the South (for whites only).

The rising mist.

    CLINTON, on the Clinch River, TENNESSEE, (. . . whites only).

The melting sun.

    CLINTON, ALABAMA, the Deep South (. . . only).

CLINTON, on the Wabash River that flows into the Ohio, the redbird state.

Why aren't you smiling?

Big Creek that flows into the Wabash, the Illinois border,—the synagogue,—Palestine Lake,—or the book "Etiquette," by Emily Post, "answers every question about what is done; how to behave, what to wear, on every occasion, intimate or formal, 671 pages illustrated."

    CLINTON.

Chapel Lake Indian Ceremonials prospectus:
"Michigan's Thrilling—New—Outdoor Live Indian Drama!
Giant Cast of Real North American Indians!
Authentic! Mysterious! Dramatic!
8:30 Nightly (Except Mondays) June 25 to Labor Day.
In the Huron National Forest near Tawas City and East Tawas in Iosco County, Michigan, just off US 23—Beauty Route to the Bridge!"

    Bear Lake.

The black and white warbler on a black larch branch.

    MILFORD, Oakland County.

"The throbbing drums of the Red Man beat again!
His ceremonial fires burn bright!
The voice of the Great Spirit calls!
The eagle—the Thunder Bird—flies again! . . ."

An apricot Nash, driven by an old Negro (65 miles),—Beaver and Big Portage Lakes.

A flame of clouds.

    HANOVER, Jackson County, MICHIGAN, Middle West,
            —the border of the Canadian province of Ontario,—the L'Anse Indian Reservation.

"From the Four Points of the Compass
– the place of the Four Winds,
– out of the reservations, the deep forest,
– as spring passes into summer,
– scores of Indians, from many tribes, gather at beautiful

> *Chapel Lake, in the Huron National Forest, in Iosco County, Michigan, to present their nightly (except Monday) spectacular, through the summer till Labor Day . . ."*

> Esso,—Big Star Lake, Carp Lake, the Chippewa Indian Reservation,—or a vaginal douche bag, "to avoid being embarrassed, buy by mail order, discreetly! The impeccable 'hygienette' is filled directly from the faucet. Patented plastic stopper at the bottom of the rubber bulb."

AUBURN, county seat of De Kalb County, IND., a hot summer state.

Why do you watch us smiling without smiling?

If you think all concentrated soups have the same taste, it's time you tried Heinz!—The Patoka and White Rivers that flow into the Wabash.

> AUBURN, Bay County. State Flower: apple blossom.

> *"In this colorful one hour and forty-five minute authentic, live Indian Pageant and Drama, will appear proud chieftains,*
> *— the glistening bronze bodies of the warriors, in their stirring dances and contests,*
> *— the beautiful maidens,*
> *— the squaws and their stoic faces,*
> *— the joyous children,*
> *— all in gorgeous costumery and regalia, presenting their Ceremonials and age-old dances,*
> *— things heretofore unseen and unknown to the White Man! . . ."*

> Coldwater and Crystal Lakes,—or a traveling douche bag, in its case, page 217 in the general catalogue, "flexible white rubber, curving, flexible tube . . ."

ALBION, county seat of Noble County.

Your not smiling hurts our feelings.

Busseron Creek that flows into the Wabash.

ALBION, Calhoun County.

"At Beautiful Chapel Lake, just a short distance from US 23 and M 55, nine miles west of East Tawas and Tawas City, on a good forest road—the famous old Plank Road, — these genuine North American Indians present their Ceremonials for your pleasure! The comfortable, picturesque open-air stadium overlooks the wooded island stage. There is a rustic refreshment stand and large lighted free parking lot . . ."

Devils Lake.

The crimson reflection on the water.

WASHINGTON.—When the sun is setting in

WASHINGTON,

WELCOME TO IOWA

its disc is still entirely above the misty horizon in
WASHINGTON.

They were certainly not the ambassadors of Europe . . .

The Upper Iowa River, tributary of the Father of Waters, "Hello, Henry!"

WASHINGTON.

Stop!

The Chicago World's Fair, 1893:
"It was deemed fitting by all the people that the four-hundredth anniversary of the discovery of America by one Christopher Columbus should be celebrated by a great World Exposition, which should spaciously reveal to the last word the cultural status of the peoples of the Earth; and that the setting for such a display should be one of splendor, worthy of its subject . . ."
                    Louis Sullivan: "Autobiography of an Idea."

The trains leaving for Sioux City.
The trains coming from Washington, D.C.

Agostino's, Neapolitan Dishes,
         Allgauer's Restaurant, German Dishes.

"Hello, Mrs. Milford!"—The Galena River, tributary of the Father of Waters.

WASHINGTON.

See how our President smiles!

Hudson Lake.

WASHINGTON COURT HOUSE.

Night on Lake Erie.

The Serpent Mound.

WASHINGTON, where you can order cherry ice cream in the Howard Johnson Restaurant, PENNSYLVANIA.

WASHINGTON, NEW JERSEY.

A Bewick's wren on a spray of ironwood.

CLINTON, county seat of De Witt County.

"Autobiography of an Idea":
". . . The crowds were astonished. They beheld what was for them an amazing revelation of the architectural art, of which previously they in comparison had known nothing. To them it was a veritable Apocalypse, a message inspired from on high. Upon it their imagination shaped new ideals. They went away, spreading again over the land, returning to their homes, permeated by the most subtle and slow-acting of poisons . . ."
Louis Sullivan.

The trains leaving for Indianapolis.
Fire.
The Anchorage, seafood specialties,
*   Bamboo Inn, Cantonese specialties.*
The trains coming from Cincinnati.

Pass!

On the highway a Lincoln whose radio is blaring "Illinois" (speed limit 65 miles), "another hour,"—Apple and Plum Rivers, tributaries of the Father of Waters.

The crimson reflection on the water.

CLINTON, Vermillion County.

Look at the way Mrs. Kennedy is smiling!

A muddy Kaiser parked beside the highway,—Clear Lake.

A light goes on.

CLINTON, Summit County, OHIO.

The woods at night.

A Kaiser (speed limit changes from 60 to 50 miles),—telephone ringing.

MARION, on the checkerboard of Linn County.

They were not sent by their princes in great state.

"Hello, I want Washington, Indiana,"—a shiny Hudson (speed limit changes from 70 to 60 miles), "get gas at the next station."

MARION, county seat of Williamson County, ILLINOIS.

Parking.

The trains coming from Cleveland.
              Collision.
"Autobiography of an Idea";
". . . A vast multitude, exposed, unprepared, they had not had time nor occasion to become immune to forms of sophistication not their own, to a higher and more dexterously insidious plausibility. Thus they departed joyously, carriers of

contagion, unaware that what they had beheld and believed to be the truth was to prove, in historic fact, an appalling calamity. For what they saw was not at all what they believed they saw, but an imposition of the spurious upon their eyesight, a naked exhibitionism of charlatanry . . ."
    Louis Sullivan, one of the greatest of all architects.
    Kidnaping.
Barney's Market Club, frogs' legs.
    Berghoff Restaurant, German accent.
The trains leaving for Pittsburgh.

Metal bridges.

Esso,—through Montgomery Ward, you can obtain old-age pills, "reinforced" variety; each one provides eighteen times the daily minimum requirements of Vitamin B1, eight times that of Vitamin B2.

    MARION, county seat of Grant County, IND.

Look how Mr. Nixon is smiling!

    Flying Service,—Riddles, Irish and Loon Lakes.

    MARION, county seat of Marion County.

The streets at night.

    Flying Service,—telephone ringing.

A pair of blue-winged warblers on two sprays of wild althea with large pink blossoms.

    MONTICELLO, wood violet state.

Metal staircases.

The trains coming from Springfield.
    Murder.

A Bit of Sweden, Scandinavian menu.
  Screams.
"*Autobiography of an Idea*":
". . . *The virus of the World's Fair began to show unmistakable signs of the nature of the contagion. There came a violent outbreak of the Classic and the Renaissance in the East, which slowly spread westward, contaminating all that it touched. The selling campaign of the bogus antique was remarkably well-managed through skillful publicity and propaganda, by those who were first to see its commercial possibilities. By the time the market had been saturated, all sense of reality was gone. In its place had come deep-seated illusions, absence of pupillary reaction to light, absence of knee-reaction—symptoms all of progressive cerebral meningitis: the blanketing of the brain . . .*"
  Louis Sullivan.
  Black Forest Restaurant, game.
The trains going to Phoenix.

No parking.

"Hello, I want Clinton, Illinois,"—or else the regular variety of old-age pills, "each one provides:
– 10 times the daily minimum requirement of Vitamin B1,

The sky is completely clear.

  – over 4 times that of Vitamin B2,

    MONTICELLO, county seat of White County, zinnia state.

– 3½ times that of Vitamin A and Vitamin D,

    Look how our President Eisenhower used to smile!

– 2½ times that of Vitamin C,

    Golden and Silver Lakes.

MOUNT VERNON, on the checkerboard of Linn County, IOWA.

– 1½ times the minimum daily requirement of iron,

They came driven from Europe by religious persecution . . .

– all the iodine you need."

"Hello, I want Washington, Iowa,"—Texaco.

MOUNT VERNON, county seat of Jefferson County, ILL.

Put on your headlights!

The trains coming from Boston.
     Police!
Black Hawk Restaurant, hot hors-d'oeuvres,
   Boston Oyster House, lobster.
"Autobiography of an Idea":
". . . Thus Architecture died in the land of the free and the home of the brave—in a land declaring its fervid democracy, its inventiveness, its resourcefulness, its unique daring, enterprise and progress. Thus did the virus of a culture, snobbish and alien to the land, perform its work of disintegration; and thus ever works the pallid academic mind, denying the real, exalting the fictitious and the false; that never lifts a hand in aid because it cannot; that turns its back upon man because that is its tradition; a culture lost in ghostly mésalliance with abstractions, when what the world needs is courage, common sense and human sympathy, and a moral standard that is plain, valid and livable. . . ."
            Louis Sullivan.
    Ear-splitting whistle.
The trains leaving for Denver.

Rusty railings.

The Greek Orthodox church,—Wonder Lake, Fox Lake,—the Illinois River, tributary of the Father of Waters,—or else the old-age tonic, for those who prefer the liquid. "One fluid ounce (two tablespoons) provides:
– 18 times the minimum daily requirement of Vitamin B1,

Another wisp of purple clouds.

    MOUNT VERNON, county seat of Posey County.

 – 10 times that of Niacinamide,

   Remember the way Mamie Eisenhower smiled!

 – over 8 times that of Vitamin B2."

   Stone Lake.

Green light.

    MOUNT VERNON.

WATERLOO. State Flower: wild rose.

They came driven from affluent Europe by poverty, by the tyranny of money . . .

Virgin Lake,—through Sears, Roebuck & Co., a tramp disguise for your children, "clever and always ready to entertain. Two-piece costume, rayon shirt. Trousers with patch. Black hat, plastic mask, cane and sack filled with treats."

   WATERLOO, county seat of Monroe County.

  Turrets, granite and rust pinnacles.

  The trains leaving for Salt Lake City.
      The ambulance.
Café de Paris, duckling,
    Charm House, chicken Maryland.
The trains coming from Las Vegas.
"*Autobiography of an Idea*":
". . . The damage wrought by the World's Fair will last for at least half a century. It has penetrated deep into the constitution of the American mind, effecting there lesions significant of dementia . . ."
             Louis Sullivan.

Turn off your headlights!

Lake Vermilion.

WATERLOO.

Two pairs of purple martins, near the hollow gourds they nest in, perched on a dead branch.

BURLINGTON.

BURLINGTON, county seat of Des Moines County, IOWA.

And had only one idea in mind, to return to Europe to take revenge by means of money, and to flout those who had driven them away . . .

Rush Lakes and Elk Lake,—or a witch's costume, page 1275, "watch out or she'll cast a spell on you! two-piece rayon . . . black cape with luminous designs . . . yellow print skirt. Hat, vinyl mask, bag of treats."

BURLINGTON.

The Winnebago Indian John Rave:
"The next night, we were to eat the peyotl again. I thought: 'Last time it almost made me sick.' But the others encouraged me, and I had to give in. I said: 'All right, I'll eat some.' And we each consumed seven pieces. The same thing happened the third night . . ."

Bone Lake.

BURLINGTON.

Chapel Lake Indian Ceremonials prospectus:
"It is an easy four-hour drive from any point in the Lower Peninsula! Enjoy the most thrilling one-night vacation and camera's delight for the entire family ever presented, at Chapel Lake Indian Ceremonials!"

Diamond Lake.

A family of red-headed woodpeckers on the dead stump where they have nested, the male bringing a caterpillar to one of the young, the female a berry.

WATERLOO, Jefferson County.

"The first night's vision was terrifying: a huge snake that came toward me, threatening.

The second night's vision was still terrifying: a half-human figure with horns and claws, that attacked me with a spear.

The third night's vision was comforting: God appeared to me in spirit and I prayed to Him with all my heart, asking for mercy, guidance, help.

O Son of God, help me. Instruct me in this religion! Help me, O medicine! Father, guide me, instruct me in this religion . . ."

The Winnebago Indian John Rave.

A shiny Dodge (speed limit changes from 65 to 55 miles),— Buckskin and Buffalo Lakes.

The evening star.

MOUNT VERNON, Dane County, WISCONSIN.

The Winnebago Indian John Rave:
". . . Many years ago, I was sick, and I feared that the sickness would be the death of me; but no sooner had I eaten some peyotl than I was completely cured. . . . The tubercular had no hope of health in those days, and now for the first time they recovered . . ."

Butternut Lake, Cedar Lake,—or the book "When You Marry," "the meaning of marriage, responsibilities and personal relations before and after marriage . . ."

The reflection of the street lamps on the chromium of the automobiles.

MARION, state of the violet.

Around 1910 another Winnebago Indian, Albert Hensley, introduced new elements of Christian origin into the peyotl religion, particularly the reading of the Bible, which he translated into his own language . . .

Clam Lake, Crab Lake,—or "Ideal Marriage" by Dr. Van de Velde, world-famous gynecologist, page 477, "a guide to that happy marriage which doctors can give their patients. Detailed and direct, written simply and clearly, it deals with every aspect of normal conjugal relations. Illustrations and diagrams. 330 pages."

The blue of the sky grows deeper.

WASHINGTON, Door County, WIS.

The Winnebago Indian Albert Hensley:
". . . Up to now you Indians have been fighting among yourselves. The goal of this new religion is to put an end to that; you will shake hands and share your meals. That is what peyotl will lead you to. Starting from today, you will love each other. Go among the nations and teach them what I tell you. Go among those of the North and teach them . . ."

Cranberry Lake,—or "Sexual Tensions in Marriage," by Dr. Van de Velde, famous gynecologist, "studies the fundamental causes of sexual tensions, and the methods of reabsorbing them. For married people and those thinking of marriage. 330 pages."

The rising of the moon.

WASHINGTON, Macomb County, MICHIGAN,

"You will see and hear:
– 'The Song of the Forest' and her woodland music,

A huge shiny Pontiac in flames beside the highway,—Duck Lake, Elk Lake.

The blinding headlights on the highway.

– *Ceremonials of the Council Fires,*

OSCEOLA. State Bird: robin.

– *the Peace Pipe Dance,*

". . . *They say that a hunter of the tribe of the Mescaleros Apaches got lost on a hunting expedition. As he wandered, he was on the point of dying of hunger and thirst. He fell to the ground, calling to death, his arms spread to the west and to the east. But then one of his hands touched something strange and cool, which he tore up and put in his mouth; it tasted good; his hunger and his thirst were satisfied. A holy spirit entered him, and he heard a voice saying to him: 'I have made you suffer so much in order to reveal the true religion to you. That is why I have made sacred the food you have just eaten. My Father has given it to me to entrust to the earth and to bestow it upon the Indians . . .'"*
The Winnebago Indian Albert Hensley.

– *the Green Corn Dance,*

Black River State Forest,—or "Overcome Arthritis," "encouraging research by thousands of specialists. Program of home treatment; return to normal life. 256 pages, illustrated."

The reflection of the signs in the lakes.

– *Legend of the Largo Springs,*

MONROE, county seat of Green County, WIS.

– *the Eagle Dance,*

The Winnebago Indian Albert Hensley:
". . . *We read in the Bible that Christ heralded the coming of a comforter (John, XIV, 16–26). A comforter came long ago for the White Men, but none had come for the Indians until the day God sent us comfort in the form of this holy food, given exclusively to the Indians. God having never allowed the White Men to understand anything about it . . .*"

　　　　　　　– Fish Dance,

　　Have you remembered to buy Kleenex?—or "Don't Worry about Your Heart" by Dr. Edward Weiss, pioneer of psychosomatic medicine, "simply written, studies the effects of emotion, anxiety, fatigue . . . What you should avoid. The problem of hypertension. How to 'live' with a heart condition. 200 pages."

The reflection of the headlights in the rivers.

　　　　　　　– Chippewa Deer Dance."
　　　　　　　Chapel Lake Indian Ceremonials prospectus.

　　　　　　　MONROE, county seat of Monroe County.

　　　　　　　Chapel Lake . . . :
　　　　　　　"Legend of the Thunder Boy,

　　　　　　　Sunoco,—Glen, Grand and Green Lakes,

The moon's reflection.

　　　　　　　– Dance of the Pleiades,

　　　　　　　CLINTON, Rock County.

　　　　　　　– Raccoon Dance,

Night over the reservations.

　　　　　　　– War Dance,

　　　　　　　Bad Axe River, tributary of the Father of Waters.

The first stars come out.

　　　　　　　–Pow Wow Dance,

　　　　　　　CLINTON.

> — *Corn Grinding Dance,*

The blue of the sky turning black.

> — *the Famous Gift Dance,*

> MONTICELLO.

> — *Indian Love Song,*

MONTICELLO. Iowa State Bird: eastern goldfinch.

> — *Ceremonial to a Dying Chieftain . . ."*

Oh, how they longed for revenge, from the first landings! . . .

Black Hawk Lake,—or the Moon-Master costume: "the man of tomorrow. One-piece, yellow rayon satin with red, black and gray stencil designs, hood and plastic space mask."

> MONTICELLO.

> *Colder.*

> Big Rice Lake.

The great blue heron, bending its head to the ground in order to fit within the limits of the page, beside a pond among low reeds.

> CLINTON, MINNESOTA.

> *Still colder.*

> A Studebaker (speed limit changes from 60 to 50 miles)— Big Rush Lake, Big Sand Lake.

Moonlight on the lake.

> PRESTON.

MONROE, Jasper County, IOWA.

They did not try to know this country, they had no desire to settle here. They were content with temporary habitations. They wanted only to survive and grow rich in order to be able to return . . .

Thirsty? Drink Coca-Cola!—or Casper the Friendly Ghost costume, "he doesn't want to scare you, just to be a friend. White rayon shroud with hood that completely conceals identity, red or black trim."

> MONROE, in the checkerboard of Turner County, like

> MARION, SOUTH DAKOTA.

> *The crimson reflection on the water.*

> The Vermilion River that flows into the Missouri.

A pair of Canada geese in front of a clump of reeds, the gander standing, looking back over his shoulder, his head black with a white neck, his open black bill showing the pointed pink tongue.

> MOUNT VERNON.

MILFORD, the Hawkeye State.

Meanwhile, until this triumphal return took place, why not reconstitute a new Europe, effacing as much as possible this continent that received but alarmed us?
                        New
                                    France,
            New
                        England,
Nova
            Scotia,
New
            Brunswick,
                        New
                                    York,
                        New
                                    Holland,
            New
                        Sweden,

New
            Orleans,
New
            Hampshire,
                        New
                                    Jersey,
                        New
                                    Amsterdam,
            New
                        London on a
New
            Thames.
Am I not still, or rather, am I not already in Europe, since I am in Milford?

Be Sociable! Have a Pepsi!—Or a Rickety Rivets the Robot Costume, "walks and talks like a person. Gray rayon costume. Trousers with a mechanical man design printed in black and gold. Robot mask."

        MILFORD.

    A light goes on.

The southern branch of the Big Blue River that becomes the Kansas River that flows into the Missouri.

A pair of ruby-crowned kinglets, in their summer plumage, on a branch of narrow-leaved kalmia.

    MONROE, on the checkerboard of Platte County.

    Another wisp of purple clouds.

A shiny, overloaded Frazer (speed limit changes from 65 to 55 miles),—Pumpkin Creek that flows into the northern branch of the River Platte.

The North Star.

    CLINTON, in huge and almost empty Sheridan County, NEBRASKA.

The evening star.

Sunoco,—or a superb rosary, "blue moonstone, beads silver plated like the lovely crucifix. Case."

The sign of the drive-in movie theater, where you watch the film in your car.

OSCEOLA, county seat of Polk County.

The reflection of the street lamps in the chromium of the automobiles.

The Nemaha and Little Nemaha Rivers that flow into the Missouri.

The illuminated face of Marilyn Monroe.

WATERLOO.

CLINTON, county seat of Clinton County, IOWA.

And since the new Europe behaved exactly like the old, they fled before a wind of hatred, intolerance, poverty and tyranny, with the firm hope of returning and making their dollars ring . . .

A pack of Lucky Strikes,—the airports of Burlington, county seat of Des Moines County, and of Des Moines, the state capital, county seat of Polk County.

CLINTON.

They left New York for Pennsylvania . . .
Good luck!

Servile old Negroes.

Crystal Caverns.

CLINTON.

*They left Virginia for Kentucky . . .
    Bon voyage!*

Arrogant young Negroes.

Brushy Mountain.

    CLINTON, LOUISIANA.

The sea,
golden waves,
        shimmer of gold,
lakes of gold,
        avalanches of gold,
puddles of gold.
        The old people's white eyebrows over their black eyes.

        Lake Pontchartrain,—telephone ringing.

A Northern water-thrush on a spray of Indian turnip, with two broken stalks and a cluster of red berries.

    WASHINGTON, Franklin County, MISSOURI.

White hair above their black foreheads.

*Driven out, fleeing, they left Pennsylvania for Ohio.
    Best wishes!*

"Hello, I want Washington, Nebraska,"—a shiny Nash (speed limit changes from 65 to 60 miles).

The Great Bear.

    WASHINGTON, Hempstead County, ARKANSAS.

A red tongue that comes out between their black lips.

They left Kentucky for Tennessee.
See you soon!

A white truck whose radio is blaring the "Arkansas Traveler" (at night 60 miles),—Petit Jean and Dutch Creek Mountains.

The illuminated face of Jayne Mansfield.

WASHINGTON.

The noise of a train.

MONTICELLO, county seat of Lewis County.

They left Ohio for Indiana.
Don't forget us!

White teeth shining in their black mouths.

"Hello, I want Clinton, Missouri,"—Shell.

The illuminated face of Rita Hayworth.

MONTICELLO, county seat of Drew County.

They left Tennessee for Arkansas.
When you come back . . .

They smell black.

B. P.,—Poteau, Muddy Creek and Missouri Mountains.

Cassiopeia.

OSCEOLA, county seat of Saint Clair County.

Their eyes burn black.
They left Indiana and Illinois for Missouri.
If you come back . . .

"Hello, I want Washington, Missouri,"—Onondaga Cave, Onyx Caverns.

The illuminated face of Jerry Lewis.

OSCEOLA.

OSCEOLA, county seat of Clarke County.

Driven on, they left Indiana and Illinois for Iowa, driving the Indians before them; and when they saw their first harvest of wheat, how they smiled!

"Hello, I want Milford, Iowa,"—the airport of Mason City, county seat of Cerro Gordo County.

PRESTON.—When it is seven P.M. in

PRESTON,

WELCOME TO KANSAS

                seven o'clock in
PRESTON.

It was not only the poisonous vines of this continent that were frightening . . .

Even when they don't look black, they're black.

Prairie Lake.

WASHINGTON, county seat of Washington County.

They're even blacker than black.

Its poison oaks, poison sumacs, venomous snakes, poisoned Indian arrows . . .

On the highway, a huge Studebaker (speed limit at night 60 miles), "get gas at the next Texaco."

        WASHINGTON.

> "Peyotl is a cactus (lophophora williamsii), small in size, shiny, carrot-shaped, that grows on the Mexican border of the United States, in the Rio Grande Valley. It can be eaten raw or sun-dried . . . Its most remarkable psychophysiological effects are an extraordinary heightening of the senses, especially with regard to the perception of colors, shapes and sounds; visual and auditive hallucinations, with some disorders in the coenesthetic sphere . . . These exceptional properties are due to its high percentage of alkaloids such as

anhaline, mescaline, lophophorine, etc. Its ingestion has no harmful consequences, but is accompanied by nausea; it is not habit-forming."
Vittorio Laternari:
"Movimenti Religiosi dei Popoli Oppressi."

They had black shoes with black laces.

Clear Creek Lake.

On a black oak branch, two female whippoorwills, the male flying above them, its mustached bill open. A caterpillar on a leaf. Two butterflies of different species in the air. In the lower right corner, a detail of the foot.

ASHLAND, OKLAHOMA.

Black spats with black buttons.

In 1890, in Darlington on the South Canadian River, the Indian Sitting Bull had convened the neighboring tribes for a great celebration of the dance of the Spirits. Among them was a half breed, John Wilson, of the Delaware tribe (half Delaware, one quarter Caddo, one quarter French), whom the ceremony sent into a trance and who, according to his own words, felt that he had entered God's heart. Later, when John Wilson was watching a ceremonial dance of the Comanche Indians, one of them offered him some peyotl and invited him to try it. He withdrew into a solitary open place, accompanied by his wife, consuming nine peyotl buds each night and renewing this repast or communion each day. His nephew Anderson recounts that the peyotl took possession of him. Under its influence, he was taken to the kingdom of the skies and there beheld celestial signs and figures, spirits of the moon, the sun and the fire, traditionally regarded by the Delawares as their ancestors and elder brothers. He also had a vision of the empty tomb of Jesus Christ, who had risen to heaven, and of the path leading from this tomb to the moon. He was told that if he followed this path, at the end of his life he would have his place in the presence of Christ and of peyotl. Further, he received various instructions for the arrangement of the holy space in the peyotl tent, the songs and all the minutest details of the ceremony . . .

An overloaded Pontiac whose radio is blaring "Oklahoma!" (at night 55 miles) "we'll be there soon."

Green light.

BURLINGTON.

BURLINGTON, county seat of Coffey County, KANSAS.

What was most frightening of all was the very existence of this continent, appearing above the horizon there where it had no reason to be at all . . .

They had black trousers with black patches.

Caltex.

BURLINGTON, COLORADO.

ASHLAND, in the sunflower state.

They were given black hats with black bands.

And the Indian—expression of this scandalous continent—inspired too much terror to be made to labor for them except in certain cases of proselytism or utopia (it would have taken all the magnificent authority of the King of Spain or of the Pope behind him); therefore, as they had been driven from Europe by an unjust poverty, and as they desired to reverse that inequality that had driven them from their country, in order to have someone still poorer than themselves beside them, making them rich, rather than attempting to domesticate the Indian, they preferred to import false natives . . .

Through Sears, Roebuck & Co., you can obtain "rotating scenic lamps of thrilling interest," "plastic cylinders, bronze-plated metal armature. The heat of the lamp makes the inner cylinder revolve, creating living scenes of a dramatic beauty. Ideal for the bedroom. Choose from:
– rocket planes: the new modern 'Jets' soaring through the sky with their vapor trails, moving clouds,
– historic trains: rediscover the age of steam locomotion . . . the smoke flows past, the wheels turn, the landscape changes,

– Niagara Falls: the thrilling cascade of water in a familiar setting, beloved by young and old alike."

ASHLAND, NEBRASKA.

They crossed Iowa to enter Nebraska.

Signal Butte.

Henslow's sparrow that often sings throughout the night, on a piece of moss-covered dead wood in front of a spray of spigelia and a sprig of phlox.

LEBANON.

Yellow light.

LEBANON, SOUTH DAKOTA.

LEBANON, Smith County, KANSAS.

Their black-Bible black preachers.

Of course the African continent was frightening, but at least its existence had been known for centuries, and above all, these imported Blacks were severed from all communication with that disquieting reservoir of power; were completely disarmed, pure of all complicity with these new rivers, these new birds; were even more out of place than we Whites. Their subjugation was quite easy; they could be made into absolute inferiors, the very image of that inequality we Whites dreamed of reestablishing in our favor in Europe . . .

The Spiritualist church.

LEBANON.

Thus they served to protect us from the Indian eyes, the Indian stare, the Indian scandal. Between this land that said, "No, you are not in Europe," and that we tried to make into Europe, and ourselves, we stretched this black screen . . .

Their black priests in black cassocks.

Lake Taneycomo.

> **LEBANON.**
>
> *Night in Chicago.*
>
> *The trains going to Baltimore.*
> *The trains coming from Wichita.*
>
> *Chez Paul, roast duck.*

Carlinville Lake.

> **LEBANON.**
>
> *The woods at night.*

Bean Blossom Lake.

LEBANON.

The lakes at night.

Telephone ringing.

A pair of worm-eating warblers, on a pokeberry branch.

> **WASHINGTON,** Franklin County.
>
> *How well they have succeeded in making our white religion black in their churches painted a white blacker than black. This screen was not only interposed between America and ourselves, but also between Europe and ourselves, between our religion and ourselves . . .*
>
> "Hello, I want Lebanon, Nebraska."

The illuminated face of Elizabeth Taylor.

> WASHINGTON, Tazewell County, ILLINOIS.
>
> *Cloud Room, pastry.*
>
> *The trains going to Miami.*
> *The trains coming from Tucson.*
>
> *Night over Lake Michigan.*
>
> A De Soto (65 miles).

Perseus.

> WASHINGTON, county seat of Daviess County, INDIANA.
>
> *The streets at night.*
>
> Lake Adams, Lake Hamilton.

The illuminated face of Burt Lancaster.

> WASHINGTON, county seat of Fayette County, OHIO.
>
> *The railroad stations at night.*
>
> *Telephone ringing.*

DANVILLE, Harper County.

Was it not hypocritical Europe who profited most of all from the slave trade?

We profited only from their labor. But Europe was scandalized when it heard its own doings discussed. Europe said: "How right we were to drive them away!" . . .

We taught them to write, out of the kindness of our hearts, and all they did was cover themselves with ink.

"Hello, I want Ashland, Kansas."

DANVILLE, Montgomery County, MISSOURI.

A screen which has even separated us from that new Europe which had been established in the northeast. They exclaimed: "We are pure, they are the ones who are guilty of these abominations! From which they profited . . ."

All books for us are tinged with black.

Esso.

       DANVILLE, county seat of Vermilion County, Lincoln's state.

The trains going to Lincoln.
    A shot!
Don the Beachcomber, world's greatest collection of rum drinks.
    A spot of blood!
The trains coming from Tulsa.
    Help!
Night over the slaughterhouses.

Flying Service.

       DANVILLE, county seat of Hendricks County.

Night over the prairies.

James, Gage and Wall Lakes.

DANVILLE, Knox County.

Night over all the churches.

Telephone ringing.

A pair of prairie warblers on a spray of buffalo grass.

    ASHLAND, Boone County.

Colors have begun to bloom on their shirts and blouses, but the word color *had started to mean black.*

They have become a multitude, and have begun to send down roots; a kind of complicity has been established between them and this continent.

"Hello, I want Washington, Missouri."

The Swan.

        ASHLAND, Cass County.

Night over the caryatids of the 1893 World's Fair, which today decorate the Museum of Natural History.
        Whistles!
The trains leaving for Santa Fe.
        Escape!
Empire Room, Creole dishes.
        Motorcycles.
The trains coming from Portland.

        Canton Lake and Springfield Lake.

The illuminated face of Kirk Douglas.

    RICHMOND.

The Lyre.

    RICHMOND.

The illuminated face of Cary Grant.

        RICHMOND.

The Charioteer.

        RICHMOND.—When it is eight o'clock in

RICHMOND,

        eight o'clock in
RICHMOND.

Night over the water.

        RICHMOND.

. The parks at night.

DANVILLE, county seat of Boyle County.

The meadows at night.

        DANVILLE, county seat of Vermilion County.

The bars at night.

LEBANON, county seat of Marion County, KENTUCKY.

The noise of the water at night.

        LEBANON, Saint Clair County, ILLINOIS.

The lights of the city at night.

ASHLAND. State Flower: goldenrod.

A cigar.

        ASHLAND. State Flower: wood violet.

A glass of beer.

        ASHLAND.

        Television.

        LIVINGSTON, ILLINOIS.

        Someone else's television.

Green light.

        LIVINGSTON, Grant County.

        Are you turning out the light?

Yellow light.

        MARION, county seat of Williamson County. State Bird: cardinal.

        They turn out the light.

The reflections of the stoplights in the chromium of the automobiles.

        MARION, Waupaca County, WISCONSIN.

        Blues.

The reflections of the stoplights in the dark shopwindows.

        PRINCETON, county seat of Bureau County.

        Echo of the blues.

The reflections of the headlights in the shopwindows.

> PRINCETON, Green Lake County.

> *They've been asleep a long time in Europe.*

The reflections of the headlights in the chromium of the other cars.

> BENTON.

The reflections of the street lamps in the shopwindows.

> BENTON.

BENTON, county seat of Marshall, KENTUCKY.

The wave of sleep that washes in from the Atlantic.

> BENTON.

> *The wave of troubled sleep that flows from Kentucky into Missouri.*

> BENTON, KANSAS.

> *The wave of haunted sleep that flows from Missouri into Kansas.*

JACKSON. State Bird: cardinal.

The heavy wave of interrupted sleep that flows from Virginia into Kentucky.

> JACKSON, MISSOURI.

> *The echo of the blues.*

> FRANKLIN.

COVINGTON, KENTUCKY.

He stirs in his sleep.

> COVINGTON.
>
> *The thick wave of contaminated sleep that flows from Ohio into Indiana.*
>
> COVINGTON.
>
> *The long wave of numbing sleep that flows from Ontario into Michigan.*

FRANKLIN, county seat of Johnson County.

Blues variation.

The Herdsman.

> DANVILLE, county seat of Hendricks County, INDIANA.

She stirs in her sleep.

The illuminated face of Jane Russell.

> LEBANON, county seat of Boone County. State Flower: zinnia.

She's dreaming.

The Lion.

> MARION, county seat of Grant County, INDIANA.

She's dreaming that she's walking alone in the dark night.

The illuminated face of Yul Brynner.

> MARION, Osceola County.
>
> *Fading blues.*

Berenice's Hair.

> PRINCETON, county seat of Gibson County.

> *That she's walking in a part of her city she's never seen . . .*

The illuminated face of Charlton Heston.

> PRINCETON, in huge, almost empty Marquette County, MICHIGAN.

> *He stirs in his sleep.*

The Smaller Lion.

> RICHMOND.

The illuminated face of Marlon Brando.

> RICHMOND, Macomb County, Wolverine State.

> *He's dreaming.*

MANCHESTER, county seat of Clay County, bourbon state.

Dreaming.

> MANCHESTER.

> *The wave of sleep that flows from Pennsylvania.*

> MANCHESTER, Washtenaw County.

> *He's dreaming he owns a car.*

JACKSON, county seat of Jackson County.

Blues coming back.

The Crab.

> JACKSON.

The sound of a car taking a curve.

> LEBANON, county seat of Warren County, OHIO.

Stirs in his sleep.

The Water Monster.

> RICHMOND, Buckeye State.

He dreams he's driving . . .

The sound of a branch cracking.

> FRANKLIN, Warren County, OHIO.

Faster than his father ever drove . . .

The Lesser Dog.

> DANVILLE. State Flower: scarlet carnation.

That the trees, the lakes, the cities rush by . . .

A dog howling.

> ASHLAND, county seat of Ashland County, OHIO.

That he has reached the shining mountains . . .

The Twins.

> COVINGTON, Miami County.

That he sees gold, and Indians around this gold, all befeathered, and that he kills them, kills them . . .

The sound of a spring.

MARION.

MARION, KENTUCKY.

That there are no more Indians, no more gold, that he is covered with blood, that he has turned black . . .

MARION.

"Notes on the State of Virginia":
". . . To these objections, which are political, may be added others which are physical and moral. The first difference which strikes us is that of color. Whether the black of the Negro resides in the reticular membrane between the skin and scarf-skin, or in the scarf-skin itself; whether it proceeds from the color of the blood, the color of the bile, or from that of some other secretion, the difference is fixed in nature, and is as real as if its seat and cause were better known to us. And is this difference of no importance? Is it not the foundation of a greater or less share of beauty in the two races? . . ."

Thomas Jefferson

        also wrote:
"*I was written to in 1785 (being then in Paris) by directors appointed to superintend the building of a Capitol in Richmond, to advise them as to a plan, and to add to it one of a Prison. Thinking it a favorable opportunity of introducing into the State an example of architecture, in the classic style of antiquity, and the Maison Quarrée of Nismes, an ancient Roman temple, being considered as the most perfect model existing of what may be called Cubic architecture, I applied to M. Clerissault, who had published drawings of the Antiquities of Nismes, to have me a model of the building made in stucco, only changing the order from Corinthian to Ionic, on account of the difficulty of the Corinthian capitals . . ."*
                                          "Autobiography."

The sea at night.

FRANKLIN, Southampton County.

The beaches at night.

"*Autobiography*":
"... *I yielded, with reluctance, to the taste of Clerissault, in his preference of the modern capital of Scamozzi to the more noble capital of antiquity. This was executed by the artist whom Choiseul Gouffier had carried with him to Constantinople, and employed, while Ambassador there, in making those beautiful models of the remains of Grecian architecture which are to be seen at Paris . . .*"
Thomas Jefferson.

"*. . . Are not the fine mixtures of red and white, the expressions of every passion by greater or less suffusions of color in the one, preferable to that eternal monotony, which reigns in the countenances, that immovable veil of black which covers the emotions of the other race? Add to these, flowing hair, a more elegant symmetry of form, their own judgment in favor of the whites, declared by their preference of them, as uniformly as is the preference of the Oran-utan for the black woman over those of his own species. The circumstance of superior beauty is thought worthy attention in the propagation of our horses, dogs, and other domestic animals; why not in that of man? . . .*"
"Notes on the State of Virginia."

The sound of an animal running.

COVINGTON, county seat of Alleghany County, VIRGINIA.

"*Notes on the State of Virginia*":
"*. . . Besides those of color, figure, and hair, there are other physical distinctions proving a difference of race. They have less hair on the face and body. They secrete less by the kidneys, and more by the glands of the skin, which gives them a very strong and disagreeable odor. This greater de-*

gree of transpiration, renders them more tolerant of heat and less so of cold than the whites. Perhaps, too, a difference of structure in the pulmonary apparatus, which a late ingenious experimentalist has discovered to be the principal regulator of animal heat, may have disabled them from extricating, in the act of inspiration, so much of that fluid from the outer air, or obliged them in expiration, to part with more of it. They seem to require less sleep . . ."

The harbors at night.

Letter from Thomas Jefferson to John Fabroni, his music teacher:
". . . If there is a gratification, which I envy any people in this world, it is to your country its music. This is the favorite passion of my soul, and fortune has cast my lot in a country where it is in a state of deplorable barbarism. From the line of life in which we conjecture you to be, I have for some time lost the hope of seeing you here. Should the event prove so, I shall ask your assistance in procuring a substitute, who may be a proficient in singing, &c., on the Harpsichord. I should be contented to receive such an one two or three years hence, when it is hoped he may come more safely and find here a plenty of those useful things which commerce alone can furnish. . . ."
June 8, 1778.

The Unicorn.

ASHLAND, Old Dominion.

Thomas Jefferson to John Fabroni:
". . . The bounds of an American fortune will not admit the indulgence of a domestic band of musicians, yet I have thought that a passion for music might be reconciled with that economy we are obliged to observe. I retain among my domestic servants a gardener (Ortolano), a weaver (Tessitore di lino e lin), a cabinet-maker (Stipeltaro), and a stone-cutter (Scalpellino lavorante in piano), to which I would add a vigneron. In a country where, like yours, music is cultivated and practiced by every class of men, I suppose there

might be found persons of these trades who could perform on the French horn, clarinet, or hautboy, and bassoon, so that one might have a band of two French horns, two clarinets, two hautboys, and a bassoon, without enlarging their domestic expenses. A certainty of employment for a half dozen years, and at the end of that time, to find them, if they chose, a conveyance to their own country, might induce them to come here on reasonable wages . . ."
June 8, 1778.

The swamps at night.

". . . A black after hard labor through the day, will be induced by the slightest amusements to sit up till midnight, or later, though knowing he must be out with first dawn of the morning. They are at least as brave and more adventuresome. But this may perhaps proceed from a want of forethought, which prevents their seeing a danger till it be present. When present, they do not go through it with more coolness or steadiness than the whites . . ."
"Notes on the State of Virginia."

The sound of a conversation.

DANVILLE, Pittsylvania County, VIRGINIA.

"Notes on the State of Virginia":
". . . They are more ardent after their female; but love seems with them to be more an eager desire, than a tender delicate mixture of sentiment and sensation. Their griefs are transient. Those numberless afflictions, which render it doubtful whether heaven has given life to us in mercy or in wrath, are less felt and sooner forgotten with them. In general, their existence appears to participate more of sensation than reflection. To this must be ascribed their disposition to sleep when abstracted from their diversions, and unemployed in labor. An animal whose body is at rest, and who does not reflect must be disposed to sleep of course . . ."
Thomas Jefferson.

"... Without meaning to give you trouble, perhaps it might be practicable for you, in your ordinary intercourse with your people, to find out such men disposed to come to America. Sobriety and good nature would be desirable parts of their characters . . ."
To John Fabroni, June 8, 1778.

The eyes at night.

Orion.

LEBANON, county seat of Russell County.

The smells at night.

"Notes on the State of Virginia":
". . . Comparing them by their faculties of memory, reason, and imagination, it appears to me that in memory they are equal to the whites; in reason much inferior, as I think one could scarcely be found capable of tracing and comprehending the investigations of Euclid; and that in imagination they are dull, tasteless, and anomalous. It would be unfair to follow them to Africa for this investigation. We will consider them here, on the same stage with the whites, and where the facts are not apocryphal on which a judgment is to be formed. It will be right to make great allowances for the difference of condition, of education, of conversation, of the sphere in which they move. Many millions of them have been brought to, and born in America. Most of them, indeed, have been confined to tillage, to their own homes, and their own society; yet many have been so situated, that they might have availed themselves of the conversation of their masters; many have been brought up to the handicraft arts, and from that circumstance have always been associated with the whites. Some have been liberally educated, and all have lived in countries where the arts and sciences are cultivated to a considerable degree, and all have had before their eyes samples of the best works from abroad . . ."

At Monticello, Thomas Jefferson built the house of his dreams.

The sound of the wind.

> RICHMOND, the state capital, where you can order chocolate ice cream in the Howard Johnson Restaurant.

> PRINCETON, county seat of Caldwell County, in the state where the gold is kept at Fort Knox, where it never leaves its vaults.

He wakes with a start . . .

> PRINCETON, WEST VIRGINIA.

> *The wave of sleep that flows from Virginia.*

> FRANKLIN.

FRANKLIN, county seat of Simpson County.

He calls . . .

> FRANKLIN.

> *The wave of soiled sleep that flows from North Carolina.*

> FRANKLIN.

> *The wave of warm black sleep that flows from Georgia.*

> JACKSON, county seat of Madison County.

> *The mountains at night.*

The Bull.

> JACKSON, Clarke County, ALABAMA.

> *The sea at night.*

They finish their dinner.

COVINGTON, county seat of Tipton County, TENNESSEE.

Continuous blues.

The Whale.

BENTON, Volunteer State.

He stirs in his sleep.

They are watching television.

LEBANON, county seat of Wilson County, TENNESSEE.

Dreaming he is lost in the woods . . .

The Ram.

MANCHESTER, county seat of Coffee County.

That the woods are inhabited by eyes . . .

They turn off the television.

MANCHESTER, Walker County.

Blues.

The Triangle.

LIVINGSTON.

They turn off the light.

LIVINGSTON.—When it is nine o'clock in LIVINGSTON,

    nine o'clock in
LIVINGSTON.

What are you afraid of?

The sea at night.

    LIVINGSTON, TEXAS.

  Tell me, what are you afraid of?

  The desert at night.

FRANKLIN, county seat of Saint Mary County.

There are almost no Indians any more; the Negroes are in bed . . .

The indigo sea, the foam of sugar and cotton.

    FRANKLIN.

COVINGTON, county seat of Saint Tammany Parish, LOUISIANA.

They play the guitar, they sing . . .

The currents of the Negro-colored Father of Waters.

JACKSON, East Feliciana Parish.

Don't be afraid, go to sleep . . .

    JONESBORO, ARKANSAS.—When it is ten o'clock in
JONESBORO,

              already eleven o'clock in
JONESBORO, Eastern Time.

The wave of sleep that flows from New Brunswick.

MANCHESTER, Kennebec County, MAINE.

The rocks, the islands at night.

             MANCHESTER, NEW HAMPSHIRE, where you can order
                      lemon ice cream in the Howard Johnson Restau-
             rant.

The wave of aerated sleep that flows from Maine.

             MANCHESTER, VERMONT.

The silent wave of sleep that flows from New Hampshire.

                    MANCHESTER, NEW YORK.

The irresistible wave of sleep that flows from Vermont.

HANCOCK, Hancock County.

He dreams he's putting out to sea.

               HANCOCK.

The fish.

               HANCOCK.

They're coming home from the movies.

                        HANCOCK.—When it is midnight in

OXFORD,

midnight in
OXFORD.

The most important religious practice of the American Europeans is the pilgrimage to the sacred city of Washington, where the principal temples and the essential government organizations are located.

The Washington Monument, illuminated.

The quasi-rectangular territory of this city (it is well known what fundamental value the American Europeans have attached to the right angle) is an enclave within the state of Maryland, but forms no part of it. It is a space apart. Its inhabitants do not participate in the "elections," the most famous of the political ceremonies of the other American citizens.

The Jefferson Memorial, illuminated.

The very name of this site without a site, District of Columbia, underlines its extraterritoriality: it refers, in fact, to a European of another language who never settled on this continent, but heralded its appearance out of the unknown.

The Lincoln Memorial, illuminated.

The name Washington actually designates the whole group of institutions and monuments. It refers to a skillful general who assumed command of operations during the War of Independence, and was quickly accorded divine status.

The Capitol, illuminated.

The man was admirable in every respect, and the pious continue to visit his lovely home, Mount Vernon; but he obviously bore little relation to the divinity which had taken him as its instrument and which is today designated by his name. Thus, if that divinity is occasionally celebrated with the latter's features, in the city of Washington itself, it is nonetheless felt that any human figuration would be almost blasphemous, and the god is represented in the form of an enormous obelisk.

The White House, illuminated.

Through this obelisk passes an east-west axis joining the palace of the Capitol to the temple of Lincoln. A little west of the obelisk passes the other branch of the cross, an axis joining the palace of the White House to the temple of Jefferson.

The Supreme Court, illuminated.

It is this arrangement, both political and symbolic, which is the soul of the United States of America.

General Lee's mansion, illuminated.

The three divinities Washington, Jefferson and Lincoln are the most important in the American pantheon; hence it is not surprising to find them carved in colossal proportions on Mount Rushmore, South Dakota. The American Europeans consider the artisan who executed this work to have given evidence of the greatest piety.

The Treasury Department, illuminated.

He added the representation of another god, Theodore Roosevelt, but most theologians today agree in regarding this as a mistake of perspective. Theodore Roosevelt certainly does not play a part comparable to that of the three great gods in the American European pantheon. The man who might be considered to come closest to them is Benjamin Franklin. His principal temple is located in Philadelphia, Pennsylvania, and is called the Franklin Institute . .

OXFORD, PENNSYLVANIA.

Treaty of William Penn with the Delaware Indians:
". . . I have already taken care that none of my People wrong you, by good Laws I have provided for that purpose, nor will I ever allow any of my people to sell Rumme to make your people drunk. If anything should be out of order, report when I come, it shall be mended, and I will bring you some things of our Country that are useful and pleasing to you. So I rest in the Love of our God that made us. I am

England 25:2$^{mo.}$: 1682.   *Your Loveing Friend,*
                                       W$^{m.}$ PENN
I read this to the Indians
by an interpreter the 6$^{mo.}$ 1682.
     Tho. Holme"

"Information to Those Who Would Remove to America":
". . . The Truth is, that though there are in that Country few People so miserable as the Poor of Europe, there are also very few that in Europe would be called rich; it is rather a general happy Mediocrity that prevails. There are few great Proprietors of the Soil, and few Tenants; most People cultivate their own lands, or follow some Handicraft or Merchandise; very few rich enough to live idly upon their Rents or Incomes, or to pay the high Prices given in Europe for Paintings, Statues, Architecture, and other Works of Art, that are more curious than useful. Hence the natural Geniuses, that have arisen in America with such Talents, have uniformly quitted that Country for Europe, where they can be more suitably rewarded . . ."
     Benjamin Franklin.

The fireflies that rose in the air at night, near Bryn Mawr.

OXFORD, NEW YORK.

MANCHESTER, Carroll County, MARYLAND.

If, in the case of Washington, the attribution of divinity was expressed by recourse to a geometric shape, in the case of Lincoln and of Jefferson, and also in the case of Franklin in Philadelphia, the pious were content to enlarge the human figure to monumental proportions.

Party at the French Embassy.

This is because with regard to Lincoln and Jefferson it was indispensable to preserve the fundamental element of the gaze, for the representatives of the various states who come to settle their differences in the palace called the Capitol (after a hill in Rome, Italy, on which stood a temple of Jupiter) do not pray to Abraham Lincoln, but it is he who, sitting in a huge armchair, his hands on a level with his shoulders, his expression one of exhaustion, continually regards them past the Washington obelisk reflected by a mirror of water.

Party at the English Embassy.

The pilgrims, who are known as tourists, come to confirm this regard, which comforts them because they mistrust their representatives, and to photograph it in order to bring its image home with them.

Party at the German Embassy.

Thomas Jefferson, standing in the center of his rotunda, stares, for his part, at the palace of the White House, residence of the President of the United States. The American Europeans doubtless believe that the President needs a still closer surveillance, or else that Thomas Jefferson's regard was less pure, less piercing than that of Abraham Lincoln, for they have arranged matters so that the monument to Washington is slightly to the east of the Jefferson-White House axis, so that it does not impede the optical trajectory.

Party at the Russian Embassy.

All these monuments are naturally of a dazzling whiteness.

Party at the Embassy of the Union of South Africa.

The most favorable time for the pilgrimage to Washington is considered to be the beginning of April, when the cherry trees, a gift to the Nation from across the Pacific, blossom around the basin in which is reflected, seen from the White House, the temple or monument to Jefferson.

     Party at the Japanese Embassy.

On this occasion, the steps of the temple are transformed into a kind of theater, where dances and songs are performed.

     Party at the Greek Embassy.

When the cherry trees have not yet blossomed on the day established for this festival, a lively consternation can be discerned on the faces of the pilgrims. It is evident that this is regarded as a bad omen. Therefore, during the last days of March, they can be seen walking among the trees, examining them with anxiety, begging them in their hearts to let their buds bloom.

     Party at the White House.

These essential organizations are extended by many other, secondary ones. Thus the sacred papers are preserved in a temple called the National Archives. The Declaration of Independence, the Constitution of the United States, the Bill of Rights are sealed within bronze vessels filled with helium; special filters protect them against the damaging effect of light rays; the reliquaries in which they are shown are constructed that they can instantaneously sink within deep vaults, safe from bombs, fire and shock . . .

    MANCHESTER.

The Dolphin.

    MANCHESTER.

MANCHESTER, Washington County.

Some believe that the extraordinary power of Abraham Lincoln's gaze must be related to the fact that he was assassinated in the very city of Washington when he was President. The murder occurred in a theater today carefully preserved. The famous whimsical comedy "Our American Cousin" was being performed. The actor John Wilkes Booth opened the door of the box, fired his pistol, leaped onto the stage, breaking his left leg, and shouted: "Sic semper tyrannis!" Now since every city in the United States was founded on some recent murder laboriously but energetically forgotten, Lincoln's murder managed to give this obscure primordial murder a stunning representation. Lincoln became, for the American Europeans, the very image of the victim, of their victim. The eyes of his statue gleam with all that blood.

Mrs. Washington.

Women play a secondary part in this system, though they are not absent from it.

Mrs. Adams.

In one of the buildings along the Lincoln-Capitol axis, borrowing the details of its architecture from various Gothic edifices, the Smithsonian Institution, the conscientious pilgrim will pause to meditate before the mannequins representing the First Ladies, that is, the wives of the Presidents, dressed in their actual gowns.

Mrs. Jefferson.

The ceremonies and sacred objects of the American Europeans are perhaps less finished than those of the Hopi or Zuni Indians, but they represent nonetheless a totality of the same order that succeeds in connecting not hundreds but millions of individuals.

Mrs. Madison.

The magical power of these monuments is such that many American Europeans, even cultivated ones, attribute architectural qualities to them.

Mrs. Monroe.

It is well known that the American Europeans also practice other religions all derived from the religion they had before having left Europe. But the schisms which had provoked the departure of the first pioneers multiplied with great rapidity in the new Europe, and this earlier religion was divided into increasingly numerous sects, of increasingly imprecise dogmatic and ritual content.

Mrs. Jackson.

The religion of Washington is the only one to be practiced by all the American Europeans.

Mrs. Lincoln.

The dust of the Christian religions, if it plays an essential part in the mental economy of this nation, is above all an expression of nostalgia for Europe.

Mrs. Theodore Roosevelt.

The inability to relate in any exact manner the two halves of their religious attitude unfortunately provokes among many American Europeans a kind of generalized numbness . . .

When it is one A.M. in

CAMBRIDGE,

132   Mobile

one o'clock in
CAMBRIDGE, where you can order strawberry ice cream in the Howard Johnson Restaurant.

The trial of Susanna Martin, held at Salem, June 29, 1692:
"1) Susanna Martin pleading Not Guilty against the accusation of witchcraft brought against her, there were produced the testimonies of numerous persons sensibly and grievously Bewitched; who all accused the Prisoner at the bar of being the one whom they believed to be the Cause of their Miseries. Then as in the other Trials, there was produced an extraordinary Effort, on the part of the Powers of Witchcraft, with cruel and frequent Outbursts, to prevent the poor Sufferers to produce their Plaints, which the Court was reduced to obtaining by long Patience, with great endurance and attention . . ."

CAMBRIDGE.

SPRINGFIELD, where you can order raspberry ice cream in the Howard Johnson Restaurant.

"2) Then a summation was given of what had passed during the first Questioning before the magistrates. Her Eye flinging to the ground those on whom she cast it, whether these latter perceived it or not; here is one of the Dialogues between the Magistrates and the prisoner at the bar:

Magistrate: What ails this people?
Martin: I do not know.

Magistrate: But what do you think?
Martin: I do not desire to spend my judgment upon it.
Magistrate: Do not you think they are bewitcht?
Martin: No I do not think they are.
Magistrate: Tell me your thoughts about them.
Martin: Why my thoughts are my own, when they are in, but when they are out they are another's.
Magistrate: You said their Master—who do you think is their master?
Martin: If they be dealing in the black art you may know as well as I.
Magistrate: Well what have you done toward this?
Martin: Nothing.
Magistrate: Why it is you or your appearance.
Martin: I cannot help it.
Magistrate: That may be your master . . . How comes your appearance just now to hurt these?
Martin: How do I know? . . . He that appeared in Sam: shape a gloryfied saint can appear in any one's shape.

Then it was discovered in her as among her kind that if the afflicted came to approach her, they were flung to the Ground. And when she was asked the reason for this, she declared: I cannot tell: It may be the Devil bears me more malice than another . . ."

SPRINGFIELD, Windsor County, VERMONT.

A male and two female nighthawks, on a white oak branch.

WARREN, Washington County.

Green light.

MANCHESTER.

MANCHESTER, Essex County, MASSACHUSETTS.

"3) The Court determined, alarmed by these Things, to continue further the Conversation with the Prisoner at the bar; and to see how the accusations might be reinforced. Upon which John Allen, of Salisbury, testified That upon his refusal, in consideration of the weakness of his Oxen, to drag off Stones at the request of this Martin, she, angered, declared: It would have been better he had, for his oxen would never serve him *more. Upon which the Witness declared: Dost threaten me, thou old witch? Resolving to throw her into the brook. To avoid this she flew over the bridge and so escaped. But as he was coming home one of his own oxn tired that he was forst to unyok him to get him home. And after they were com home, put the sd oxn to Salsbury beach where several other oxn usually are putt where they had Long rang of meadow to feed on and where catl did use to gett flesh, but in a few days all the oxn upon the beach we found by their tracks were gon to the mouth of the River Merrimack but not returned from whence we thought they were run into the sd river. Those that sought them they did use all immaginall Gentleness to them to some acquaintance which some of them seemed to attend, being found, but all on a sudaine away they all ran with such violence as if theyr motion had been dyabolical till they came neer the mouth of the Merrimack River and then turned to the right hand and ran right into the sea all but two old Oxn. And then one of them came bak againe with such swiftness as was amazing to the beholders who stood redy to receive him and help his tired carcase up, but letting him Loose away he ran up into the island, and from there through the marshes up into Newbury towne and so up into their woods and there was after a while found near to Amesbury. So that of: 14 good oxn only that was saved the rest were all cast up some at Cape Anne some in one place and some in other, they only had their hides . . ."*

MANCHESTER, where you can order gooseberry ice cream in the Howard Johnson Restaurant, NEW HAMPSHIRE.

A pair of saw-whet owls, the male on a branch, head turned to the right, the female on a small mound, bill open, a mouse held in her right talon.

WARREN.

WARREN, Worcester, Bay State.

"4) John Atkinson testified that he Exchanged a cow of his with a Son of Susanna Martin, that she muttered and was unwilling that this deponent should have ye Cow. I came to bring the cow home notwithstanding hamstringing of her and halting her she was so madd thatt we could scarce gett her along, butt she broke all the ropes fastened to her we putt the halter two or three times round a tree which she broke and ran away which could only be Witchcraft . . ."

WARREN, RHODE ISLAND.

The long-eared owl with its orange eye.

WARREN.

A pair of burrowing owls.

MANCHESTER, where you can order plum ice cream in the Howard Johnson Restaurant, CONNECTICUT.

Yellow light.

CLINTON.

CLINTON, Worcester County.

"5) Bernard Peache testified that Being in bed on a Lord's Day night he heard a scrabbling at the window he this deponent saw Susanna Martin come in at the window and jump down upon the floor. Coming up to this deponents feet and took hold of them and drew up his body into a hoope and lay upon him about an hour and a half or two hours in all which time this deponent could not stir nor speak but feeling himself beginning to be loosened or lightened he beginning to strive he put out his hand among the clothes and took hold of her hand and brought it up to his mouthe and bitt three of the fingers (as he judged) to the breaking of the bones which done the said Martin went out of the Chamber downe the stairs and out of the door. This deponent called to the people of the house and told them what was done and did also follow her, but the people did not see her. But without the door there was a buket on the left hand side and there was a drop of blood on the handle too and more upon the snow for there was a little flight of snow and there were the print of her two feet, about a foot without the threshall but no more footing did appear.

He further deposeth that some time after this as he supposeth about three weeks after the said Martin desired this deponent to come and husk corn at her house the next Lord's Day night, saying that if I did not come it were better that I did. But this deponent did not go being then

Living with Nahum Osgood of the said Salisbury and that night Lodged in the barne upon the hay and about an hour or two in the night the said Susana Martin and another came out of the shop into the barne and one of them said here he is and then came towards this deponent, he having a quarter staff made a blow at them but the rooff of the barne prevented it and they went away but this deponent followed them and as they were going toward the window made another blow at them and struck them both down but away they went out at the shop window and this deponent saw no more of them.

And the Rumor went that the said Martin had a broken hand at that time but the deponent cannot speake to that upon his own knowledge.

The said Peache testified also of the Bewitchment unto death of the Catl, due to the anger of said Martin . . ."

   CLINTON.

The European little owl, the bird that for more than two thousand years has been associated with Pallas Athena, goddess of wisdom.

   MANCHESTER, NEW YORK.

Red light.

   CAMBRIDGE.—When it is two A.M. in

OXFORD,

OXFORD.   two o'clock in

Long night.

OXFORD.

A pair of pygmy owls.

CLINTON, Rock County.

SPRINGFIELD, Calhoun County.

He's asleep.

SPRINGFIELD, Walworth County, WISCONSIN.

Then, from all the reservations, tremendous accumulators, spread waves of dreams . . .

JACKSON, county seat of Jackson County, MICHIGAN.

Sleep.

JACKSON, Washington County.

The short-eared owl.

WARRENS.

WARREN, Wolverine State.

The rustling of the reeds at night.

    WARREN.

RICHMOND, Macomb County, MICHIGAN.

Start.

    RICHMOND, county seat of Wayne County.

    RICHMOND.

PRINCETON, apple blossom state.

Sleep.

    PRINCETON, county seat of Gibson County, INDIANA.

    He smiles in his sleep.

        PRINCETON, county seat of Caldwell County.

NEWPORT, Monroe County, MICHIGAN.

Eye.

    NEWPORT, county seat of Vermillion County.

        NEWPORT, county seat of Campbell County, KENTUCKY.

    NEWPORT.

A pair of screech owls with their young on a branch of Jersey pine.

    CLINTON.

Algol.

CLINTON, county seat of Hickman County.

Red light.

CLINTON, county seat of Anderson County, TENNESSEE.

The glow of a factory.

CLINTON, ALABAMA.

CLINTON, Lenawee County.

Murmurs.

CLINTON.

A pair of great horned owls.

JACKSON, county seat of Jackson County.

JACKSON, county seat of Breathitt County.

JACKSON, county seat of Madison County.

JACKSON.

The barred owl, on a branch, threatening a gray squirrel.

NEWPORT, Shelby County, and

NEWPORT, Madison County, OHIO.

Eye.

The silence of the night.

RICHMOND, Buckeye State.

Horns.

Vega.

        SPRINGFIELD, OHIO.

    Teeth.

Altair.

        SPRINGFIELD.

Arcturus.

            SPRINGFIELD.

Betelgeuse.

      WARREN, county seat of Trumbull County. State Flower: scarlet carnation.

Aldebaran.

      OXFORD, Butler County.

Regulus.

      MONTROSE.—When it is three A.M. in

MONTROSE,

        still two o'clock in
MONTROSE, Central Time.

        MONTROSE, SOUTH DAKOTA.

SPRINGFIELD, Brown County.

        SPRINGFIELD.

WARREN, county seat of huge and almost empty Marshall County,
    MINNESOTA.

I'm frightened.

RICHMOND, Gopher State.

No, don't be frightened, go back to sleep . . .

NEWPORT, MINNESOTA.

Eye,
        horns,
                muzzles,
                        hair,
                                lips,

a black tongue,
 a black hand approaching,
  I'm paralyzed by that stare,
the whirling waters,
 a field in flames,
  horses crossing the lake,
they're waiting for me,
 they want to make me dive into that mud,
and they're sneering . . .

PRINCETON, Benton County. State Flower: moccasin flower,—White Earth Indian Reservation.

Sneering . . .

    PRINCETON, IOWA.

A pair of snowy owls on the trunk of a dead tree, against a stormy night sky with a single moonlit edge of cloud.

    MONTROSE.

The murmurs at night.

    MONTROSE, MISSOURI.

CLEVELAND, Le Sueur County.

    CLEVELAND, NORTH DAKOTA.

The great gray owl, with its concentric circles around the eyes.

    CLEVELAND, WISCONSIN.

A pair of Richardson's owls, the male in profile with its yellow eye accented by a tuft of hair near the bill.

    JACKSON.—When it is three A.M. in

JACKSON,

three o'clock in
JACKSON.

They're asleep.

Old River Lake at night, former meander of the Father of Waters.

    JACKSON, LOUISIANA.

A pair of monkey-faced barn owls, the male pinioning a chipmunk with its left talon, against a black sky above a meandering, crepuscular river seen from a great height.

    CLINTON.

CLINTON, Hinds County.

They're not all asleep, they're prowling. I catch sight of one looking at me through the window, and his eyes gleam so brightly that my sheets burn . . .

Lake Bolivar and Lake Lee at night, former tributaries of the Father of Waters.

    CLINTON, ARKANSAS.

        CLINTON, OKLAHOMA.

Sea-surge at night.

    CLINTON, TENNESSEE.

        CLINTON, KENTUCKY.

            CLINTON, INDIANA.

                CLINTON, MICHIGAN.

The sea, a hurricane of dreams from the sea, a shoal of dreams that flows up the Father of Waters.

    JACKSON.

The sighs of the night.

        JACKSON.

The desires of the night.

            JACKSONS.

The terrors of the night.

                JACKSON.

The screams of the night.

    JACKSON.

All the feathers of the night.

        JACKSON, GEORGIA.

All the scales of the night.

            JACKSON, SOUTH CAROLINA.

Men covered with feathers,
> men covered with scales,
>> men covered with hair,
men covered with tar that smells so strong . . .

CLEVELAND, county seat of Bolivar County, MISSISSIPPI.

It's not possible, he's opening the window, stepping in, and I cannot scream in my nightgown, I can't take a step, I try to pull up the sheet to cover myself. Outside a million mosquitoes hum . . .

Beulah, Horseshoe and Moon Lakes at night, former meanders of the Father of Waters.

FULTON, county seat of Itawamba County.

Each of his footsteps leaves a print of ashes; his nails are green as carabid beetle wing-cases; his teeth shine like turquoises in his black mouth. I smell his breath approaching me, scorching me. I smell in his odor all the odor of the woods, the swamps and the river. Then I can no longer even hold the sheets over my breast; despite all my efforts, I know that my fingers are loosening. His face is just over mine. Outside, the magnolia blossoms are opening. He lays his hand on my nightgown; it makes a great, burning patch there. My heart beats in my breast, so fast. He opens his trousers. I tell him: "I love you, I love you, I've never loved anyone but you." Tears fall from his eyes. That mouth presses against my mouth, and I am devoured by flames. That horrible mouth . . .
I'll tell my father to kill you.
There's nothing, only the eddies of the river and the swaying of the magnolia.
That hand burns me, these lips burn me, this whole room burns me.
I can never look at him again without burning.
I'll tell my father to kill him.
There's nothing.
Sleep.

Flower Lake and Swan Lake at night, former meanders of the Father of Waters.

FULTON, Clarke County, ALABAMA.

A howl.

        CLINTON, Greene County.

A whinny.

                GREENVILLE.

A whine.

          GREENVILLE.

A groan.

        GREENVILLE.—When it is four A.M. in GREENVILLE,

four o'clock in
GREENVILLE.

My husband is sleeping beside me.

Fairy Cave.

TROY, county seat of Lincoln County.

He doesn't know my dreams.

Crystal Caverns, Marvel Cave.

      TROY.

A shudder in the grass.

Turns.

      TROY.

Shudder in all these beds.

Tracery.

      TROY.

Loops.

> *A shudder on the lake water.*

> TROY, PA.

> *On the river water.*

Meanders.

> TROY, N.Y.

> *A shudder from the sea.*

Charms.
At night right angles begin vibrating.
The hissing of serpents echoing from square to square.

> HAMILTON, Hancock County.

Green light.

> HAMILTON, IND.

Yellow light.

> HAMILTON, OHIO.

Red light.

> DIXON, county seat of Lee County, ILL.

> *A wave of anxiety from a black district.*

> Through Montgomery Ward you can obtain the "Rhythm Method of Family Happiness," latest edition, by Dr. John P. Murphy, "natural method of planned parenthood. Approved by doctors and churches. Complete information, questions and answers. Easy method to determine cycles. Graphs, tables, illustrations. 212 pages."

The lights of a plane in the sky.

> FULTON, on the Father of Waters, Whiteside County.

The glow of an airport.

> FULTON.

The glow of a fire.

> FULTON.

A lighted window in the country.

> LEXINGTON.

> LEXINGTON, on the Missouri, county seat of Lafayette County, MISSOURI, the Middle West.

My wife is sleeping beside me, I see she's dreaming.

Jacob's Cave, Onondaga Cave, Round Spring Caverns.

> LEXINGTON, where the Howard Johnson Restaurant must be closed still.

> LEXINGTON, VA., Atlantic Coast.

GLASGOW, Show-Me State.

My wife is sleeping beside me, I won't tell her my dreams. She'd say . . . She'd think . . .

Bluff Dwellers Cave, Truitt's Cave,—through Sears, Roebuck & Co., an arsenal of plastic missiles: "31 scale models of American rockets, missiles, satellites . . . With a special 32-page booklet: 'Know Your Missiles,' by the famous Willy Ley . . . and a subscription to the Space Newsletter by the same Willy Ley."

> GLASGOW, Barren County.

The planet Mars.

> GLASGOW.

The planet Jupiter.

> JACKSON, county seat of Breathitt County, KY., the South.
>
> *Don't walk around in the Negro districts; from each of their looks might sprout a hideous dream, and you'll need to drink . . .*

The planet Saturn.

> FULTON.

FULTON, county seat of Callaway, MO.

She'd think I'm not normal; she'd tell me to go see a psychoanalyst. I know she doesn't tell me all her dreams, she'd be afraid that . . .

Meramec Caverns,—or a group of surface-to-surface missiles, page 1038, including an Air Force Snark, and a Marine Regulus, with tractors, launching platforms, officers.

> FULTON.

Over all the hospitals of the prairie flows a long wave of insomnia.

> TROY, county seat of Doniphan County, KANS., Middle West.

The planet Neptune.

> HAMILTON, Greenwood County.

The planet Pluto.

> BUFFALO.

BUFFALO. State Flower: hawthorn.

If only it were possible to start everything over from the beginning, if only the frontier were still open and we could escape this new Europe and found new cities in a different way . . . I'll have to keep quiet before my colleagues and my bosses. They'd think that . . . They'd suspect me of . . . I have a wife and children; they're asleep, dreaming; I see that she's smiling, things are all right in her dream, it's a good night; if only I could sleep; if only . . .

The church of the Latter-Day Saints, called the Mormons,—or a plastic space kit: "space taxi created from the drawings of Willy Ley, with baggage locker, pilot's cabin, hatches fore and aft for guiding the taxi into the space station . . . Plus the model Jupiter C and Vanguard rockets."

   BUFFALO, OKLA.,—the Osage Indian Reservation.

The muffled roar of a bomb test.

   LEXINGTON.

HAMILTON, Caldwell County, MO., Ozark Mountain state.

I'm dreaming of buffalo, herds of horses, Indians of the plains, Latter-Day Saints and their trek across the states to new lands . . . But I'll tell them, even my wife, I'll tell them that I'm dreaming of having money; and if ever . . . , if ever I had money, if ever my bank teller . . . "What's the matter? Why aren't you asleep? What's wrong? You're not acting normal. Why are you looking at me like that? It's almost as if you were looking at me like a . . ."

"Shut up. It's nothing. I'm just the way I always am. Go to sleep, it's only . . ."

Shawnee National Forest.

   HAMILTON, IOWA,—the Tama Indian Reservation.

The dew.

   BUFFALO.

BUFFALO, MINN.,—Leech Lake Indian Reservation.

JACKSON, county seat of Cape Girardeau County.

For a moment I thought . . . He was looking at me; it was just the way it was in my dream. In his eyes there was such greed, such despair; I thought he was going to take me in his arms, bite me, that something in him was going to burst and then what could I have done? He's closed his eyes. His breathing is calmer now. He's white, he's recovered his White Man's face, he's making an effort to smile, he's managed to smile. It happens less and less often. He won't say anything. He won't tell his dreams, he won't guess my dreams; he'll say he's dreaming of money. How scared I was! It was nothing, it was only one of those waves from the Negro districts and the reservations. We have to be more careful. I'll smile, I know I'll manage to smile, so no one will be able to tell . . . The alarm clock will go off soon. If only I could sleep some more, if only . . .

Deer Run State Forest.

JACKSON.

JACKSON, WYO., Far West,—Wind River Indian Reservation.

Scarves of mist.

LEXINGTON, NEBR., Middle West.

The smells of the night.

DIXON.

The slowness of the night.

DIXON.—When it is five A.M. in

DIXON,

        still four o'clock in
DIXON, Mountain Time.

Gold! There's gold!

Custer National Forest.

        DIXON, WYOMING, Far West.

        They say they've found gold!

        Bighorn National Forest.

A rustle of leaves in the wind.

        BUFFALO.

BUFFALO, Fergus County.

The ghost towns.

Shell,—Gallatin and Beaverhead National Forests.

GLASGOW, in enormous Valley County, MONTANA,—Fort Belknap Indian Reservation.

I had wandered for months searching for gold, and when I returned to the city it was absolutely empty. The wind blew through the broken windowpanes. The snow drifted in the cold stoves.

A Volkswagen going much faster than the authorized fifty-five night speed limit passes a trailer,—Lewis and Clark, Deer Lodge and Helena National Forests.

TROY, Treasure State,—Fort Peck Indian Reservation.

Then I walked through the streets all night searching for a survivor. All the bottles in the old inn were empty . . .

Thunderbird glacier,—Bitterroot and Lolo National Forests.

    TROY.

    They say they've found gold!

    Saint Joe National Forest.

A shifting of dust in the wind.

    RAYMOND, IDA.,—Fort Hall Indian Reservation.

    I'll have a gold beltbuckle, gold spurs, and I'll come back to Europe covered with gold!

    Salmon and Clearwater National Forests.

    RAYMOND, WASH., Pacific Coast,—Spokane Indian Reservation.

A tumble of pebbles in the wind.

    FAIRFIELD.

The sound of streams in the night.

    FAIRFIELD.

FAIRFIELD, Teton County, MONT.—State Flower: bitterroot,—Blackfeet Indian Reservation.

But in one bedroom with dusty sheets there was still a Bible under the bed, and a supply of wood beside the stove. The rain had flooded the floor, and there were little puddles with moss . . .

Rainbow glacier,—Kootenai National Forest.

    FAIRFIELD.

    They set off, tormented by gold fever . . .

    The Blue Buttes.

The roof cracks in the night.

    HAMILTON, N.D., the Middle West,—Fort Berthold Indian Reservation.

    And it's true that one came back tossing gold around him.

    Black Butte, White Butte.

The sound of the wind in the night.

    BUFFALO.

        BUFFALO, MINN.,—White Earth Indian Reservation.

A call echoing from valley to valley, from river to river in the night.

    BUFFALO, S.D.,—Standing Rock Indian Reservation.

    Rivers of gold . . .

    Black Hills National Forest.

Not a sigh in this night, except for the wind.

RAYMOND.

RAYMOND.

RAYMOND, Sheridan County.

I had lost all recollection of the road that might lead to another city. Shivering, I waited for morning in order to set off, without hope of gold, across the mountains, the deserts, the prairies. There wasn't a single bullet left in the gunmaker's store, but I found a good knife in the restaurant kitchen . . .

Vulture glacier.—When it is five A.M. in

LINCOLN,

the sun is rising in
LINCOLN, Central Time.

The deserted streets.

Crescent Lake,—across the southern state border,

        LINCOLN, KANSAS, Middle West (for whites only),—the Iowa, Sac and Fox Indian Reservation.

NELSON, county seat of Nuckolls County.

The empty fields.

Mobil,—Island Lake, Swan Lake,—across the Missouri, tributary of the Father of Waters,

        NELSON.

        A pedestrian.

        "Sleep,"—Mark Twain National Forest.

A pair of pearl-gray Canada jays with white heads, white-edged wings and tails, on a leafy branch of white oak on which a wasp's nest is hanging.
        A mockingbird on a branch of flowering locust.

LINCOLN, MISSOURI (. . . whites only).

The newspaper vendor arrives at his stand.

"Another two hours,"—the Clark and Shawnee National Forests,—continuing east,

LINCOLN, ILLINOIS.

A sunbeam through the pane.

Pomona Natural Bridge.

A yellow-throated vireo on a branch of swamp snowball, head tipped back to catch a wasp.
A male pigeon hawk, named "the Little Corporal" by Audubon.

FAIRFIELD.

The red clouds.

FAIRFIELD.

FAIRFIELD, Clay County, NEBRASKA.

A sunbeam over the prairie.

A huge yellow Pontiac passes an old orange Ford, which is already going much faster than the daytime speed limit,—Bean, Alkali and Goose Lakes,—across the Missouri, but farther north,

FAIRFIELD, IOWA,—the Tama Indian Reservation.

He's still asleep, I don't want to wake him.

The old Indian mounds.

MINDEN, county seat of Kearney County, Cornhusker State.

He's still asleep, it's high time to wake him.

Eagle Nest Butte,—Storm and Sandbeach Lakes.

    MINDEN.

RAYMOND, Lancaster County.

He turns over in his bed.

McCarthy Lake,—across the recessed southwest corner,

    RAYMOND, COLO., Far West,—Ute Indian Reservation.

    The dawning day.

    Great Sand Dunes National Monument.

On a sarsaparilla creeper, three male indigo buntings of different ages and at different stages of their magnificent blue plumage, the beige female below them, walking head down along a branch.
    Cuvier's regulus, on a branch of flowering broad-leaved kalmia, a bird discovered by Audubon; no similar bird has ever been seen since.

    GENOA.—When it is seven A.M. in
GENOA,

                    still pitch dark in
GENOA, Pacific Time.

Gold!

Wowoka was born around 1856 in Mason Valley among the Paiute Indians. Adopted by a farmer, David Wilson, he was given the name Jack Wilson. During a serious illness in 1886 he had a vision. In 1888 there was a solar eclipse. Wowoka fell into a trance and saw the Great Spirit amid the spirits of the dead, Who assigned him the mission of spreading a new religion called the Dance of the Spirits. The dead will return, the White Men will leave, swept away by a tremendous wind; the houses, the cattle, the property of the White Men will remain in Indian hands. The buffalo will return. Disease, poverty and death will cease . . .

I divorce you,
          you divorce me,
he divorces her,
          she divorces him,
let's get a divorce!

King Lear Peak.

MINDEN, county seat of Douglas County, NEVADA, Far West,—the Lake Pyramid Indian Reservation.

I have divorced him,
 we were getting a divorce.
Gold scattered by the wind.

She will divorce him,
 let him divorce her!
The jingling of silver dollars in pockets.

Let's get a divorce!

Flying Service,—Paradise Peak, Golconda Summit.

NELSON, Clark County.

He should get a divorce.
 Gold!
The crystal chandeliers, the operas in the desert . . .
 Why doesn't he get a divorce?
What if we were to get a divorce . . .
 Gold!
I shook the handle of the machine, and look at the avalanche of coins that fell out into my hand! . . .
 They will have got a divorce by now,
let's get a divorce!

A Chrysler whose radio is blaring "Home Means Nevada" passes a huge old Ford parked beside the highway,—Emigrant, Pearl and Antelope Peaks.—When the day breaks in

LEE,

WELCOME TO NEW HAMPSHIRE

        long since broad daylight in
LEE, Eastern Time.

Atlantic puffins,
      razor-billed auks,
           northern phalaropes,
     Atlantic murres,
black guillemots.

Lake Winnipesaukee, "Hello, Jerry!"—Across the southern state line,
      LEE.

    The trial of Susanna Martin, Salem, June 29, 1692:
"6) Robert Downer testified that the Prisoner, several years ago being brought to Court for a witch the said Downer having some words with her among other things told her he believed that she was a witch, at which she seemed not well affected and said that a she devel would fetch him away shortly at which this deponent was not much moved. But the next night as he lay in his owne house alone there came at his window the likness of a catt and by and by come up to his bed took fast hold of his throat and Lay hard upon him a Considerable while and was like to throttle him at Length he minded what Susana Martin had thretened him with the Day before he strove what he could and said avoid thou she devil in the name of the father and the son and the holy Ghost, and then it Let him go and jumpt down upon

the floor and went out at window againe. He further sayth that the next morning before ever he had say'd anything of it some of that family asked him about it (as from her owne)."

Trappist Preserves, made and packed by the monks of Saint Joseph's Abbey, Spencer, Massachusetts (prospectus):
"For 1400 years, since the founding of Monte Cassino in the sixth century, monks following the Rule of Saint Benedict have prayed and worked in common and lived by the labor of their hands. They have tilled the land and lived upon its fruit . . . They have tended cattle and from their milk made butter and cheese . . . They have cultivated vineyards and made fine wines . . . They have gathered berries and fruits and made tempting preserves to brighten the meals of traveler and guest . . ."

The sea,
   washes,
rinses,
   rewashes,
rinses,
   delivers.

"Hello, Mrs. Nelson!"—Plum Island.

HANOVER, on the Connecticut River, Vermont border, Grafton County.

Whistling plovers,
 mallards,
   three-toed gulls,
 hooded mergansers,
rosy gulls.

Esso,—Sunset and Merrymeeting Lakes.

  HANOVER, Plymouth County.

The sea,
  let the sea wash me,
let the sea purify me,
  let the sea take me away,

let the sea bring me back,
   let the sea change me.

Salem, June 29, 1692:
"7) John Kimball deposed that Susanna Martin, upon a Causeless offense, had threatened him concerning a certain Cow of his, That it had been as good you had for she will never do you any more good (and so it came to pass) for the next Aprill following that very Cow lay in the dry yard with her head to her side (but stark dead) and when she was flayed no Impediment did appear in her for she was a stout Lusty Cow. And in another while another cow died and then an ox, and then other cattle to the value of thirty pound that spring. But the said John Kimbale further deposeth that the same year he needed to get a Dog and hearing that the wife of said George Martin had a bitch that had whelps and this deponent went to her to get one of her but she not letting him have his choice he did not absolutely agree for any but said he heard on Blesdell had a bitch by which he may supply. But being upon that accompt at said Blesdalls and marked the whelp agreed for, George Martin coming by esked him whether he would not have his wifes whelpes to which this deponent made answer on the negative. The same day Edmond Elliat said that he was at the house of the said Martins and heard the said Martin asked his wife why this deponent were not to have one of her puppies, and she said he was then said he have got one at Goodman Blesdells and he saw him choose it and mark it, to which his said wife said If I live Ill give him puppies enough. Within a few days after this deponent coming from his Intended house in the woods and there did arise a little black cloud in the northwest and a few drops of Raine and the wind blew pretty hard, and as this deponent came by several stumps of trees by the wayside he by Impuls he can give no reason of that made him tumble over the stumps one after another though he had his ax upon his shoulder which put him in Danger and made him resolved to avoid the next but could not. And when he came a little below the Meeting House there did appear a little thing like a puppy of a darkish color it shott betweene my Legs forwards and backwards as on that were Destracted. And this deponent being free from all fear used all possible

endevers to cut it with his ax but could not hurt it and as he was this belaboring with his ax the puppy gave a little Jump from him and seemed to go into the ground. In a little further going there did appear a black puppy someut bigger than the first but as black as a coal to his apprehension which came against him with such violence as its quick motions did exceed his motions of his ax. Do what he could and it flew at his belly and away and then at his throat and over his shoulder one way and go off and up at it again another and with such quicness seized his throat or his belly while he was without fear. But at last I felt my heart to fayle and sink under it that I thought my life was going out and I recovered myself and gave a start up and calling upon God and naming the name Jesus Christ and then it invisibly away. But this deponent made it not known to any body for fretting his wife.
The next morning Edmond Eliat (as he told abroad and in his own house) said that he going toward the house of said Martin to Look at his oxen went in to light his pipe and the said Martin's wife asked him where Kembal was, said Eliat said abed with his wife for ought he knew, said she, they say he was frighted Last night, with what said Eliat, she said with puppies, Eliat replyed that he heard nothing of it and Asked where she heard of it and she said about the Town. John Kimbale made oath to the truth of all that is written on both sides of this paper."

Trappist Preserves:
"Hospitality is as monastic as work or prayer . . . and what is more hospitable than a cheering meal . . . what more cheerful than clear sparkling jelly or colorful flavorful preserves? Monks have prepared them for centuries . . . prepared them from the finest ingredients and with conscientious care that only the best might be placed before their guests. In the spirit of this tradition the monks of Saint Joseph's Abbey in Spencer, Massachusetts, have blended conscientious workmanship with the finest of ingredients . . . we have patiently followed tested, time-tried recipes to produce these different preserves . . . monastic preserves . . . Trappist preserves that bring to you the warmth of hospitality and the integrity of age-old tradition . . ."

"Still another hour,"—Nantucket and Monomoy Islands.

BERLIN, in huge Coos County, N.H., New England,—the border of the Canadian province of Quebec.

Great black-backed gulls,
   Wilson's snipe,
      Brünich murres,
   American eiders
white-eyed scoters.

A yellow Studebaker bumps an old overloaded yellow Kaiser that is already going much faster than the authorized speed limit,—Winona, Waukewan, Winnisquam Lakes.

BERLIN, Worcester County, MASS.

"*. . . These Trappist Preserves are packed in attractive gift boxes . . . and are also available in individual family-size jars:*

– apricot-pineapple,
– blackberry jelly,
– cherry-pineapple conserve,
– cranberry conserve,
– strawberry jelly . . ."

The sea,
   let the sea cleanse me
of all this mud,
   of all this grease,
of all this soot,
   of all this sugar.

The trial of Susanna Martin:
"8) William Brown testifying saith that his wife Elizabeth being a very rational woman and Sober and one that feared God did one day meet with Susana Martin and just as they came together the said Susana Martin vanisht away out of her sight which put the said Elizabeth into a great fright. After which time the said Martin did many times afterward appear to her at her house and did much trouble her and when she did com it was as birds pecking her Legs or prick-

ing her with the motion of their wings and after that would rise up to her throat in a bunche like a pullets egg and then she would tern back her head and say, Witch you shant choke me. In the time of this extremity the church appointed a day of prayer to seek God on her behalf and thereupon her trouble ceased and she saw Goodwife Martin no more for a considerable time for which the Church instead of the day of humiliation gave thanks for her Deliverance. But longtime after the said Elizabeth told this deponent that as shee was milking of her cow the said Susanna Martin came behind her and told her that she would make her the miserablest creature for defaming her name at the Court. About two months after this and from that time to this very day have been under a strange kind of distemper frenzy uncapible of any rational action though strong and healthy of body, the Doctor declaring her distemper was supernatural and no sickness of body but that some evil person had bewitched her . . ."

A huge red Mercury passes a bright tan Nash whose radio is blaring "Mahogany Hall Stomp,"—Tuckernuck, Muskeget and Chappaquiddick Islands,—through Montgomery Ward you can obtain the "royal gold medal set," "no need to be an artist, from now on all you need to do is paint by numbers: create a charming picture, even if you have never held a brush in your life! It's fun . . . And so easy! Just fill in the numbered areas on the canvas with the corresponding colors. Finish off your work in an elegant oak frame. With this set you receive two Rembrandt water-colors. Panels in pairs. 40 oil-colors in vacuum-sealed glass jars, four superior-quality, washable brushes. Net weight: six pounds. . . ."
Or, through Sears, Roebuck & Co., an assortment of seven knitted nylon or rayon panties artistically embroidered with the days of the week:
". . . Choose from
– white for Sunday,
    – The Last Supper, with The Sermon on the Mount,
– yellow for Monday,
    – Autumn Landscape, with The End of the Day,
– blue for Tuesday,
    – Sunset at Sea, with Homecoming,
– pink for Wednesday,
    – Thoroughbred, with The Foxhunt,

– white for Thursday,
  – Scenes from Swan Lake (Ballet),
– green for Friday,
  – Venus and Adonis."
– black for Saturday,
"please include hip measurements,"—continuing south,

        BERLIN, CONN., New England.

        The suburbs of New York City.

        The sea,
                dirty papers,
        cigarette butts,
                paper plates,
        odd sandals,
                bottletops

        Lake Candlewood.

ANDOVER, Granite State.

Arctic terns,
      horned grebes,
            Leach's petrels,
      European cormorants,
Wilson's petrels.

Salmon Mountain,—Newfound Lake, Canaan Street Lake,—or a man's ring with a three-carat imperialite, "the artificial stone that looks like a diamond," or a Sandran floor covering, "you've seen it on television,
        you've seen it in the newspapers. Now have it in your home.
        Choose from:
        – gold and rust squares,
        – irregular crushed cork check,
        – rust with gold stars,
        – textured gray,

        ANDOVER, Essex County, where you can order pistachio
            ice cream in the Howard Johnson Restaurant.

— textured taupe,
— white with gold stars,
— beige with gold stars,
— marbled beige with gold threads,
— vinyl pinewood,
— marbled gold and white squares."

Salem, June 29, 1692:
"9) Sarah Atkinson testified that Susanna Martin came from Amesbury to their house at Newbury in an Extraordinary dirty season when it was not fit for any Person to travell she then came on foot when she came into our house I asked her whether she came from Amesbury affoot she said did I asked her how she could come in this time affoot and bid my children make way for her to come to the fire to dry herself she replyed she was as dry as I was and turned her coats on Side and I could nott perceive that the Soule of her shoes were wet I was startled at it yet she should come so dry and told her that I should have been wet up to my knees if I should have come so far on foot she replyed that she scorned to have a drabled tayle . . ."

The monks of Saint Joseph's Abbey:
"— pineapple preserve,
— pineapple-mint jam,
— grape jelly,
— red currant jelly,
— red raspberry jam,
— rhubarb-orange conserve,
— strawberry jam,
— wild elderberry jelly,
— fig jam,
— peach preserves,
— Seville orange marmalade . . ."

The sea,
       the sea's great washing,

let the sea strike me,
       let the sea enter me,
let the sea awe me,
       let the sea open my eyes.

Nashawena and Cuttyhunk Islands.

ANDOVER.

A nest of robins, on a branch of chestnut oak; the female holds a red berry in her beak.

FRANKLIN.

A pair of bobolinks on two branches of red maple.

FRANKLIN, on the Merrimack River, N.H., a skiing state.

Royal eiders,
    Icelandic gulls,
        great puffins,
    purple sandpipers,
Sabine's gulls.

The church of the Assemblies of God,—Mount Washington, Mount Lincoln,—Silver Lake,—or a talisman seal ring, page 692, synthetic stone and two rose-cut diamonds,
    or a "Scintillating Sandran" floor covering, page 571, "millions of metallic sparks. The patterns are printed with vinyl inks on an impregnated plastic surface, then millions of tiny sparkles are scattered and sealed in by a layer of transparent vinyl. Neither your feet nor your hands ever touch the shimmering beauty of this floor covering:
"choose according to your month of birth:
– garnet red for January,
    – scattering of stars on beige, gold sparkles,
– amethyst purple for February,
– aquamarine for March,
    – rust and beige checks, gold sparkles,
– sapphire blue for April,
– emerald green for May,
    – scattering of stars on beige, gold sparkles,
– alexandrite violet for June,
– ruby red for June,
    – scattering of stars on white, gold and silver sparkles,
– zircon rose for October,

FRANKLIN.

– topaz gold for November,
   – marbled taupe, bronze, gold and silver sparkles . . ."
– zircon blue-green for December,"—across the eastern state line,

> *ivory gulls,*
>   *solitary sandpipers,*
>   *Isle of Man puffins,*
>   *barnacle geese,*
> *harlequin ducks.*

> *The sea,*
>   *islands,*
> *channels,*
>   *narrows,*
> *straits,*
>   *reefs.*

Mount Desert Island.

On a black-gum branch covered with berries, three black-capped warblers.

ANDOVER, Oxford County.

Two ring-billed gulls, one adult, one young, both simultaneously looking behind them on the bank of a lake or channel; two shells and some pebbles.

> *The sea,*
>   *outboards,*
> *water-skiing,*
>   *diving boards,*
> *toboggans,*
>   *buoys,*
> *Holboell's grebes,*
>   *Audubon's puffins,*
>   *land plovers,*
>   *common terns,*
> *blue-winged teal.*

Sears and Pickering Islands in the Atlantic.

MILFORD, Hillsboro County. State Flower: purple lilac.

Laughing gulls,
>> *stormy petrels,*
>>>> *American gold-eyes,*
>>> *white-winged crossbills,*
glaucous gulls.

White Mountain National Forest,—the church of the Seventh-Day Adventists,—Mount Patience.

MILFORD, on the Penobscot River, Penobscot County, ME., —the border of the Canadian provinces of Quebec and New Brunswick,—the Penobscot Indian Reservation.

Red-breasted mergansers,
>> *Barrow's gold-eyes,*

the sea,
>>> *waterspouts,*
>>>>> *semi-palmated sandpipers,*
caves,
>>> *archipelagoes,*

capes,
>>> *American puffins,*
Forster's terns,
>> *jetties.*

A huge garnet-colored shiny trailer passes an overloaded cerise trailer,—Eagle Island, Butter Island, Monhegan Island,—or "Ambassador" folding doors, super-resistant plastic, steel frame, oak-bark or toast shades.

On a peeling treetrunk, three three-toed Arctic woodpeckers.

LEE, Penobscot County.

Or an assortment of three panties with "feminine ruffles," page 255, "a touch of delicate lace on these silky nylon briefs is enough to give you that impression of femininity . . . ; elastic at the waist and leg holes; one white, one pink, one blue or all white . . ."

A pair of white-fronted geese on the shore of a lake; the gander, standing, turns his head and neck over his back, his mate, sitting, catches the sepia feathers of her half-extended right wing in her pink bill.

>*The sea,*
>>*ebb,*
>
>*Trudeau's terns,*
>>*gull-billed terns,*
>
>*detour,*
>>*flow,*
>>>*gold-winged warblers,*
>
>*roar,*
>>*Cape May warbler,*
>
>*hairy woodpeckers,*
>>*spatter.*

Bois Bubert and Petit Manan Islands.

The rising tide.

NEWPORT.

NEWPORT, county seat of Sullivan County.

Winter wrens,
>*bank swallows,*
>>*Bohemian waxwings,*
>*pine grosbeaks,*

house wrens.

Fox State Forest,—across the Connecticut River,

NEWPORT.

Quilts of the Shelburne Museum:
No. 182: Jacob's Ladder:
"The design of this quilt represents Jacob's dream during his wanderings, when he lay down on the earth with a stone for

a pillow and dreamed of a ladder that was 'set upon the earth, and the top of it reached to heaven, the Angels of God mounting and descending it . . .' The large maple leaf sewn on one of the white squares derives from a superstition of uncertain origin, but probably inherited from the Oriental belief that only the supreme gods could create perfection, and that man would be presumptuous to try to produce faultless works. In order to avoid punishment for her audacity in attempting to imitate the divinity, the woman who created a quilt deliberately destroyed the symmetry of her pattern, thus warding off bad luck . . ."

Green Mountain National Forest,—continuing west,

NEWPORT, N.Y.,—the border of the Canadian provinces of Quebec and Ontario,—the Cattaraugus Indian Reservation.

The Indian Handsome Lake was born around 1735 in a Seneca family belonging to the Wolf Clan, in a village near Avon, N.Y., which he was forced to leave in 1799, with the entire population, for Tonawanda, under the pressure of the white invaders who set fire to the houses, fields, and villages. Handsome Lake was then one of the Seneca chiefs, belonging to the Council of the Iroquoi League, a confederation of the five nations speaking the Iroquois language: the Onondagas, Senecas, Oneidas, Cayugas and Mohawks. For some time Handsome Lake had been living as an invalid in the house of his brother-in-law Cornplanter. He had given up all hope of survival when, on June 15, 1799, he fell into a trance and heard a voice calling him. Outside he found three men, or rather three spirits in human form, who presented him some branches laden with fruit and told him to pick them, assuring him that he would be miraculously cured. They informed him that the Great Spirit greatly deplored the intemperance of men, particularly the abuse of alcohol, and made him a prophet of the new doctrine of salvation. They showed him the paradise destined for the blessed, faithful to this true religion, and the inferno where the evil one ruled, loading canoes with casks of whiskey.

Freedomland prospectus:
"In New York City,
Just 30 minutes from Times Square,
This is Freedomland, U.S.A.
A $65,000,000 extravaganza.
205 acres of colorful Americana.
35 rides never seen before.
Parking facilities for 10,000 cars.
Shelter, shade and rest accommodations.
Restaurant and snack bar facilities.
2,000 costumed performers and service personnel specially trained to provide a friendly, courteous atmosphere . . ."

325,000 Austrians,
15,000 French Canadians.

Fisherman's Net, seafood,
Baroque, French cuisine,
Golden Horn, Armenian specialties.

The planes leaving for London.
The planes coming from Paris.

WABC, Turkish broadcasts,
WNBX, French broadcasts,
WBYN, Ukrainian broadcasts.

The boats sailing for Rotterdam.
The boats coming from Le Havre.

Testimonial:
Photograph of Nelson A. Rockefeller, Governor of the State of New York (smiling).
"Freedomland is the ultimate expression of the effort to dramatize our history and to bring it

176   Mobile

> *home vividly to everyone who sees it . . . We welcome Freedomland for itself, and as an entertainment center which will attract visitors from all over the world . . ."*

>> *The Arabs who read "As-Sameer,"*
> *The Armenians who read "Gotchnag,"*
The Chinese who read the "China Tribune."
>>> *Barney's, steaks,*
>> *Kismet, Armenian dishes,*
Hapsburg House, Austrian specialties,
>>>> *The planes leaving for Stockholm.*
>>>> *The planes coming from Rome.*
>>> *Antique shops: along Second and Third Avenues between 47 and 57 Streets.*
>>>> *The ships sailing for Bremen.*
>>>> *The ships coming from Puerto Rico.*

>> *Press release:*
>> "*Freedomland ranks as the world's largest outdoor family entertainment center; situated in a 205-acre arena, the U.S.-shaped park spans 85 acres, with the remainder devoted to parking and service facilities. Previous world's largest—in California—covered 65 acres . . ."*

>> The Adirondack Mountains.

A pair of catbirds on a blackberry bush.

>>> FRANKLIN, VT., New England,—the border of the Canadian Province of Quebec.

A black myrtle warbler, on a variegated iris, with two of its young on a vine with black berries.

>> *Quilts of the Shelburne Museum:*
>> *No. 10: The Civil War:*
>> "*This quilt was found in New Jersey and was traditionally made by a Civil War veteran. A descendant of his tells the following story: This quilt was made by a wounded, discharged*

Union soldier toward the end of the Civil War in order to soothe his shattered nerves. He could not escape entirely the effects of the war as his quilt has silhouette figures of armed soldiers on horse and afoot marching grimly around an intermediate border; in the central group foot soldiers surround women who appear to be offering refreshment on trays. Their outlines recall the trademark figure on the box of a well-known brand of chocolate. This trademark was adopted by the manufacturers in 1780 and had its origin in a contemporary French painting called 'La Chocolatiere.' Crescent moons, hearts and fat complacent doves may have been introduced to the militant picture to humor a wife or sweetheart."

Mount Mansfield and Camel's Hump State Forests.

Ripples on the lake.

    FRANKLIN.

Wind in the woods.

    BERLIN.—When it is ten o'clock in

LEBANON,

WELCOME TO NEW JERSEY

                ten o'clock in
LEBANON.

Chimney swifts,
              golden-crowned kinglets,
                          red-throated divers,
        Virginia rails,
lesser bitterns.

The sea,
            white hats,
wrists,
            straw hats,
thighs,
            beige hats.

The outskirts of New York City:
Newark has approximately 160 Protestant churches, 41 Catholic churches, 32 synagogues and over 60 churches of various other denominations.

The Kittatinny Mountains, "Hello, Jim!"—across the Delaware River,

LEBANON, where you can ask for pear ice cream in the Howard Johnson Restaurant.

"Information to Those Who Would Remove to America":
". . . Of civil Offices or Employments, there are few; no superfluous ones, as in Europe; and it is a Rule establish'd in some of the States, that no Office should be so profitable as to make it desirable. The 36th Article of the Constitution of Pennsylvania, runs expressly in these Words: "As every Freeman, to preserve his Independence, (if he has not a sufficient Estate) ought to have some Profession, Calling, Trade, or Farm, whereby he may honestly subsist, there can be no Necessity for, nor Use in, establishing Offices of Profit; the usual Effects of which are Dependence and Servility, unbecoming Freemen, in the Possessors and Expectants; Faction, Contention, Corruption, and Disorder among the People. Wherefore, whenever an Office, thro' Increase of Fees or otherwise, becomes so profitable, as to occasion many to apply for it, the Profits ought to be lessened by the Legislature . . ."
Benjamin Franklin.

"Hello, Mrs. Franklin!"—Bald Eagle Mountain,—continuing west,

LEBANON, OHIO, Middle West.

In Toledo, Hungarians read the weekly "Hungarian-American Weekly." In Cleveland, Hungarians read the daily "Szabadsag."

Campbell Hill, highest point in the state—continuing west,

LEBANON, IND.

Smile!

Hindustan Falls,—continuing west,

LEBANON, ILL.

> *The splendid cast-iron ornaments created in 1900 by Louis Sullivan to decorate the Schlesinger Meyer department store, today Carson Pirie Scott, the last major work he produced in Chicago: spirals, volutes, darts, sprouts, themes, answers, echoes.*
>
> The population center of the United States,—telephone ringing.

BERLIN, Camden County.

The outskirts of New York City:
In Newark, Hungarians read the weekly "Newarki Hirlap."
Whistling plovers,
        green-winged teal,
the sea,
        green sandals,
                sooty terns,
ankles
        sooty sandals,
heels,
        black coots,
snowy egrets,
        white sandals.

"Hello, I want Lebanon, New Hampshire,"—Texaco,—Jenny Jump and Mohepinoke Mountains.

> BERLIN, PENN.,—the Cornplanter Indian Reservation.
>
> *". . . These Ideas prevailing more or less in all the United States, it cannot be worthy any Man's while, who has a means of Living at home, to expatriate himself, in hopes of obtaining a profitable civil Office in America; and, as to military Offices, they are at an end with the War, the Armies being disbanded . . ."*
>
>   *Benjamin Franklin.*

"We'll be there soon,"—Wills and Evitts Mountains.

HANOVER, Essex County, N.J., the smallest state after Rhode Island, Delaware, Connecticut and Hawaii.

The sea,
        bags,
black ducks,
        common terns,
black hats,
        chaises longues,
            spotted sandpipers,
        white pelicans,
yellowlegs,
        white scarves,
the outskirts of New York City:
in Newark, Italians read the weekly "Italian Tribune."

A dusty, overloaded lemon-yellow DS19 parked alongside the highway. A fire truck passes, driven by a Negro,—Scotts, Pohatcong and Schooley Mountains.

HANOVER.

The sunlight on the white housefronts.

HANOVER.

The sunlight on the windshield.

HANOVER.

The sunlight on the lakes.

HANOVER.

NEWPORT, the Garden State.

Some Italians in Newark prefer the "New Jersey Italian-American."
The outskirts of New York City.

Laughing gulls,
        beach puffins,

the sea,
                    little terns,
          little pails,
little spades,
          little rakes,
little mussels,
          black skimmers,
Bonaparte gulls,
          little black sieves.

Lake Hiawatha,—Green Pond and Bearfort Mountains,—through Sears, Roebuck & Co., you can obtain a nylon and wool "Harmony House, Carvex" carpet, "pile so deep it looks much more expensive than it really is."

FRANKLIN, N.J., a beach state.

> Or, through Montgomery Ward, a "Modern Fantasy" shower curtain, "a lovely dream: modern abstract pattern on a new, 'brushed silk' three-dimensional semi-opaque plastic; looks almost like satin."

The sea,
          striped towels,
buffleheads,
          green herons,
the outskirts of New York City:
in Jersey City Poles read the weekly "Glos Narodu,"
                    black-bellied plovers,
solid green towels,
          green and black checked towels,
towels with letters,
          American gold-eyes,
stilt-plovers,
          American eagle towels.

The Lutheran church,—Hopatcong and Shawnee Lakes,—Pochuck Mountain,—or a "Nylsurf" carpet, page 753:
> Or a "Sandran Scintillating Crown" floor covering, "exceptional resistance to acids, alcohol, oil. The non-porous surface sheds dust and humidity:

"spice brown and ivory,
   – green with gold pebbles,

ANDOVER, Sussex County. State Flower: violet.

   – gray terrazzo with gold and silver sparkles,
– ivory and parchment brown,
   – rust terrazzo with multicolor sparkles,

The sea,
   ice cream,
the outskirts of New York City.

   – white and black terrazzo with gold sparkles,
– aquamarine and smoke gray,
   – taupe-turquoise-rose with multicolor sparkles,

Black rails,
   marsh hawks,
      American magpies,
   sharp-shinned hawks,
gull-billed terns.

   – rust and gold pebbles,
– spice brown and shell beige,
   – ivory-cream-gray terrazzo with silver sparkles."
– desert sand and beige."

Unguents,
   tubes,
bottles,
   salves.
In Newark, Portuguese read the weekly "Luso-Americano."

Jenny Jump State Forest,—the Baptist church,—Lake Denmark.

MILFORD, on the Delaware River, the Pennsylvania state line, Hunterdon County.

The sea,
   dark glasses,

American brants,
> *orchard orioles,*
green glasses,
> *red-shouldered hawks,*
>> *purple glasses,*
brown glasses,
> *field sparrows,*
whistling plovers,
> *mirror glasses,*
the outskirts of New York City.

Lebanon State Forest,—across the northern state line,

> MILFORD, N.Y.,—the Tuscarora Indian Reservation.

> Two pairs of white-breasted black-capped nuthatches on a dead branch covered with various kinds of lichen.

Two crested flycatchers, one shedding its tailfeathers with which the other is playing.—To the east,

> MILFORD, CONN., where you can order apple ice cream in the Howard Johnson Restaurant.—When it is eleven o'clock in

COLUMBUS,

WELCOME TO NEW MEXICO

           still nine o'clock in
COLUMBUS, Mountain Time.

While the Anasazi in the north were beginning to build their houses under the cliffs, various civilizations developed in the southern deserts; the Hohokam—a Pima term meaning "those who have vanished"—invented ingenious irrigation systems, made mother-of-pearl jewelry and cotton fabrics . . .

Cibola National Forest,—"Hello, Joe!"—across the southeast state line,

        COLUMBUS, TEX. (for whites only),—the border of the Mexican states of Chihuahua, Coahuila, Nuevo León and Tamaulipas,—the Alibamu and Koashati Indian Reservation.

HANOVER, Grant County, N.M., the largest state after Alaska, Texas, California and Montana, on the border of the Mexican states of Chihuahua and Sonora,—the Zuñi Indian Reservation.

Early in the fourteenth century, the Anasazi of the north moved south to escape a drought and settled mostly in the valley of the Rio Grande; only the Hopis and the Zuñis preferred to travel farther west . . .

Sunoco,—Apache and Gila National Forests.

CLAYTON, county seat of Union County.

In 1536, Cabeza de Vaca crossed the Southwest. In 1539, after the expedition of Esteban the Moor, killed by the Zunis, Fray Marcos de Niza began talking about the Seven Cities of Cibola, of the land "so rich in gold, silver and other precious metals that even the women there wore golden garments." In 1540, Francisco Coronado set out to find them with an army of 1,500 men, accompanied by many missionaries, including Fray Marcos de Niza, and he reached the Zuni pueblo of Hawiku quite disappointed with what he found there. The following year, however, he set out again in search of Quivira, another mythical land of abundance. In 1598, Juan de Onate, equipped with six suits of armor, set out with 130 families, 270 armed men, chariots, and 7,000 head of cattle; he founded San Gabriel de Yunque, the first capital of New Mexico. Then he wandered for ten years in search of Quivira, the city of gold. In 1640 the Spaniards counted 700 pueblos; today there are no more than 30. In 1680, the Pueblo Indians rebelled against the Spanish domination; twelve years later they were reconquered, and the Jesuits established their series of missions . . .

A huge plum-colored old truck, driven by a white man, whose radio is blaring "O Fair New Mexico," going much faster than the speed limit, passes a brown Nash driven by a Negro woman,—Santa Fe, Carson and Lincoln National Forests,—across the eastern state line, but farther north,

    CLAYTON, OKLA. (. . . whites only),—Osage Indian
      Reservation. When it is ten o'clock in

SALEM,

WELCOME TO NEW YORK

noon chimes in
SALEM, Eastern Time.

The three angels announced to the Seneca Indian Handsome Lake the imminent appearance of another person who had sent them before him. In a final vision appeared the Great Spirit himself, touched by Handsome Lake's sufferings. In the trance, he saw his own dead son and a dead niece come to him, both deploring the intemperance of the living. The Great Spirit made him promise to abjure alcohol and gave him all the precepts of the new religion. In particular, he was to give up certain profane traditional dances and celebrations, but not the Dances of the Cult, which, according to an ancestral seasonal succession in relation to the work of the fields, constituted the kernel of the most important religious festivals of the Iroquois culture . . .

Freedomland prospectus:
"Now you and your family live the fun, the adventure, the drama of America's past, present and future! Now for the first time anywhere, journey across a continent—across 200 years—to enjoy the entertainment thrill as big as America itself!
Open seven days a week.
Enjoy the gaiety of Mardi Gras!
See the Chicago Fire!
Thrill to the Wild West!
Live through History's adventures!"

Have you been in New York long?

57,000 Englishmen,
  30,000 Chinese.

Hearthstone, American specialties,
  Brussels, French cuisine,
    Palace d'Orient, Armenian cooking.

The planes leaving for Lisbon.
  Customs officers.
The planes coming from Madrid.

WBNX, Irish broadcasts.
  WEVD, Armenian broadcasts,
    WFUV-FM, French broadcasts.

The ships leaving for Rio de Janeiro.
  Stevedores.
The ships coming from Hamburg.

The Empire State Building: 655 windows to wash twice a month.

Freedomland testimonial:
Photograph of Robert F. Wagner, Mayor of New York City (smiling). "New York City is proud to welcome this new member of the community, and we are happy to extend the friendliness and civic cooperation for which our city is justly famous . . ."

The Arabs who read "Meraat-ul-Gharb,"
  the Chinese who read the "Chinese Journal,"
    the Czechs who read the "New Yorkske Listy."
Lindy's, Broadway atmosphere,
  Viennese Lantern, Austrian cooking,
    House of Chan, Chinese dishes.
  The planes leaving for Vienna.
    Check your passports.
  The planes coming from Istanbul.
Automobile showrooms: Broadway, above 50 Street, Park Avenue between 47 Street and 60 Street.
  The ships leaving for Buenos Aires.
    Porters.
  The ships coming from Copenhagen.

The Empire State Building: 60 miles of water pipes.

Press release:
"*Many natural wonders have been transplanted to Freedomland. There are scale-size forests, a rebuilt Rocky Mountains in perspective, a miniature Great Lakes, the panorama of the Great Western Plains. Natural foliage includes live squash growing on the vine; desert planting in Arizona and New Mexico; magnolias and oleanders around New Orleans . . .*"

Lake Oneida, "Hello, Johnny"—Across the southern state line,

       SALEM.

       Gull-billed terns,
              lesser terns,
                     common terns,
              sooty terns,
       black coots.

       The sea,
              picnics,
       French-fries,
              Coca-Cola,
       newspapers,
              tin cans.

       "Hello, Mrs. Clayton"—Rainbow Lake.

CLAYTON, on the Saint Lawrence, border of the Canadian province of Ontario, Jefferson County.

The Great Spirit told the Seneca Indian Handsome Lake that the chief festivals to preserve in the new religion were those of the New Year, when a white dog was sacrificed, the strawberry festival, the maize-harvest or feather festival, with the dance of thanksgiving to the Great Spirit, to the mythical Ancestor, to the ancestors of the tribe, to the three sisters, and the other figures of the pagan tradition, and finally the festival of the green grain, that of the winter solstice, and the medicine ceremonials . . .

Freedomland prospectus:
"The 65 million dollar extravaganza as big as America itself! Where you and your family live the unforgettable fun, adventure and excitement of our great American heritage! . . ."

58,000 Czechs,
        16,000 Danes.
The Arabs who read "Al Bayan,"
        the Chinese who read the "Chinese Nationalist,"
              the Estonians who read the "Vaba Eesti Sona."
NEW YORK TIMES NEW YORK TIMES NEW YORK TIMES NEW YORK TIM

Forum of the Twelve Caesars, new, superb menu and setting,
        Chambord, French cuisine,
              Ruby Foo's, Chinese dishes.
The planes coming from Cairo.
        Taxi!
The planes coming from Caracas.
WBNX, German broadcasts,
        WEVD, Irish broadcasts,
              WLIB, Greek broadcasts.
The ships coming from Ostend.
        The green water.
The ships sailing for Alexandria.
The Empire State Building: 3,500 miles of telephone and telegraph wires.

And how long will you be in New York?
        Shhh!

Testimonial:
". . . We feel that Freedomland will be right at home in our midst. As the world's largest outdoor entertainment attraction, it fits quite naturally into the world's greatest tourist and business metropolis . . ."
        Robert F. Wagner, Mayor of New York City.

Grand Central Oyster Bar, seafood,
        Sun Luck, Chinese cuisine,
              Liborio, Cuban specialties.
The planes leaving for Rio.
        Stamp machine.
The planes arriving from Buenos Aires.

Second-hand books, East 57 St. and Fourth Avenue from Astor Place to 11 St.
The ships leaving for Piraeus.
The black water.
The ships arriving from Panama.
The Empire State Building: 365,000 tons.
One way.
Astor Theater,
Bijou Theater,
Capitol Theater,
Criterion Theater.
Freedomland press release:
"*Among the more exotic plants are buffalo grass and rare water lilies, palm trees, birds of paradise, New Zealand flax, orchids and banana plants—all blossoming in their 'natural habitats.' The duplicated Kansas farm area has a full-size corn field, complete to ears of corn on the stalks . . .*" "*. . . Chicago will be re-created as it was in 1871, the year of the great fire. The city will burn down every 20 minutes, despite the volunteer companies that will rush down its streets with hand-drawn hose carts and manually operated pumps. You may be one of those who help fight the fire to a standstill. As the call goes up for volunteers, maybe you'll rush forward bravely to aid in manning the hose or pumping the water that douses the flames. Later, as you sail farther and farther from Chicago, suddenly you see the towering flames of the city on fire reflected in the water . . .*"

Shell,—Lake Seneca, Lake Cayuga.

CLAYTON, N.J., Atlantic Coast.

The sea,
fires on the beach,
laughing gulls,
Bonaparte gulls,
black ducks,
the smoke,
the ashes,
the smells,
green herons,
swallow-tailed hawks,
the dunes.

"We're there,"—Silver Lake, Lake Palatine, continuing south,

CLAYTON, DEL.

A bluejay with two females, one holding an egg in its bill, the other crushing one with its claw, so that its contents drip into the open mouth of the male on a dead branch garlanded with birthwort.

FRANKLIN.

A pair of brown-headed nuthatches on a bare branch.

FRANKLIN, Delaware County, N.Y.,—the border of the Canadian provinces of Quebec and Ontario,—the Onondaga Indian Reservation.

The cult of the Good Message, or Evangel, preached by the Seneca Indian Handsome Lake is still a fervent one on the New York State reservations where descendants of the five nations who had formed the Iroquois league still survive.

Freedomland prospectus:
"Excitement! Adventure! Education!
Cross the centuries from Colonial New England to the pioneer West, from Mexican border towns to Great Lakes ports, from Cape Canaveral to the Northwest Passage! Chug through the picturesque Old West on an early iron horse, explore the Northwest in a fur trapper's canoe, soar 70 feet above the earth in a mine oar bucket . . . tour through America's waterways and wilderness on the most thrilling new rides ever designed!
Over forty authentic themes to make history live *again at Freedomland! . . ."*

150,000 Englishmen,
   17,000 Finns.

The Arabs who read "Al Hoda,"
  the Chinese who read the "United Journal,"
    the Finns who read the "*New Yorkin Uutiset.*"
NEW YORK HERALD TRIBUNE NEW YORK HERALD TRIBUNE NEW YORK

Black Angus, steaks,
> *Chateaubriand, French cuisine,*
>> *Lee's, Chinese dishes,*

Patricia Murphy, American specialties,
> *Lum Fong, Chinese cuisine,*
>> *La Barraca, Cuban cooking.*
> *The planes leaving for Lima.*
>> *Racetracks.*
> *The planes arriving from Manila.*

WBNX, Greek broadcasts,
> *WEVD, German broadcasts,*
>> *WLIB, Hungarian broadcasts.*
> *The ships coming from Halifax.*
>> *Piers.*
> *The ships leaving for Antwerp.*

The Empire State Building: 2,000,000 kilowatt-hours per month.

Testimonial:
". . . We wish Freedomland good luck in achieving its high-level aims and trust it will help spread the message of Americanism, as well as the spirit of New York, throughout the nation and the world.
> *Very truly yours,*
>> *Robert F. Wagner, Mayor of New York City."*

> *Are you coming?*

And what do you think of New York?
> *Baby!*

The planes leaving for Tokyo.
> *Coca-Cola machines.*

The planes coming from Hong Kong.
> *Bridal gowns, on Grand Street.*

The ships sailing for Liverpool.
> *The garbage floating on the water.*

The ships coming from Singapore.
> *The Empire State Building: 1,860 steps to the 102d floor.*

Globe Theater,
> *Holiday Theater,*
>> *Mayfair Theater,*
>>> *Rialto Theater.*

The subway from the far end of the Bronx:
  East 241 Street,
  East 238 Street,
  East 233 Street . . .

Press release:
"Over eight miles of navigable rivers, lakes and streams flow through Freedomland; there's half a million yards of paving, 15,000 trees and plants. Roadways, walkways, shade areas, rain shelters and rest rooms are designed to accommodate 32,000 persons at any given time. Restaurants and other eating places can serve 30,000 persons an hour . . ."
". . . In Freedomland's Northwest, dummy Indians concealed in the bushes fire harmless bullets and shoot teleguided arrows . . ."

An old tomato-colored Pontiac, parked beside the highway. A huge yellow Plymouth passes, driven by a yellowish white man,—Keuka, Canandaigua and Honeoye Lakes,—across the eastern state line,

FRANKLIN, VT., a New England state bordering on the Canadian province of Quebec, the least densely populated of all the states after Alaska, Nevada, Wyoming and Delaware.

Quilts of the Shelburne Museum:
No. 140: Ann Robinson:
"Ann Robinson of Connecticut began this quilt on October 1, 1813, and finished it exactly three months and twenty-seven days later, as she carefully cross-stitched on her work. Border of blue saw-tooth triangles on a white ground. Multicolor calico laurel boughs. Horns of plenty spill out a profusion of tulips and other flowers, other bouquets filling the spaces between them. Two trees grow out of calico mounds at the bottom; between them, a lithe cat leaps onto another low mound, pursued by two dogs. Other dogs bark at birds carefully cut out of printed chintz, preening their wings in the branches . . . At the top, three circles surmounted by an imperial crown doubtless allude to the trinity."

Iroquois Lake,—continuing east,

FRANKLIN, N.H.

>
> *Duck hawks,*
> *blue-headed vireos,*
hermit thrushes,
> *chestnut-sided warblers,*
> *swamp sparrows.*

> Bow Lake,—continuing east,

> > FRANKLIN, ME.,—the border of the Canadian provinces of Quebec and New Brunswick,—the Indiantown Indian Reservation.

> > *The Labrador duck, extinct since 1878.*

> > *The sea,*
> > > *the salt,*
> > *drops,*
> > > *rime,*
> > *ripples,*
> > > *glimmers.*

> Beau Lake,—telephone ringing.

A pair of Blackburnian warblers on a branch of dwarf maple; a male, in another plate, in front of a flowering spray of spotted phlox.

> **MANCHESTER.**

A Maryland yellowthroat with its little black Venetian mask, on a branch of wild olive, and its mate on a bitterwood branch.

A little wind.

> MANCHESTER, where you can order plum ice cream in the Howard Johnson Restaurant.

A whirlwind of dust.

MANCHESTER.

MANCHESTER, Ontario County, Empire State,—the Allegany Indian Reservation.

On Hill Cumorah, near Manchester, New York, Joseph Smith discovered in 1823 the gold tablets that are the source of the Book of Mormon and of the religion of the Latter-Day Saints. . . .

Freedomland prospectus:
"Take the wheel and tour the countryside of Colonial New England!
— Board an authentic space ship!
— Ride a side-wheeler!
— And many more!
— See the Chicago Fire!
— Be there when the Pony Express comes pounding into the old stockade!
— Enjoy the New Orleans Mardi Gras!
— Witness the San Francisco Earthquake!
— Travel from coast to coast!
— The greatest entertainment your family has ever known!
— Relive historic adventures! . . ."

40,000 Frenchmen,
the Arabs who read "Al-Islaah,"
Reuben's, Broadway atmosphere,
        495,000 Germans,
        the French who read "France-Amérique,"
        Café Chauveron, French cuisine,
                the Germans who read "Aufbau,"
TIME TIME TIME TIME TIME TIME TIME TIME TIME TIME TIME TIME
                Peking, Chinese cuisine,
Four Seasons, new, exquisite menu and decor,
        Bohemian National Hall, Czech dishes,
                Copenhagen, Danish cooking.
        The planes leaving for Frankfurt,
                for Sydney.
        The planes arriving from Geneva,
                from Auckland.
WBNX, Hungarian broadcasts,
        WEVD, Greek broadcasts,
                WOV, Italian broadcasts.
        The ships leaving for Genoa.

The screams of the gulls.
The ships arriving from Calcutta.
The Empire State Building: 60,000 tons of steel, enough to make a double railroad track from New York to Baltimore.

Testimonial:
Photograph of Milton T. Raynor, President of Freedomland.
Smile.
"For us, that big day is here! The final dab of paint, the final geranium is in place and the final rehearsal of our costumed cast of 3,000 is over. The curtain is up today and our show is on!"

Bronze and copper ware, especially on the east side of Allen Street.
    The ships leaving for Casablanca.
    Eddies.
    The ships coming from Santiago.
The Empire State Building: 37,000,000 cubic feet.
    One way.
Rivoli Theater,
    Loew's State Theater,
        Victoria Theater,
            Paramount Theater.
The subway from the far end of the Bronx:
    East 225 Street,
    East 219 Street,
    Gun Hill Road.
The subway from the far end of Brooklyn:
        Brighton Beach,
        Sheepshead Bay,
        Neck Road,
        Avenue U.

    Excuse me . . .
        Are you coming in?
Have you seen the show at the Museum of Modern Art?
    It's late . . .

Freedomland press release:
"Fifty thousand hamburgers, hot dogs, sandwiches, soda, milk and coffee can be served each hour at specially designed snack stands . . ."
". . . On the Freedomland train, just around the turn of a bend—just

where is a guarded secret—a great surprise awaits the riders; one characterized by masked men, blazing sixguns and suddenly disappearing mail bags . . ."

"Hello, I want Clayton, New York,"—Gull Island in the Atlantic,—Cuba Lake, Silver Lake,—across the eastern state line, but farther south,

MANCHESTER, MASS., New England, the smallest state after Rhode Island, Delaware, Connecticut, Hawaii and New Jersey.

The trial of Susanna Martin, Salem, June 29, 1692:
"10) John Pressy testified that upon a Saturday in the evening near about the shutting in of the daylight he was bewildered and lost his way a little beyond the field of George Martin and having wandered a while he came back againe to the same place which he knew by stooping trees in that place. And in Less than half a mile going he saw a Light stand on his Left hand about two rod out of the way it seemed to be about the begness of a half bushell, and he having a stik in his hand did with the end of it indeverred to stir it out of the place and to give it some small blows with it and the Light seemed to brush up and move from side to side as a turkey cock when he spreads his tayle but went not out of the place. He further sayth that after striking it and his recovering himself and going on his way when he had gone about 5 or 6 rod he saw Susana Martin standing on his Left hand as the light had done that she stood and lookt upon him and turned her face after him as he went along but said nothing, but that he went home as aforesaid, but knowing the ground that he was upon returned and found his owne house but being then seized with feer could not speake till his wife spake to him at the door. The next day it was upon inquiry understood that the said Goodwife Martin was in such a miserable case and in such pain that they swabbed her body. This deponent further sayth that some years after the said John Pressy had given his evidence against the said Susana Martin she the said Martin came and took these deponents to do about it and reviled them with many foule words saying wee had took a false oathe and that we should never prosper and that we should never

prosper for our so doing particularly that we should never have but two cows and that if we were never so likely to have more yet we should never obtain it. We do further testify that from that time to this day we have never exceeded that number but something or other has prevented it, though never so likely (to obtain it) though they had used all ordinary means for obtaining it . . ."

Trappist Preserves, made and packed by the monks of Saint Joseph's Abbey, Spencer, Massachusetts (prospectus):
". . . Trappist wine jellies are not merely flavored with wine, but are made with the pure wine. Careful timing in preparation maintains the full-bodied bouquet and perfect clarity of the wine itself. No longer an item found only on the formally set dinner table, wine jelly has become a favorite accompaniment for meat, fish, and fowl.
– Port: cheese dishes, chicken pie, ham,
– Tokay: on ice cream, fruit cake, toast,
– Sherry: hors d'oeuvres, fish, lobster,
– Claret: lamb, veal, chicken, cheese soufflé,
– Burgundy: roast beef, roast duck, venison,
– Muscatel: fish, scallops, lobster, shrimp."

The sea,
    let the sea take me,
let the sea be revenged upon me,
    let the sea swallow me,
let there be no trace of me left,
    let the sea drown me . . .

Billingsgate Island, in Cape Cod Bay.

A pair of Wilson's warblers on a flowering stalk of chelone glabra.

    CANTON, where you can order vanilla ice cream in the Howard Johnson Restaurant.

A pair of song sparrows, each about to swallow a spider.

Cirrus clouds in the sky,—across the eastern state line, but still farther south,

CANTON, CONN.

The sea,
                  plastic ducks,
plastic seals,
                  plastic dragons,
plastic swans,
                  plastic whales.

The outskirts of New York City.

Lake Shaw.

A pair of Connecticut warblers on a spray of blue gentian.

MANCHESTER, where you can ask for apricot ice cream in the Howard Johnson Restaurant.

A pair of goldfinches on a stalk of common thistle with pink blossoms.

The clouds spread,—across the southeast state line,

MANCHESTER.

"Information to Those Who Would Remove to America":
". . . Much less is it adviseable for a Person to go thither, who has no other Quality to recommend him but his Birth. In Europe it has indeed its Value; but it is a Commodity that cannot be carried to a worse Market than that of America, where people do not inquire concerning a Stranger, What is he? but, What can he do? . . ."
                                              Benjamin Franklin.

Veiled Lady Cave.

A raven with bluish plumage on a branch of thick shell-bark hickory heavy with fruit.

FRANKLIN, PA.—the Cornplanter Indian Reservation.

A pair of Cooper's hawks, the male on a dead branch, the female pursuing a small blue bird with a red throat.

"... If he has any useful Art, he is welcome; and if he exercises it, and behaves well, he will be respected by all that know him; but a mere Man of Quality, who, on that Account, wants to live upon the Public, by some Office or Salary, will be despis'd and disregarded . . ."
Benjamin Franklin.

Penn's Cave, Alexander Cavern.

The sun is overcast.

CANTON.—When it is one o'clock in

CANTON,

WELCOME TO OHIO

                one o'clock in
CANTON.

In Cleveland, Poles read the "Wiadomosci Godzienne."
In Cincinnati, Germans read the "Freie Presse."

Leesville Dam Lake, "Hello, Ken!"

        CANTON.

        "Information to Those Who Would Remove to America":
        ". . . The Husbandman is in honor there, and even the Mechanic, because their Employments are useful. The People have a saying, that God Almighty is himself a Mechanic, the greatest in the Universe; and he is respected and admired more for the Variety, Ingenuity and Utility of his Handyworks than for the Antiquity of his Family . . ."
                                                    Benjamin Franklin.

        "Hello, Mrs. Franklin!"—Indian Caverns.

BRIDGEPORT, on the Ohio River, the West Virginia state line, tributary of the Father of Waters, Belmont County.

In Cleveland, Germans read the "Wächter und Anzeiger."
In Akron, Hungarians read the "Akroni Magyar Hirlap."

Mobil,—Dover and Clendening Dam Lakes.

BRIDGEPORT, PA.,—the Cornplanter Indian Reservation.

". . . *They are pleas'd with the Observation of a Negro, and frequently mention it, that Boccarorra (meaning the White men) make de black man workee, make de Horse workee, make de Ox workee, make ebery ting workee; only de Hog. He, de hog, no workee; he eat, he drink, he walk about, he go to sleep when he please, he libb like a Gentleman . . ."*
Benjamin Franklin.

Lincoln Caverns and Seawra Cave.

A pair of wood thrushes on a branch of dogwood covered with berries.

MANCHESTER, on the Ohio, the Kentucky state line, Adams County,
    OHIO, the Middle West, one of the most heavily populated states.

An alder flycatcher at the top of a sweet gum branch, the bark spreading into broad, flat blades.

In Dayton, Hungarians read the "Magyar Hirado."
In Cleveland, Lithuanians read the "Dirva."

A huge shiny tan De Soto, driven by a very dark white woman, passes a tan Plymouth driven by a very dark white man,—Milton, Berlin, and Mogadore Dam Lakes.

MANCHESTER.

Chapel Lake Indian Ceremonials prospectus:
"You will see and hear:
— a Mother's Lullaby,
— Sunrise Chant,
— Tom Tom Dance on the Giant Drum,
— the Mysterious Flute Player,
— Log Rolling,
— Canoe Jousting,
— the drama of the White Scout's Capture and his Trial by Fiery Gantlet,
— the Blood Brotherhood and Tableau of Peace!"

*In Detroit, Greeks read the "Athenaï,"
    Italians read the "Tribuna Italiana,"
        Hungarians read the "Detroit Ujsag."*

Lake Saint Helen.

A pair of slate-colored juncos on bare branches of great swamp ash.

        LEXINGTON, MICH.,—the border of the Canadian province of Ontario,—L'Anse Indian Reservation.

In a cloudy sky, a pair of tree swallows, accompanied by a floating down-feather.

*In Detroit, Hungarians read the "Southwest Journal,"
    Italians read the "Voce del Popolo,"
        the Flemish read the "Gazette van Detroit."*

"Surprises and thrills galore!"

The two Long Lakes.

A gust of wind.

        COVINGTON.

COVINGTON, Buckeye State.

In Toledo, Poles read the "Ameryka Echo."
In Cleveland, Rumanians read the "American Rumanian News."

The Serpent Mound,—Pleasant Hill and Charles Mill Dam Lakes,—through Sears, Roebuck & Co. you can obtain an electric blanket with double thermostat security, permitting husband and wife to choose their own preferred temperature.

        COVINGTON, IND.

Or through Montgomery Ward, white down-filled pillows imported from Europe, "buy pillows in pairs, cheaper at

Ward's! Can't you already feel the downy softness of a pillow stuffed with pure white European goose down?"

Keep smiling!

Marengo Cave.

A pair of kingbirds, on a cottonwood branch, the male, with his red and gold crest, holding a bee in his bill.

GREENFIELD.

A pair of olive-sided flycatchers, on a balsam pine branch.

GREENFIELD, ILL.

GREENFIELD, MO. (for whites only).

GREENFIELD, OKLA. (. . . whites only)—Arapaho Indian Reservation.

GREENFIELD, OHIO, a livestock state.

In 1830, Joseph Smith organized the Church of the Latter-Day Saints, known as the Mormons; he had set out for Missouri, but preferred to stop at Mentor, Ohio, where he gained many converts, including Brigham Young, who was to succeed him . . .

Chief sects of Cincinnati:

Baptists,
    Roman Catholics,
        Christian Scientists,
            Episcopalians,
Evangelists,
    Greek Orthodox,
        Jews,
            Lutherans,
Methodists,
    Presbyterians . . .

Mound City Group National Monument and Seip Mound,—Loramie Dam Lake,—or a single thermostat electric blanket in assorted colors, choose from:
"Ming blue,
>   or an anti-allergic, anti-mildew, anti-mite, anti-dust pillow, page 415, stuffed with foam rubber,

LEXINGTON, Richland County. State Flower: scarlet carnation.

– ice pink,
>   or a pillow stuffed with Dacron Polyester Fiberfill made by Du Pont, red label,

In Toledo, 300 churches of 31 denominations.

– Savannah green,
>   – or a low-cost pillow stuffed with crushed chicken feathers,

Seven Caves,—the Newark Mounds.

– parchment beige,
>   or a pillow stuffed with whole duck feathers.

>   LEXINGTON, where you can order plum ice cream in the Howard Johnson Restaurant.

– canyon orange.

>   *In Louisville 500 churches of 45 denominations.*

– sun yellow," 11 different degrees of heat.

>   *Negro voices.*

Mammoth Cave National Monument.

>   LEXINGTON.

>   *In Nashville, 643 churches:*
>   *Baptist,*
>   >   *Roman Catholic,*

Presbyterian,
             Episcopalian,
Nazarene,
             Lutheran,
Seventh-Day Adventist . . .

Negro songs.

Rattlesnake Falls.

LEXINGTON.

The sea,
the laundress,
             foam,
linens,
             laces,
plumes,
             banners.

Our syllables that they have turned black.

Amicalola Falls,—telephone ringing.

A crow on a black-walnut branch heavy with fruit, above the tiny nest of a ruby-throated hummingbird.

COVINGTON, KY., the South (. . . only).

Our words that they have turned black.

"Hello, I want Greenfield, Indiana,"—Cascade and Onyx Caves.

The sunshine on the white clouds.

COVINGTON, TENN. (. . . only).

They have taken our pianos and made black music on them, if you can call it music . . .

> Ozone and Marcella Falls.

The glittering needle of a plane.

> COVINGTON, GA., the Deep South (. . . only).
>
> *They bewitch us, bind us by that black melopoeia.*
>
> *Bird of paradise flowers.*
>
> *The sea,*

laps,

> *licks,*

gnaws,

> *polishes,*

flattens.

> Estatoah and Tallulah Falls,—telephone ringing.

Cirrus clouds between the cumulus.

> MANCHESTER.
>
> *There's not one of our tunes that they don't take, distort, and gradually force us to sing the way they do.*
>
> "Hello, I want Lexington, Kentucky."

A sunbeam passes over the fields.

> MANCHESTER.

A sunbeam reflected in a windshield.

> MANCHESTER.

SALEM, Columbiana County.

In 1800, in Etna, Ohio, Johnny Appleseed planted his first apple tree. For forty years he wandered through the wilds of Ohio, handing out Swedenborg's books and handfuls of appleseeds, dressed in rags, barefoot, in all weather, with his buckskin knapsack . . .

"Hello, I want Greenfield, Ohio,"—Old Man's Cave.

    SALEM, W. VA., the beginning of the Middle West.

    I fled, I fled the South, the beautiful South, the marvelous South . . .

    Organ Cave.

        SALEM, VA., the South.

A flock of red crossbills, males and females, young and mature, around their nest hanging from a long hemlock bough.

A pair of blue-gray flycatchers on a black walnut branch.

        BRIDGEPORT.—When it is two o'clock in

LOVELAND,

WELCOME TO OKLAHOMA

                still one o'clock in
LOVELAND, Central Time.

According to the Kiowa Indians, two young men who had set out on an expedition of war to the south had left their sister, who waited vainly for their return. Sure they were dead, she gave way to her despair until she fell to the ground, overcome by sleep. In a dream she had a vision, or rather heard a voice which said: "The brothers whose death you mourn are actually alive. When you waken, you will find beside you what will take you to them again." When she awakened she dug in the ground and found a peyotl plant. She called the priests and instituted the first peyotl ritual. The celebrants solemnly ate the peyotl and had dreams that showed them the two brothers wandering, starved, in the mountains of the Sierra Madre in Mexico. Immediately a relief expedition was organized, which succeeded in finding them safe and sound . . .

A Negro walk.

Lake of the Cherokees.

        LOVELAND, COLO., the Far West,—the Ute Indian Reservation.

ELGIN, Comanche County.

Black, they lounge along our walls.

The Oto Indian Jonathan Koshiway founded a Christianized version of the peyotl religion, which spread among the Omahas and the Winnebagos. He organized the Firstborn Church, which flourished so well among the Negroes that in the nineteen-twenties the Negro John Jamison organized the Negro Firstborn Church, while the Koshiway establishment turned into the Native Church of America, whose intertribal and pan-Indian character was emphasized by the Winnebago Indian Jesse Clay . . .

Flying Service,—Murray and Texoma Lakes,—"Hello, Lou!"

    ELGIN.

    It wasn't gold they found here, but oil . . .

    Black, they stare into our shopwindows.

    "Hello, Mrs. Loveland!"—The Sierra Tinaja Pinta.

BRIDGEPORT, Caddo County, OKLAHOMA, Middle West (for whites only),—the Osage Indian Reservation.

Charter of the Native Church of America:
"... *The goal of the Peyotl Church is to cultivate and promote among those who believe in the omnipotent God and follow the tradition of the Indian tribes, the religion of the Heavenly Father; to develop the moral virtues, that is, sobriety, zeal in action, charity, rectitude, mutual respect, brotherhood and unity among the members of the various Indian tribes of the United States of America; all by means of the sacramental use of peyotl . . ."*

Black, they stroll along our streets.

A shiny indigo Volkswagen stalled alongside the highway; a green truck passes, driven by a fat, pink white man,—Comanche, Duncan and Clear Creek Lakes.

    BRIDGEPORT, Wise County.

    Black, they sleep on our sidewalks.

Thousands of horses in the dust . . .

    Esso,—the Sierra Vieja and the Sierra Diablo.

A pair of turkey vultures.

        CANTON, Van Zandt County seat, TEX., the largest state after Alaska, on the border of the Mexican states of Chihuahua, Coahuila, Nuevo León and Tamaulipas

(. . . whites only),—Alibamu and Koashati Indian Reservation.

A yellow-throated warbler on a chestnut branch.

Thousands of horns in the dust.

Their black arms, their black foreheads covered with dust . . .

A red truck whose radio is blaring "Texas, Our Texas," driven by a fat, dark white man, passes a shiny yellow one driven by a thin, red white man,—Delaware, Apache and Davis Mountains,—through Montgomery Ward you can obtain the relaxing vibrator-armchair with radiant heat: "Let your cares and tensions fly away. Stretch out and relax after a hard day,—whether your efforts have been mental or physical. Sink into the luxury of the most comfortable armchair ever invented. The double action of Ward's relaxing armchair sets your legs at the most comfortable angle. . . . It is the weight of your own body that controls the inclination. Even the foot support is lined with latex foam to afford you supreme comfort . . ."

TAFT, Sooner State (men, women, colored people),—Arapaho Indian Reservation.

Or through Sears, Roebuck & Co., a bottle of "Vita-Plenty," "our best all-round formula . . . Each of these pleasant-tasting, sugar-coated tablets is filled with 11 vitamins, 12 minerals, plus liver extract for strengthening the blood . . ."

Black, they gather.

The Delaware Indian Flowing Mane: "Peyotl will be the new religion of the Indians. It will prevail among all the Indians, and only among them . . ."

Kiamichi Mountain,—Lakes Tecumseh and Wewoka,—or the "American Cook Book," "one of the largest and completest . . . Over 1,500 recipes tested by the Institute of Culinary Arts."

TAFT, San Patricio County.

Or a 100-piece "Encanto" china service for twelve, decorated with a rose and gilt-edged, made in Japan.

Black, they murmur.

Thousands of derricks in the dust . . .

Christmas and Wild Horse Mountains.

The sunshine on the highway.

LEXINGTON.

LEXINGTON, on the South Canadian River that flows into the Arkansas, tributary of the Father of Waters, Cleveland County, OKLA., an oil state ("These premises are restricted"),—Kenwood Indian Reservation.

The Delaware Indian Flowing Mane: "I feel compassion for all men, that is what peyotl has taught me . . . I suffer for any man who commits a sin . . . I pray for the rich and poor alike. All are equal; each of us waits for God. When we die the same place waits for all of us . . . From today on I must prepare myself to enter the beyond. I pray God and peyotl to make my mind clear so that I may learn the practice of the good . . ."

Black, they begin laughing.

Methodist church,—Sans Bois and Pine Mountains,—Lake Altus,—or the "Betty Crocker Cook Book," page 1032, "over 2,200 tested ways of preparing nourishing, tasty and attractive meals. 1,276 illustrations."

LEXINGTON.

Or the "Tempo" service, page 520, "modern, distinguished, with an abstract black spiral and platinum edges," made in Japan.

In 1838, Joseph Smith founded the Mormon village of Adam-ondi-Ahman, near Trenton, Missouri, which he was forced to abandon a year later because of the persecutions of the gentiles . . .

I tell you those Negroes are laughing at us!

Lake Niangua.

    LEXINGTON.

The city of Chicago, like a spatter of ink on the map.

Empire Room, Creole dishes,
Golden Ox Restaurant, German specialties,
Guey Sam, Cantonese cooking.

The Lithuanians who read the "Draugas,"
the Germans who read the "Abendpost,"
the Swedes who read the "Svenska Amerikanaen Tribunen,"
the Italians who read the "Italia,"
the Poles who read the "Dziennik Chicagoski."

The trains coming from Saint Louis.
The trains leaving for Oklahoma City.

In 1824, Captain White bought a village from the Sac and Fox Indians for two hundred sacks of corn. In 1830 a post office was established in the new village named Venus, which was soon absorbed into the slightly older locality called Commerce. When Joseph Smith was forced to abandon Adam-ondi-Ahman in Missouri, he came and settled there, changing the name of Commerce by special charter to Nauvoo (which in Hebrew means Pleasant Land). In 1841 he began the construction of a great temple that was never completed. A group of the Latter-Day Saints, rebelling, under pressure from the neighboring gentiles, against Smith's authority, published a tract, "Expositor," which the latter had destroyed as well as the press on which it had been printed. The leaders of the opposition took advantage of this move and had Joseph Smith and his brother Hyrun arrested and locked up in the prison of Carthage

> *county seat of Hancock County. On June 27, 1844, a furious crowd broke into the prison and assassinated the prophet and his brother. It was then that Brigham Young assumed leadership of the church. He sold all its property and set out with his flock toward Great Salt Lake . . .*

> Lake Pana.

GREENFIELD, mistletoe state.

Black, they undress all our daughters with a nostalgic glance.

According to the Delaware Indian Flowing Mane, during a hunting expedition across the plains, a young man, eager to give proof of his valor, separated from his party and set off alone. In vain they sought for him far and wide, day after day. Finally, in fear and trembling, his sister began to search for him. Alone, she crossed an endless territory; her effort and despair, hunger and thirst were such that finally, at the end of her strength, she prayed to God to let her die. Prostrate, her head to the east, she suddenly felt something cool in the mud, and at the same time a young man appeared to her who declared: "Why are you so distressed? Look at me. All your family is safe, your brother is safe; I have assured the safety of all." The human figure vanished, but a voice was heard, and it was the peyotl itself that spoke, the plant she had pulled out of the mud, which gave her the precepts of the new cult, made her "see" her brother safe and sound, and lastly ordered her to teach the people the new religion. "Take the peyotl, with it, you will have salvation and be distressed no more."

The Chikaskia River that flows into the Arkansas,—the Roman Catholic church,—Jackfork Mountain,—or the "New Cookbook" in the "Better Homes and Gardens" series, "1,403 thrice-tested recipes . . . Deep-freeze charts, buffet settings, picnic ideas, seasoning, diets, methods of measuring, preserving calendars, foreign dishes."

> GREENFIELD, MO. (. . . only).

> Or the "Rose Chintz" service, made in Japan, "romantic setting of regularly spaced rose buds; sparkling platinum rims."

Black, they have a grin that shows their teeth.

Montrose and Lotawana Lakes.

GREENFIELD, ILL.

In 1849, the Icarian French, under the leadership of Etienne Cabet, took possession of the deserted city of Nauvoo, Illinois, on the Mississippi, the Iowa border, but soon the hostility of the neighboring people and internal dissensions led to a new desertion. Today Nauvoo is famous for its vineyards . . .

The Poles who read the "Dziennik Zwiaskowy,"
the Czechs who read the "Denni Hlasatel,"
the Greeks who read the "Hellenic Free Press."
The trains coming from Kansas City.
The Chinese who read the "San Min."
The Lithuanians who read the "Naujienos,"
The Norwegians who read the "Viking."
The trains leaving for Tulsa.
Taxi!
Henrici's, steaks, chops,
Harding's Colonial Room, organ music,
How Kow Restaurant, Cantonese dishes.

Mattoon and Charleston Lakes.

GREENFIELD, IND.

GREENFIELD, OHIO.

A pair of red-breasted nuthatches.

CANTON.

A pair of Savannah sparrows on two horizontal branches, in front of a thin curtain of tall, dead grass, among which are blooming a spigelia and a phlox.

Cirrus clouds in the sky.

CANTON.

CANTON, Blaine County, OKLA., cotton belt.

According to the Delaware Indian James Webber, during the hostilities between the Comanche Indians and the Mexican tribes, in 1860, it happened that one group was pursued by its enemies. One squaw, who had long suffered from some sickness, in order not to hold the warriors back, was left in a tent with a little boy to help her, until they could come back for her. During the night, the frightened child ran off after the riders. Finding herself abandoned, despairing that the boy could ever find safety in the huge prairie, she threw herself down on the ground to pray to the Great Spirit and fainted away. Then there appeared to her a person resembling a great Indian chieftain who advised her not to worry any longer about the child, who was safe, nor about herself, for she would recover on condition that she found a certain plant with medicinal properties and ate it, and that then she would receive the precepts of a new religion. The woman found and ate the peyotl, who appeared to her in person in a second vision in order to teach her the rites, songs and rules of the new cult which she founded among the nations . . .

The laughter of their black children.

If you think all dehydrated soups taste the same, it's time you tried Heinz!—Red Rock and Black Bear Creeks that flow into the Arkansas.

CANTON.

A black attraction.

Lake Anthony.

A pair of black vultures, tearing at the head of a Virginia deer.

ELGIN, Chautauqua County, KANS. (. . . only),—the Pottawatomie Indian Reservation.

A pair of loggerhead shrikes quarreling on a dead, lichen-covered branch spiraled with round-leaved smilax with small black berries.

A black obsession.

Afton and El Dorado Lakes.

ELGIN, NEBR.

They left Nebraska for Wyoming.

Lamb's Lake.

A pair of fox sparrows on a clump of moss, grass, berries and dead leaves.

BRIDGEPORT, Saline County.

A pair of cedar waxwings on a branch of red cedar.

You say we hate them, but just look at them! Don't you see that they're invading us, and that they won't forgive us?

Caltex,—a blue Lincoln, driven by a dark, fat white woman, sideswipes an old blue Kaiser parked beside the highway, its radio blaring "Home on the Range,"—Lakes Sabetha, McKinney and Inman.

An invasion of clouds in the sky.

BRIDGEPORT.

The air grows sultry.

MANCHESTER.

MANCHESTER, Grant County.

Like an array of black clouds.

The state capitol, surrounded by oil wells, built over an oil deposit.

The Cimarron River that flows into the Arkansas.—When it is two P.M. i̇
BEAVER,

WELCOME TO OREGON

        noon in
BEAVER, Pacific Time.

Varied thrushes,
        water ouzels,
                sage grouse,
                        Swainson's hawks,
                evening grosbeaks,
    purple martins,
red-winged blackbirds.

The sea,
        Pacific pink scallops,
Pacific jewel boxes,
        Lewis' moon shells,
eroded periwinkles,
        sunset clams.

Umpqua National Forest, "Hello, Mike!"

        BEAVER, WASH.,—the border of the Canadian province of British Columbia.—the Makah Indian Reservation.

In 1855, the Indian chief Seattle, who gave his name to the largest city in Washington, formerly called New York, declared to the European negotiators: "Every bit of this land is sacred . . . Every hill, valley or plain, every woods has been sanctified by some glorious or horrible event in the past. Even the rocks that seem mute and dead when they bake in the sun, tremble with extraordinary events linked to the life of my people . . . When the children of your chil-

dren will suppose themselves alone in the fields, the shops, on the roads or in the silent forests, they will not be alone at all . . . At night, when all sound has died away in the streets of your villages, and when you think they are empty, they will swarm with the host of those who once lived there, faithful to that sublime site. The white man will never be alone."

The sea,
        murmur,
lamentation,
        echo,
roar,
        murmur.

In 1881, the Squaxon Indian John Slocum, after a serious illness, fell into a trance one morning at dawn and remained unconscious until evening. He was believed to be dead. When he awakened he announced that he had indeed been dead, but that he had revived, that he had traveled to heaven, that the angels there had forbidden him to enter because of his bad actions on earth. From on high he had seen his own body and realized how badly he had acted hitherto. The angels had given him the rules of a new religion, and given him the mission of teaching them to men . . .

"Hello, Mrs. Grant!"—Gifford Pinchot National Forest.

NEWPORT, on the Pacific, county seat of Lincoln County.

The sea,
    Oregon tritons,
yellow-headed blackbirds,
    Bullock's orioles,
giant Pacific scallops,
    sea perches,
        meadowlarks,
            Townsend's warblers,
starred plaice,
    pilchards,
        Western bluebirds,
    lazuli buntings,

clay-colored sparrows.

B. P.,—Fremont and Siskiyou National Forests.

NEWPORT.

LEXINGTON, Morrow County, ORE.,—the Klamath Indian Reservation.

Oregon juncos,
    black-throated green warblers,
        MacGillivray's warblers,
            Western tanagers,
the sea,
    Northern anchovies,
lings,
    red-tailed perch,
sea elephants,
        red-breasted mergansers,
    ancient murrelets,
eared grebes,
    Pacific mackerels.

A huge bright purple Hudson, driven by a fat pink white man, passes a purple Studebaker driven by a thin dark white man, "go straight ahead," —the Siuslaw, Willamette and Mount Hood National Forests.

ELGIN, Beaver State,—the Siletz Indian Reservation,

The sea,
    gray whales,
whistling swans,
    Baird's cormorants,
        Brandt's cormorants,
            valley quail,
Pacific humpbacks,
    blue whales,
rorquals,
    sperm whales,
        pygmy nuthatches,
    Lewis' woodpeckers,
dwarf hermit thrushes.

Crater Lake National Park,—Deschutes and Ochoco National Forests,—through Sears, Roebuck & Co., you can obtain an oval sports rug "that can also be hung on the wall to keep up your team spirit; perfect for game rooms, dens, bedrooms, dormitories, anywhere you want a bright, sports accent; your name, that of your school or team, woven in the rug . . . Any colors you specify, or monocolor if you prefer," soccer, basketball or baseball models.

 WARREN, Columbia County, ORE., crater state,—the Warm Springs Indian Reservation.

  Or through Montgomery Ward, a "Beautyrest" mattress, "try Beautyrest for thirty days at home . . . Prove to yourself Beautyrest's comfort. Choose any style, degree of firmness, size. After having slept on your Beautyrest thirty days, if you aren't completely satisfied, send it back to Ward and your money will be refunded. The mattress will be returned to Simmons who will destroy it in accordance with the law."

American bitterns,
  pine grosbeaks,
    Bohemian waxwings,
      common linnets,
the sea,
  inlets,
rocks,
  creeks,
ponds,
  puddles,
short-tailed grouse,
  bank swallows,
hairy linnets.

The Methodist church,—Cultus and Winopec Lakes,—Malheur National Forest.

  WARREN, IDA., the Far West,—the border of the Canadian province of British Columbia,—the Coeur d'Alene Indian Reservation.

TAFT, on the Pacific, Lincoln County.

> TAFT, CALIF., Pacific Coast, the largest state after Alaska and Texas, the most heavily populated after New York,—the border of the Mexican state of Baja California,—the Los Coyotes Indian Reservation.

White pelicans,
    spotted sandpipers,
        common terns,
the sea,
    kelp,
slipways,
    cabins.
canoes,
    currents,
                pied-billed grebes,
            black coots,
        green-winged teal,
red-throated divers.

> *A member of the French department of the University of California at Los Angeles asked me if I preferred seeing something beautiful or something ugly. "Ugly, of course!" "I'm going to take you to Clifton's Cafeteria . . ."*

Sparkle Lake.

> *Prospectus: "The Influence of One Life":*
> *"Millions have perished in war and terror . . .*
>> *Another prospectus: "Views of the Holy Land":*
>> *"Edmond J. Clinton was born in Missouri in 1872, came to California in the '80's with his father. He and his wife were both Salvation Army captains . . .*
>>> *A third prospectus: "Views of Clifton's Cafeteria":*
>>> *"Clifton's Pacific Seas on Olive Street has a façade with waterfalls and tropical foliage . . .*

We survive . . .
>   Later he established himself in the restaurant business in San Francisco, became proprietor of the Puritan Dining Rooms, the Quaker Dining Room, and later the Clinton Company . . .
> >   The rock portico, beneath the front waterfalls and neon floral patterns, where the passer-by may rest . . .

Millions are homeless . . .
>   His desire was always to serve others in the name of Jesus Christ. Twice he and his family went to China, supported in their mission work by his business . . .
> >   A fantastic neon palm by a Polynesian grass hut . . .

We are sheltered . . .
>   In 1928 he sold his San Francisco business interests. He later came to Los Angeles to unite his efforts with those of his son who had established Clinton's . . .
> >   Overlooking the main dining room where throughout the day fresh flower leis and corsages are presented to guests . . .

This night in all the world, for every man well nourished, three are hungry . . .
>   Since then, until a few days before his death, he was to be seen on the floor of Clifton's Pacific Seas Cafeteria, helping and visiting with guests and associates . . .
> >   Guests provide birthdays and Clifton's provides the birthday cake, free . . .

We are fed . . .
>   Because his life was an exemplification of the message of The Garden, it was decided that the project should be a memorial to him . . .
> >   The main dining room looking toward the waterfalls . . .

The world's abundance should have blessed mankind. Instead the finger of the bitter past points to a bloody page . . . 'and we shall meanly lose or nobly save the last best hope of earth' . . .
>To those who espouse the philosophy that 'business is business' and nothing more, the idea of combining a place for meditation and reverence with a commercial enterprise may seem incongruous . . .
>>Tropical jungle scene is the motif of this muraled wall . . .

Each life is tested by its answer to the question first asked in the world's beginning: 'Am I my brother's keeper?'
>Many guests welcomed the installation of The Garden, a place for reverence and meditation. At first a simple room with some beautiful pictures was contemplated. One picture suggested was that of the artist Hoffman: "Christ in the Garden' . . . Then the thought was suggested by Dr. William Evans that this scene be revealed as a garden diorama with the figure of Christ in sculptured form. The Garden as it exists today evolved from this idea.
>>A view of the dining room through one of the neon trees . . .

One Life was lived in answer. 'Twas such a little span of years in such a far-off lonely little land.
>The sculptor Marshall Lakey was commissioned in November, 1943. Then arose the problem of the text for the recording which was to present the challenge of Christ's example. The meaning of Christ's life and His spiritual and historic influence should, it was felt, be presented with theological restraint . . .
>>Rain-hut, in the mezzanine dining room, where it rains every twenty minutes . . .

This Life began in a village stable. No birth could be lowlier, hence none need despair because of lowly birth. No wife, no child—yet, He showed each lonely heart its deepest need.

Since this is not a project of any religious denomination it should not presume to assert a creed. It should not presume to tell any visitor what to believe. Sufficient if it should challenge him to make his own answers on the basis of the evidence presented. Whatever else may be disputed within or without the Christian faith, there is no dispute about the tremendous influence of Christ's life. The most skeptical cannot dismiss it as without meaning beyond human understanding . . .

Organ and piano music are presented from this central stage. Guests' request numbers are gladly played . . .

For thirty years He grew and learned His simple trade, shaping the native wood to serve the wants of home and craft . . .

Before being inscribed and recorded 'The Influence of One Life' was rewritten many times after being submitted to many thoughtful adherents of Jewish, Catholic and Protestant faiths. . . .

From the entertainment platform we see this grass hut . . .

Three years He wandered, teaching, shaping the native hearts to service of truth and love . . .

To those who ask why Christ was not mentioned by name in the recording, the answer is that not one of all the millions who have heard it has failed to identify Him . . .

Figure of Jesus, the Christ (Marshall Lakey, sculptor) in the Garden for Meditation, where a recording of 'The Influence of One Life' is heard . . .

He held no earthly rank or office, wrote no book, no song; painted no picture, builded no monument . . .

To those who ask:—'Why did you leave Christ in the tomb and not proclaim the Resurrection?' the answer is that the existence of the Garden and

countless other evidences of Christ's influence after two thousand years proclaim that He was not left 'in the tomb.' In the Garden we engage in no theological controversy . . .
> The room of the weavers acts as a reception room to the Garden . . .

While still in the flush of youth, His own people turned against this Man who strangely taught that evil can only be overcome by good . . .
> Christ is 'left in the tomb' only to the mind and heart in which He does not live. He is resurrected for each man or woman who believes, lives and acts in response to His teachings . . .
>> This 5-foot parchment scroll hangs in the 'Vaulted Archway' opposite the 'Grotto of the Rock' where the words of 'The Influence of One Life' are heard on a recording before entry into the Garden . . .

He was denied . . . deserted . . . betrayed . . .
> The Garden projects no quarrel with any sincere believer, seeks to impose no belief. It is not a church or a shrine. We offer to all reverent persons a presentation of Christ's influence . . .
>> Multi-Purpose Food (MPF). Clifton's completely balanced, nutritionally adequate five-cent meal (no charge to those without funds). . . .

One dark hour He knelt in the Garden, His hour of decision . . .
> Personal salvation is a personal problem. We do not presume to present its solution. True faith cannot be imposed from without. It must come from within. The test of that faith lies in the life that is lived, not in the creed professed . . .
>> Multi-purpose food being used with the noonday meal at the Nakamura Day Nursery, in Yokohama, Japan (U.S. Signal Corps photo) . . .

He gave Himself over to His enemies, was tried and condemned in mockery, spat upon and lashed, nailed to a cross between two thieves . . .
>   *Since the opening of the Garden at Clifton's on January 21, 1945, there have been many requests for a written description of its various features* . . .
>   *Clifton's Brookdale Cafeteria, 7th and Broadway, Los Angeles. One of the largest of its kind in the world* . . .

He died asking forgiveness for His persecutors . . .
>   *Public interest has exceeded all expectations. Visitors have averaged about a thousand daily. When crowds of upwards of three thousand tax the Garden's capacity on Sundays, it is necessary to turn away many hundreds.*
>   *Brookdale in the Redwoods—the main dining room* . . .

He was laid in a borrowed tomb . . .
>   *Comments of visitors are varied. They reveal an inward hunger not to be satisfied by 'bread alone.' Many questions are asked to which receptionists often have no time to give adequate answers:—*
>   *Little Chapel, Brookdale. Among flowing brooks and redwood trees you may pause for a moment's meditation in the little stone Chapel. A redwood forest scene made of 10,000 miniature pieces lights up while a recording of 'Parable of the Redwoods" plays* . . .

Nearly two thousand years have passed and none has reigned or wrought or served or dreamed who has so touched and moulded human life. He is the ideal—the example—the greatest unalterable, wholesome, growing influence in a world of blood and tears . . .
>   *Why should a commercial cafeteria go to this expense to create this scene from the Garden of Gethsemane?* . . .
>   *Old rock fireplace, in the dining nook below organ ledge* . . .

He who was friendless would be Friend of all. Homeless, He dwells in countless homes. Books on His life fill libraries. His Gospels cover the earth. Song and music in His praise fill the heavens. Pictures, spires and monuments proclaim His influence . . .
    What are the business principles of Clifton's?
    Main dining room from one of the upper terraces . .

The names of Pharaohs, Caesars, emperors and kings of all the ages that have come and gone are but ghosts upon a printed page. Their legions dust upon the land; their proud armadas rust upon an ocean floor . . .
    This is the question which most puzzles visitors to the Garden; this 'mixing of religion with business'. . .
    Dining terraces overlooking the main dining room, Wishing Well . . .

But this one solitary Life surpasses all in power. Its influence is the one remaining and sustaining hope of future years . . .
    Business is many things to many men. To some 'business is business' and nothing more. To some it is a game, to others an intellectual exercise, to some a social service or a way of life. To some it is just an unpleasant necessity, a means to other ends. Some like to get away from their business to devote their major interest to some outside social, religious, political or cultural activity . . .
    Your photograph in beautiful surroundings while you dine . . .

Where does such power dwell?
    To us business is not a compartment shut off from our other interests. It is a part of our life. We see no reason why our other interests and ideals should not be a part of our business. We see no reason why, in serving our guests food for their body we should not also give them food for mind and spirit . . .

> Pine room—one of several newly decorated group meeting rooms. Brookdale's special rooms can accommodate any size gathering . . . from 3 to 300!

'Be therefore not anxious . . . But seek ye first His kingdom and His righteousness—and all these things shall be added unto you . . .'
> Must we only enjoy art in an art gallery, politics in the voting booth, religion in the church, books in a library, education in a school, music in the concert hall, business in our offices? Since each of these is a part of life, why not so organize our daily existence as to express all these interests in our common daily tasks? . . .
>> Gift and souvenir shop, found below street level at the Brookdale . . .

In a Roman court nearly twenty centuries ago, Pontius Pilate asked . . .
> We believe that everything that contributes to a better life should be applied to business . . .
>> Clifton's Lakewood, third and newest unit, depicting its modern, 'California Casual' surroundings . . .

'What shall I do with this Man?'
> It is only when the best fruits of religion are assimilated into our business, our pleasure, our politics, our lives that they have complete moral and spiritual justification . . .
>> Nelda and Clifford E. Clinton, founders of Clifton's, in the patio of their Hollywood Hills home . . .

Today each troubled heart must meet the challenge when the Pilate-within asks:
> For further particulars on Clifton's, its policies and practices, ask for Clifton's 'In Your Service,' free at information desks."

Los Angeles and Clifton's will always welcome you."

'What shall I do?'
By Ernest R. Chamberlain as suggested by Clifford E. Clinton."

Los Padres National Forest.

On a spray of bittersweet, a pair of Audubon's warblers, a pair of hermit warblers, a pair of black-throated gray warblers.
A pair of towhees on a blackberry bush.

OAKLAND.—When it is one o'clock in

OAKLAND,

WELCOME TO PENNSYLVANIA

           already four o'clock in
OAKLAND, Eastern Time.

"Information to Those Who Would Remove to America":
"According to these Opinions of the Americans, one of them would think himself more obliged to a Genealogist who could prove for him that his Ancestors and Relations for ten Generations had been Ploughmen, Smiths, Carpenters, Turners, Weavers, Tanners, or even Shoemakers, and consequently that they were useful Members of Society; than if he could only prove that they were Gentlemen, doing nothing of Value, but living idly on the Labour of others, mere "fruges consumere nati," and otherwise good for nothing, till by their death their Estates, like the Carcass of the Negro's Gentleman-Hog, come to be cut up . . ."
                                                                        Benjamin Franklin.

"The Gospel of Wealth":
"When visiting the Sioux, I was led to the wigwam of the chief. It was like the others in external appearance, and even within the difference was trifling between it and those of the poorest of his braves. The contrast between the palace of the millionaire and the cottage of the labourer with us today measures the change which has come with civilization . . ."
Andrew Carnegie (1835–1919, "American philanthropist" born in Dunfermline, Scotland).

Blue Mountain, "Hello, Sam!"

           OAKLAND, N.J., one of the smallest states.

Brown thrashers,
　　　　　gull-billed terns,
　　　　　　　　　American brants,
　　　　　marsh hawks,
black rails.

The sea,
　　　　　footprints on the sand,
sand on the thighs,
　　　　　streams in the sand,
sand in the shoes,
　　　　　bird tracks on the sand.
The outskirts of New York City.

"Hello, Mrs. Taft!"—Beaver Lake.

A Bachman's sparrow on a branch of flowering pinckneya.

NEWPORT.

A pair of seaside sparrows on a reed among Cherokee roses.

NEWPORT, on the Juniata River, tributary of the Susquehannah, Perry County.

". . . But this change, however, is not to be deplored, but welcomed as highly beneficial. It is well, nay, essential for the progress of the race that the houses of some should be homes for all that is highest and best in literature and the arts, and for all the refinements of civilization . . ."
　　　　　　　　　　　　　　　　　　　Andrew Carnegie.

"In short, America is the Land of Labour, and by no means what the English call Lubberland, and the French Pays de Cocagne, where the streets are said to be pav'd with half-peck Loaves, the Houses til'd with Pancakes, and where the Fowls fly about ready roasted, crying, Come eat me! . . ."
　　　　　　　　　　　　　　　　　　Benjamin Franklin.

B. P.,—Brush and Shade Mountains.

　　　NEWPORT.

Fire!

The airport at Columbus, county seat of Franklin County, the state capital.

NEWPORT.

Smile!

The airport at Indianapolis, county seat of Franklin County, the state capital.

A pair of rusty song sparrows with two of their young on a black hawthorn branch.

MIDDLETOWN, Butler County.

A male and two female long-billed marsh wrens beside their spherical nest on the top of a clump of reeds.

The fire engine siren.

"How much longer? An hour?"—The airport at Cleveland, county seat of Cuyahoga County, and at Akron, county seat of Summit County.

The shadows grow longer.

MIDDLETOWN, Henry County, IND., the Middle West.

Smile, please!

The airport at Terre Haute, county seat of Vigo County, and at Lafayette, county seat of Tippecanoe County.

WARREN, on the Allegheny River that flows into the Ohio, tributary of the Father of Waters, county seat of Warren County, PA.,—the Cornplanter Indian Reservation.

"Who then are the kind of Persons to whom an Emigration to America *may be advantageous? And what are the Advantages they may reasonably expect? . . ."*

Benjamin Franklin.

". . . Much better this great irregularity than universal squalor . . . The 'good old times' were not good old times. Neither master nor servant was as well situated as today . . ."

Andrew Carnegie.

An old black Chevrolet parked beside the highway. A purple Chevrolet passes, driven by a young, fat, red-faced white woman, "turn left," —Tuscarora, Bald Eagle and Stone Mountains.

>WARREN, county seat of Trumbull County, OHIO, one of the most heavily populated states.

Charred beams.

>B.P.,—a shiny, overloaded indigo Cadillac, driven by an old, skinny, dark white man, passes a yellow Chevrolet driven by an old, skinny, almost white Negro,—the airport at Dayton, county seat of Montgomery County, at Newark, county seat of Licking County, at Zanesville, county seat of Muskingum County,—through Montgomery Ward, you can obtain a nursing service including:

or through Sears, Roebuck & Co., a bottle of "Perlettes," little easy-to-swallow capsules "ideal for every member of the family:
– 15 milligrams of iron,
>"8 bottles, nipples and tops,

– 46 milligrams of calcium,
>– one box of nipples, two tops,

– 35 milligrams of phosphorus,

>WARREN, on the Salamonie River that flows into the Wabash, Huntingdon County.

– one nylon swab,
– one milligram of manganese,
>– one graduated measuring pot,

– five milligrams of potassium,
>– one straining funnel,

They left Indiana for Illinois.

— .5 milligrams of molybdenum,
  — one pair of metal tweezers,
— one milligram of copper,
  — one nylon nipple brush,
— .15 milligrams of cobalt,

> Caltex,—a huge old red Dodge driven by a young, very dark Negro woman, going much faster than the speed limit, collides at a red light with a green Oldsmobile,—the airport at Kokomo, county seat of Howard County, at Marion, county seat of Grant County, at Muncie, county seat of Delaware County.

  — four measuring spoons,
— .15 milligrams of iodine,
  — one aluminum stirring rod."
— 1.4 milligrams of zinc."

WARREN, ILL.

BEAVER, the Keystone State.

"The price we pay for this salutary change is, no doubt, great. We assemble thousands of operatives in the factory, and in the mine, of whom the employer can know little or nothing, and to whom he is little better than a myth . . ."
Andrew Carnegie.

". . . Land being cheap in that Country, from the vast Forests still void of Inhabitants, and not likely to be occupied in an Age to come, insomuch that the Propriety of an hundred Acres of fertile Soil full of Wood may be obtained near the Frontiers, in many places, for Eight or Ten Guineas, hearty young Labouring Men, who understand the Husbandry of Corn and Cattle, which is nearly the same in that Country as in Europe, may easily establish themselves there . . ."
Benjamin Franklin.

Indian Caverns,—Tussey and Terrace Mountains,—or a hooked rug, "sculptured elegance," "Delightful, original! the pattern forms a classic Greek key design, comes in

– black,
>> or a pot of "Lo-luster" paint, "better for six reasons:
>> 1) saves time, work, money,

– white,
>> 2) keeps its color longer,

– Federal gold,
>> 3) dries faster,

– cherry red,
>> 4) resists rust and dirt,

– dawn gray,
>> 5) doesn't scale,

– mint green,
>> 6) concealsimperfections in the surface covered;

– charcoal gray,
> comes in
> – white,

– parchment beige,
> – driftwood gray,
> – pebble beige,

– Ming blue,
> – patio turquoise,

> BEAVER, Pike County, Buckeye State.

> – marigold yellow,

– parchment brown,
> – bamboo ivory,

> *A refrigerator among the embers.*

> – smoke gray,

– frosty pink,
> – desert rose,

> Kelleys Island in Lake Erie,—the airport at New Philadelphia, county seat of Tuscarawa County, and at Woodsfield, county seat of Monroe County.

> – cream,

– spice brown,"
> – mirage green,

> – canyon red,
> – charcoal gray,
> – elf green." Or a Johnson & Johnson selection of presents for the newborn baby, page 298:
> "soap,"

or a bottle of "the most popular of our formulas, the famous 'Vita-Perles,' rich in vitamin power . . . more vital minerals . . . in each energy-packed capsule. Made to exceed the daily minimum requirements in essential vitamins,

> – jar of cold cream,

– iron,
> – bottle of lotion,

> JAMESTOWN, Greene County.

> – jar of oil,

– iodine,
– more generous rations of important calcium
– and phosphorus,
> – can of powder,

> *Some bottles, some cans, charred, split open and blackened.*

Excellent nutritive supplement for all the members of the family over twelve years of age."

> – 54 cotton swabs."

The sky is overcast.
> The airport at Wilmington, county seat of Clinton County.

A sunbeam through the clouds.

> JAMESTOWN.

The sky closes over.

> HARRISVILLE.

HARRISVILLE, Butler County, PA., an Appalachian state.

". . . A little Money sav'd of the good Wages they receive there, while they work for others, enables them to buy the Land and begin their Plantation, in which they are assisted by the Good Will of their Neighbors, and some Credit . . ."
Benjamin Franklin.

". . . All intercourse between them is at an end. Rigid castes are formed, and, as usual, mutual ignorance breeds mutual distrust . . . Under the law of competition, the employer of thousands is forced into the strictest economies, among which the rates paid to labour figure prominently . . ."
Andrew Carnegie.

The Presbyterian church,—Wonderland and Lincoln Caverns, the Kittatinny Mountains.

HARRISVILLE, W.VA.

JAMESTOWN, Mercer County.

". . . But, whether the law be benign or not, we must say of it: it is here; we cannot evade it; and while the law may be sometimes hard for the individual, it is best for the race, because it insures the survival of the fittest in every department . . ."
Andrew Carnegie.

At the end of his life, Andrew Carnegie sold his Pittsburgh steel mills to John Pierpont Morgan and devoted himself to good works.

". . . Multitudes of poor People from England, Ireland, Scotland, and Germany, have by this means in a few years become wealthy Farmers, who, in their own Countries, where all the Lands are fully occupied, and the Wages of Labour low, could never have emerged from the poor Condition wherein they were born . . ."
Benjamin Franklin.

Woodward Cave.

JAMESTOWN.

Freedomland prospectus:

"Ride the Iron Horse!
Take your seat on the old Iron Horse!

Chug across the continental divide as she wends her way through the Pioneer West to San Francisco and back again to Chicago.

Chicago Fire!
Roaring flames racing through the city!
The pounding hooves and clanging wagons of an entire fire force turned out to stem the raging blaze! A dramatic page of history comes to life before your eyes—in a thrill you'll never forget!

Space Ride
Board an authentic space ship in Satellite City!
Blast off for a thrilling trip into orbit around the earth! See the world's wonders from thousands of feet above!

Crossfire in the Civil War!
You ride a correspondents' wagon to the front lines! Suddenly shot and shell ring out around you! You're caught in 'no man's land'—in the battle of the Blue and Gray!"

55,000 Greeks,
       125,000 Hungarians,
the Arabs who read "As Sayeh,"
       the Germans who read the "Staats-Zeitung und Herold,"
          the Poles who read the "Czas."

LIFE LIFE LIFE LIFE LIFE LIFE LIFE LIFE LIFE LIFE LIFE LIFE LIFE

Harvey's Seafood House, fish,
    Colony, French cuisine,
        Holland House Tavern, Dutch cooking,
Christ Cella, steaks,
    Brauhaus, German dishes,
        Pantheon, Greek food.

The planes leaving for Honolulu,
    for Lima,
The planes coming from Montevideo,
        from Johannesburg.

WBNX, Italian broadcasts,
        WFUV-FM, German broadcasts,
                WWRL, Arab broadcasts.

The ships coming from Recife.
The ships leaving for Las Palmas.

The Empire State Building: 35,000 visitors a day.

       Will you have some?
              No, thanks.
Didn't you see it on television?
          Going down?
     You're welcome.

Testimonial:
Photograph of Mary Martin, star of the hit Broadway musical "Sound of Music." Smile.
"It is my pleasure to extend a triple salute to Freedomland today on the occasion of its official opening . . ."

Jewelry, 47 Street between Fifth and Sixth Avenues.
       The ships leaving for the Azores.
             The wind.
     The ships leaving for Bermuda.
The Empire State Building: millions of postcards sold yearly.
     No Parking.
Radio City Music Hall,
    Winter Garden Theater,
        Warner Theater.
The subway coming from the far end of the Bronx:
Burke Avenue,
Allerton Avenue,
Pelham Parkway.
The subway coming from the far end of Brooklyn:
    King's Highway,
    Avenue M,
    Avenue J,
    Avenue H.
The subway coming from the far end of Queens:
        179 Street,

*169 Street,
Parsons Boulevard,
Sutphin Boulevard,
Van Wyck Boulevard.*

Press release:

". . . Jule Styne, noted American songwriter, who composed the 'Freedomland' album, was born in London, England; was a fine classical pianist before he was ten. His Freedomland tunes were written to capture the spirit of Little Old New York, the Chicago Fire, Mardi Gras, old-fashioned New England, the rugged West and Satellite City. These songs will be played continually in the park in the area they dramatize . . .

In the forests of Freedomland, mechanical dummy bears growl and move realistically, while a mechnical cub 'climbs' a tree . . ."

Mount Marcy, highest point in the state.

A female yellow-throated vireo in her nest on a dogrose branch, the male bringing her a worm. Two other males in the air in various flight positions.

HARRISVILLE, Lewis County, N.Y.,—the Onondaga Indian Reservation.

On two wild almond branches, a pair of cardinals, the male blood-red, the female reddish-brown and olive.

Freedomland prospectus:

"Pirate Ride!
Sabers clash! Cannons boom! You journey through the action-packed era of the old buccaneers! Fierce duels rage around you as swashbuckling pirates battle for treasure!

Northwest Passage!
Adventure in unexplored wilds! Ride a fur-trapper's canoe through uncharted waters! The air crackles with the danger of Indian ambush—the peril of wild animals stalking the underbrush!

Ride a 1901 Cadillac!
Take the wheel and tour the countryside of Colonial New England! A family-fun outing past farms, homes and fishing villages, re-created to make a delightful trip for young and old!

Little Old New York!
Stroll through the shops, the streets, the gaiety and atmosphere of New York as it was 100 years ago! Singing waiters, horse and buggies, costumes . . . policemen . . . everything is here to recapture an era!"

475,000 Irish,
the Arabs who read "Caravan,"
Red Coach, American specialties,
WBNX, Polish broadcasts,
Sardi's, Broadway atmosphere.
       1,100,000 Italians,
       the Chinese who read the "United Journal,"
       l'Armorique, French cuisine,
       WEVD, Italian broadcasts,
       Debrecen, Hungarian cooking.
              The Letts who read "Laiks,"
              Café Tokay, Hungarian cuisine,
              WHOM, German broadcasts,
              Passy, French cuisine.
COLLIER'S COLLIER'S COLLIER'S COLLIER'S COLLIER'S COLLIER'S COLLI
       Apple machine.
The planes coming from Saigon,
       from Manila,
     leaving for Manila,
       for Bangkok.
Expensive clothes for women, Fifth and Madison Avenues.
     The ships leaving for Lisbon.
       Smokestacks.
     The ships coming from Amsterdam.
The Empire State Building: the tallest television tower in the world, a quarter of a mile above street level.

Freedomland testimonial:
"First, as hostess of New York City's 'summer festival,' I am

proud the exciting activities of this gigantic attraction have been added to a program of events which is unmatchable in any other city in the world. Headed by Freedomland, New York is truly 'the city with everything . . .'"

Mary Martin.

Can I take you home?
I have my car.
Don't dawdle.
And you won't rather have Chesterfields?
No, I'm going straight home . . .
Psst!

The Empire State Building: the observatory staff speaks eight languages.
    The ships sailing for Jamaica.
    Cranes.
    The ships coming from Puerto Rico.
New Yorker Theater,
    R.K.O. Palace Theater,
        Sutton Cinema.
The subways coming from the far ends of the Bronx, Brooklyn and Queens:
Bronx Park,
    Newkirk Avenue,
        Union Turnpike,
East 180 Street,
    Cortelyou Road,
        Puritan Avenue,
177 Street.
    Beverly Road,
        Continental Avenue,
    Church Avenue.
        67 Avenue,
        Rego Park.
Museum of Natural History: the equestrian statue of Theodore Roosevelt, the statues of Boone, Audubon, Lewis and Clark.

Press release:
"Freedomland scouts scoured the country for herds of live buffalo, wild mustangs, mountain burros, trained mules and

pinto ponies which visitors will see in action at Freedomland. Among the unusual animals are the seals who live on the duplication of Seal Rock in the park's 'San Francisco Bay'. . . ," ". . . On a 400-passenger stern-wheeler, you'll sail through the 'Great Lakes,' and on board your ship all is gaiety. There's music and singing, a jangling piano and banjo. Original strains composed by America's top tunesmiths; your steamer passes a real Indian village on the banks. In the distance the towering flames of burning Chicago are reflected in the water . . ."

Heart and Cascades Mountains.

It's going to rain.

NEWPORT, on West Canada Creek that flows into the Mohawk River, tributary of the Hudson, Herkimer County.

Prospectus:
"Plantation Restaurant!
Gracious dining in a setting of the Old South. All across Freedomland you'll find interesting restaurants with menus and decor of their individual locales and time periods. The Steak House in Chicago, both Chinese and Italian restaurants in San Francisco, Mexican Restaurant in Tucson and the Dairy Restaurant in the Midwest. Also numerous snack bars prepared to serve you with a light bite in sparkling clean, cheerful surroundings . . ."

20,000 Latin Americans,
the Greeks who read the "Atlantis,"
Trader Vic's, new, exciting menu and decor.
WBNX, Spanish broadcasts.
The planes leaving for Fairbanks,
                for Singapore.
King of the Sea, fish.

"Pony Express!
Be there when the Pony Express comes pounding into the old Cavalry stockade! Post your own letter! You'll pick it up yourself when you get to Tucson!"

> 55,000 Northern Irish,
> the Jews who read the "Hadoar,"
> Pavillon, French cuisine,
> WEVD, Lithuanian broadcasts,
> The planes coming from Teheran,
>   from Damascus.
> Karachi, Indian dishes.

"Old West:
'O.K., pardner, it's a showdown!' Guns blaze! Bullets whiz past you! You're right smack in the middle of the wild and woolly West!"

> The Lithuanians who read the "Darbininkas."
> Cavanagh's, Irish cuisine,
> WFUV-FM, Italian broadcasts,
> The ships leaving for Miami, coming from Nassau,
> Angelo's, Italian cooking.

READER'S DIGEST READER'S DIGEST READER'S DIGEST READE

"Tornado Ride:
A howling Tornado roars across the Kansas prairie! See the awesome spectacle of homes and trees uprooted right before your eyes!"

Less expensive women's clothes, West 34 Street.

"Ore Bucket Ride!
Soar through the air 70 feet above Freedomland! A breathtaking panoramic view! An unforgettable ride in this exciting new version of the old mine ore bucket!"

The Empire State Building: from the observatory, you can see the rainclouds gathering, red sometimes, and the ships at sea often as far as forty miles away.

Freedomland testimonial:
"Next, as one who has spent her life in the entertainment world . . . And lastly, as a parent, I welcome such a wholesome, significant project. Freedomland offers a program of pleasure for children and adults alike. It will also renew in

all of us the pride and understanding of America which is so important for each of us to appreciate to the fullest at this time . . ."

Mary Martin.

The ships sailing for Houston.
    Newspapers floating.
The ships coming from New Orleans.
    Newspapers blown away.
Fine Arts Theater,
    Park Avenue Cinema,
        Loew's Canal Street Theater.
The subways coming from the far end of the Bronx, Brooklyn and Queens:
    Parkside Avenue,
East 174 Street,
        Woodhaven Boulevard,
    Prospect Park,
Freeman Street,
        Grand Avenue,
    Seventh Avenue,
Simpson Street.
        Elmhurst Avenue,
    Atlantic Avenue.
        Roosevelt Avenue,
        65 Street.

Museum of Natural History: over 760,000 specimens of shells catalogued.
    Bronx Zoo: 1,000-pound American elk.

    All alone?
        Shocked?
    No, you don't understand.
That was on television the other day.
    Careful!
        He's staring at me.
    Why is he staring at me like that?

Freedomland press release:
"Five thousand original costumes of 300 styles have been

designed for historical areas. Chief costumer Gordon Weiss and staff researched more than 1,000 photos and museum pieces for realism. Costumes run the gamut of early America: 'Keystone' cops of the 1850's, early firemen and railroad men, pioneers, Indians, cowboys, Civil War soldiers in both Blue and Gray. Fully equipped spacemen of the future roam Satellite City . . ."

A photograph from "Life," August 1, 1960, caption: "Children gasp with fright as a stalactite almost falls on them in Freedomland's underground promenade, where they learn a touch of the United States' geological history." All the anguish of this country painted on the young, convulsed faces . . .

Caltex,—a gray jeep driven by a young, almost yellow Negro passes a bright green one driven by an old, skinny Chinaman,—Cathead, Bullhead and Panther Mountains.

The first drops.

    MIDDLETOWN.

The road changes color.

    MIDDLETOWN, MD.

The flags of all the embassies in Washington, D.C.

The sea,
        a peacock of drops,
an eagle of foam,
        a rose of glass,
a fan of salt,
        a mane of noise.

Calvert Cliffs.

A pair of short-billed marsh wrens on their spherical nest among reeds.

    OAKLAND.

A pair of American redstarts on a branch of scrub elm, to which is attached a wild bees' nest.

The windshield wipers begin working.

    MIDDLETOWN, DEL.—When it is five o'clock in

MIDDLETOWN,

WELCOME TO RHODE ISLAND

                five o'clock in
MIDDLETOWN.

"After twenty-two years of nightmare and terror, sustained solely by the conviction that certain impressions of mine are purely imaginary, I refuse to guarantee the veracity of what I believe I have discovered . . ."
                                                                                H. P. Lovecraft.

The sea,
                all it hides,
rejects,
                imbibes,
transforms,
                takes back.

Chapman Pond, "Hello, Steve!"

        MIDDLETOWN, CONN.

JAMESTOWN, Newport County.

The sea,
                all those it tempts,
pursues,
                seduces,

ravishes,
        changes.

"West of Arkham the hills rise wild, and there are valleys with deep woods that no axe has ever cut. There are dark narrow glens where the trees slope fantastically, and where thin brooklets trickle without ever having caught the glint of sunlight. On the gentler slopes there are farms, ancient and rocky, with squat, moss-coated cottages brooding eternally over old New England secrets in the lee of great ledges; but these are all vacant now, the wide chimneys crumbling and the shingled sides bulging perilously beneath low gambrel roofs . . ."
                                                                             H. P. Lovecraft.

Esso,—Watchaug and Worden Ponds.

HARRISVILLE, Providence County, R.I.

"My knowledge of the thing began in the winter of 1926–27 with the death of my granduncle, George Gammell Angell, Professor Emeritus of Semitic Languages in Brown University, Providence, Rhode Island . . . The professor had been stricken whilst returning from the Newport boat; falling suddenly, as witnesses said, after having been jostled by a nautical-looking Negro who had come from one of the queer dark courts on the precipitous hillside . . ."
                                                                             H. P. Lovecraft.

The sea,
        thousands of claws,
thousands of fangs,
        thousands of tongues,
thousands of suckers.

An old red truck driven by a skinny young very black Negro in a white shirt, going much faster than the speed limit, passes a pineapple-colored Nash driven by a thin young red-faced white woman in a gray dress, her radio blaring "Bugle Call Rag," "keep going straight ahead,"—Quidnick, Coventry and Flat River Reservoirs.

WARREN, Bristol County.

The sea,
        thousands of shrouds,

moving corridors,
     halls of silk,
suffocations,
     wrecks.

"That glimpse, like all dread glimpses of truth, flashed out from an accidental piecing together of separated things—in this case an old newspaper item and the notes of a dead professor. I hope that no one else will accomplish this piecing out; certainly, if I live, I shall never knowingly supply a link in so hideous a chain. I think that the professor, too, intended to keep silent regarding the part he knew, and that he would have destroyed his notes had not sudden death seized him . . ."
                                                              H. P. Lovecraft.

The Scituate and Westconnaug Reservoirs.—When the sun sets at

NEWPORT,

WELCOME TO TENNESSEE

                    it is six o'clock in
NEWPORT, Eastern Time.

You reproach us for hating them, but our hatred is nothing to that which rises at evening in their black eyes.

The airport at Knoxville, county seat of Knox County,—across the Father of Waters,

                NEWPORT, ARK., the South (for whites only).—But it is only five o'clock in

TRENTON, Central Time, county seat of Gibson County.

And if we are so determined to maintain barriers, it is because we feel only too deeply the power that lurks in their darkness.

Mobil,—the airport at Jackson, county seat of Madison County, and at Memphis, county seat of Shelby County, "Hello, Tom!"—Across the Great Smoky Mountains,

      TRENTON.

    The sea,
                silver scales,
    silver feathers,
                silver pearls,
    silver clouds,
                silver lips.

The Creek Indians adopted the alphabet of the Cherokee Sequoyah. The missionaries decided it was high time to print the Bible in the Creek and Cherokee languages . . .

Because, you know, it's not true that these Negroes prefer our white women, actually it's our white women who prefer . . .

"Hello, Mrs. Warren!"—Lake Apalachia.

A pair of broad-winged hawks on a pig-nut branch.

NEWPORT, Carteret County.

The sea,
    gold scales,
gold tiles,
    gold mail,
gold lashes,
    gold pupils.

And these Negroes, they can tell just what complicity in the bellies of our white women wakens at nightfall the ember of their breath and their muddy eyes . . .

The Creek and Cherokee Indians began publishing a newspaper and drew up a constitution . . .

"How much longer? Two hours?"—Lakes Hiwassee and Santeetlah.

The purple clouds.

CLEVELAND, Rowan County, N.C. (. . . whites only),— the Cherokee Indian Reservation.

And if they walk that way, these Negroes, if they laugh, if they murmur that way, it's to make them feel that cunning domination in which we know they hold them only too well . . .

The sea,
    purple scales,

purple skeins,
> *purple enamels,*
purple shells,
> *purple threads.*

But gold was found in the Creek and Cherokee territories; those who had called themselves the five civilized tribes were driven into Oklahoma, then called Indian Territory . . .

Flying Service,—a maroon Pontiac, driven by a young thin Chinese girl in a purple dress with green polka dots, passes a maroon Ford driven by an old, almost white Negro woman in an indigo dress with yellow polka dots,—Fontana, Aquone and Glenville Lakes,—through Montgomery Ward, you can obtain a complete recording of the New Testament, "a blessing for those with failing sight, old people, invalids. Twenty-five hours of listening. Imitation-leather cover. Protestant version: 26 records at $16\tfrac{2}{3}$ rpm."

The street lamps come on.

> JAMESTOWN, Old North State (men, women, colored people).

We don't make the mistake of thinking those Negroes are weak, we don't think they're going to disappear, blend like a little stream into the ocean of whiteness . . .

Every means was used, corruption, threats, force. Certain Creek or Cherokee chiefs from whom the Europeans had managed to buy the territories of their tribes were massacred by their own people . . .

The sea,
> *glass scales,*
jade cascades,
> *emerald beds,*
onyx pages,
> *mint lenses.*

The airport at Winston-Salem, county seat of Forsyth County,—Logan and Waterville Lakes,—or the Challoner-Rheims Catholic version, page 620, in 30 records.

Twilight.

        LEXINGTON, where you can order vanilla ice cream in the Howard Johnson Restaurant, county seat of Davidson County, N.C., a swamp state ("These premises are restricted").

The five civilized tribes then set off on the path of tears, and thousands of them were massacred by the European soldiers who drove them on, before they reached Oklahoma. Only a few managed to take cover in the mountains, where the Cherokee Indian Reservation is located today . . .

Therefore, when they act too big, these Negroes, when they make us feel too deeply this coming power we are so afraid of, a little of their own rage explodes in us, and there is a riot, sometimes a murder, a kind of splatter of black ink on the page of our South . . .

The sea,
        sapphire scales,
foreign sails,
        indigo eddies,
cobalt damasks,
        lapis panes.

The Episcopalian church,—The airport at Charlotte, county seat of Mecklenburg County, and at Fayetteville, county seat of Cumberland County,—Summit Lake,—or Bible History, "excellent for Sunday School, and as a present; 26 high spots of the New Testament, and 21 of the Old, in all, four records."

The automobile headlights come on.

        FRANKLIN, county seat of Macon County.

And in Oklahoma, the five civilized tribes established a new government, printed newspapers and books again, organized schools, but made the mistake of siding with the Southern side in the Civil War; therefore, upon the victory of the

North, they were reduced to a new servitude, and some time later, the Federal Government declared that Oklahoma was no longer Indian Territory . . .

The sea,
                    obsidian scales,
jade plumage,
                    tillage of the swell,
fields of fresh ink,
                    rosewood shells.

Of course these outbursts are mistakes, since ultimately it's those Negroes who derive all the advantage from them, since world opinion is aroused, since even the North is beginning to regard us once again as dogs, but it's their own contagion that possesses us then like a demonic spirit in which they enjoy making us function . . .

The airport at Wilmington, county seat of New Hanover County.

The green sky.

ARLINGTON.

ARLINGTON, Shelby County, TENN. (. . . only).

But at least for a while they keep to the sidelines, they know their hour is not yet come, they no longer strut around in the same way, for a little while, a very little while; they feed on the shadows . . .

A huge plum-colored Cadillac, driven by an old, yellow-skinned, fat white man in a blue shirt with orange polka dots, passes an old maroon Buick driven by a fat young white man in a green shirt and red polka dots, his radio blaring "O Tennessee!," already going much faster than the daytime speed limit, "we took the wrong road, we have to go back," —the airports at Dyersburg, county seat of Dyer County, at Nashville, county seat of Davidson County, the state capital, at Chattanooga, county seat of Hamilton County,—across the northern state line,

ARLINGTON.

Then they put on those martyred looks, and our women, those of our women who were the most determined, who screamed the loudest, tremble even more at approaching their black districts, and gradually you see a new, secret smile at the corners of their black lips, for they don't even need to look at them, their backs, their hands secrete this venom, this disturbance . . .

The Tennessee that flows into the Ohio,—continuing northeast,

ARLINGTON.

I fled the South!

The Miami River that flows into the Ohio.

A red-eyed vireo, perched on a branch of honey locust, straining toward a yellow-haired spider hanging from the center of its web.

FRANKLIN, county seat of Simpson County.

So despite these obstructions, we lose ground every day before this huge threat, and if we cover ourselves with opprobrium in this way, at least it forces our governments to strengthen the segregation laws that protect us . . .

The Cumberland and Tradewater Rivers that flow into the Ohio.

The indigo sky.

FRANKLIN, Warren County.

New lynchings in the South! I escaped . . .

The Little Miami River and Owl Creek that flow into the Ohio.

The evening star.

LEXINGTON, where you can order plum ice cream in the Howard Johnson Restaurant, county seat of Fayette County, KY. (. . . only).

Northerners tell us: You should be nice to the Negroes; and they send them help; and then they proclaim: See how friendly they are, all they ask is a little good will. They don't suspect this unfathomable deceit . . .

Shell,—a tomato-colored De Soto, driven by a very black, skinny old Negro in a cerise shirt with maroon polka dots, sideswipes a huge plum-colored Dodge parked beside the road,—Green, Kentucky and Licking Rivers that flow into the Ohio,—or else a "faith" type edition of the Bible, "If ye have faith as a grain of mustard seed" (Matthew, XVII, 20), "faith is represented by a transparent plastic marble which enlarges a grain of mustard seed enclosed within it . . . attached to the zipper fastening of the binding. Illustrations, eight color plates."

The illuminated signs.

LEXINGTON, Richland County, OHIO, the Middle West.

Lynchings? You ran away? How could such a thing be possible? We thought that no longer existed, that it was over at last, a bad dream, one of those bad dreams; we didn't even think about it any more! . . .

Sunoco,—a pistachio Dodge, driven by a fat old Negro in a chocolate shirt, sideswipes a pistachio Ford driven by a fat old yellow white woman in a lemon-yellow dress with strawberry polka dots, —the Scioto and Muskingum Rivers and Raccoon Creek that flow into the Ohio.

The drive-in theaters are filling up.

NEWPORT, on the Ohio, Campbell County.

They don't suspect that desire for vengeance . . .

The two branches of the Big Sandy River, border of West Virginia, that flows into the Ohio.

The moon.

NEWPORT, Shelby County, and another

NEWPORT, Madison County.

My God! In this day and age! In our country! We have to do something! We admit your innocence, your good will, your martyrdom . . . Aren't we white men; aren't the White Men the Negroes in the South . . .

Polson Creek that flows into the Ohio, and Grand River that flows into Lake Erie.

Green light.

JAMESTOWN.

Yellow light.

JAMESTOWN.

JAMESTOWN, Volunteer State (. . . colored people).

They suppose it would be enough to grant them equality, and that then everything would be all right, but what they don't understand is that the Negroes do not want any such equality . . .

Chickamauga Dam Lake,—the airport at Paris, county seat of Henry County, and at Clarksville, county seat of Montgomery County,—through Sears, Roebuck & Co., a china service imported from Japan, serves eight, 53 pieces, "Corinthian" pattern, "a design of ears of corn, artistically inspired, gleaming with 22-carat gold, gray accents. Brilliant white background bordered with 22-carat gold. Ultra smart . . ."— Across the Father of Waters, but farther north,

JAMESTOWN.

They suppose, on the other side of the Mississippi, but farther north, in Illinois, that it would be enough for these Negroes that the white man, who has considered himself their superior for centuries, from the height of the present superiority left to him, as from a balcony, in his tremendous generosity toward this poor darker brother, should condescend to let down to the depths of his misery a kind of rope ladder so that he can climb up to his own level, it being understood that he could never reach it by himself, that he is therefore really inferior and that it was actually right to treat him as he has been treated . . .

The airport at Springfield, county seat of Greene County,— continuing west,

JAMESTOWN, KANS. (. . . only),—the Iowa, Sac and Fox Indian Reservation.

HUNTSVILLE, county seat of Scott County, TENN., cotton belt (". . . restricted").

But they don't want any such thing, these Negroes, and we know that they are much stronger than the Northerners suspect . . .

The Baptist church,—Great Falls and Center Hill Dam Lakes,—the airport at Crossville, county seat of Cumberland County,—or the "Gold Wheat" style, page 952, "the simplicity, grace and elegance of 22-carat ears of wheat, swaying against white background enriched with a 22-carat gold border. Gleaming beauty to embellish any table. Modern shape . . ."

HUNTSVILLE, county seat of Randolph County.

We know perfectly well that charity isn't enough for them . . .

The airports at Clinton, county seat of Henry County, and Nevada, county seat of Vernon County.

Red light.

LEXINGTON, on the Missouri, county seat of Lafayette County, MO. (. . . only).

Of course they gladly accept what we give them, they will use it in their own way, but it's no use expecting from them, especially from their children, that gratitude you count on . . .

A lime Studebaker, driven by a very black young Negro woman in a lime dress with maroon polka dots, sideswipes an old raspberry-colored Studebaker parked beside the road, —the airports of Saint Louis, De Soto and Crystal City,— or a box of "Regimen" tablets, "begin today to control your weight with Regimen tablets! Helps keep your weight normal without any special dieting. Eat what you like, without being tempted to overeat. Regimen tablets help satisfy your appetite" . . .

The moon above the screen.

JASPER, Jasper County.

They want to make you feel eventually that the situation is reversed. They want to admit you some day to that civilization you envy them . . .

The airport at Houston, county seat of Texas County, and at Versailles, county seat of Morgan County.

The moon above the Coca-Cola sign.

FRANKLIN.

FRANKLIN, county seat of Williamson County. State Flower: iris.

That is why that future civilization of our United States in which we will be their equals can only be invented by them . . .

Dunbar Cave,—the Lutheran church,—Dale Hollow Dam Lake,—or the "Cretonne" pattern, "dramatic dogwood shaded in Tuscan maroon, dawn gray and sun yellow. Brown foliage, or parchment and sage green. Gleaming palladium edges,"—across the northeast border,

FRANKLIN.

"Notes on the State of Virginia":
". . . The Indians, with no advantages of this kind, will often carve figures on their pages not destitute of design and merit. They will crayon out an animal, a plant, or a country so as to prove the existence of a germ in their minds which only wants cultivation. They astonish you with strokes of the most sublime oratory; such as prove their reason and sentiment strong, their imagination glowing and elevated. But never yet could I find that a Black had uttered a thought above the level of plain narration; never saw even an elementary trait of painting or sculpture . . ."
Thomas Jefferson.

At Monticello, Thomas Jefferson invented a music stand to permit five musicians to play together.

The sea,
        everything left on the beach,
footprints,
        wrappings,
forgotten clothes,
        someone.

Stone Mountain,—continuing northeast,

    FRANKLIN, W.VA., beginning of the Middle West,—northeast,

        FRANKLIN, PA., the Atlantic Coast, —the Cornplanter Indian Reservation,—northeast,

        FRANKLIN, N.Y.,—the border of the Canadian provinces of Quebec and Ontario,—the Tonawanda Indian Reservation.

A pair of barn swallows, blue above, rust below, on their nest hanging from a rafter.

    NEWPORT, Giles County.

The sea,
> our footsteps at night,
that comes from the sea,
> effaced by the sea,
alone,
> in the warm wind.

". . . In music they are more generally gifted than the whites with accurate ears for tune and time, and they have been found capable of imagining a small catch. The instrument proper to them is the Banjar, which they brought hither from Africa, and which is the original of the guitar, its chords being precisely the four lower chords of the guitar. Whether they will be equal to the composition of a more extensive run of melody, or of complicated harmony, is yet to be proved . . ."
Thomas Jefferson.
At Monticello, the walls of the salon were covered with paintings bought in Paris.

Copper and Moccasin Ridges.

The moon above the steeple.

CLEVELAND, Russell County, VA., the South.

At Monticello, Thomas Jefferson had installed above the main doorway a huge clock which functioned by means of two cannonball weights which slowly descended for a whole week in the two corners on each side, thus indicating the days inscribed on the wall, from Sunday to Saturday . . .

The sea,
> *you're black,*
you're moist,
> *like a fish,*
no one can see us,
> *the beach is empty.*

". . . Misery is often the parent of the most affecting touches in poetry. Among the blacks is misery enough, God knows, but no poetry. Love is the peculiar oestrum of the

poet. Their love is ardent, but it kindles the senses only, not the imagination. Religion, indeed, has produced a Phyllis Wheatley, but it could not produce a poet. The compositions published under her name are below the dignity of criticism. The heroes of the Dunciad are to her, as Hercules to the author of that Poem . . ."   *Thomas Jefferson.*

B.P.—a maroon Mercury driven by an old white man in a yellow shirt passes an old maroon Packard driven by a young Negro in a white shirt going much faster than the 55-mile speed limit,—Sinking, Bald and Sweet Springs Mountains,—or a silver service of 50 pieces, "Paul Revere" pattern by Oneida Ltd., "eternal simplicity,—truly American . . ."

A cloud passes over the moon.

LEXINGTON, county seat of Rockbridge County.

". . . Ignatius Sancho has approached nearer to merit in composition; yet his letters do more honor to the heart than the head. They breathe the purest effusions of friendship and general philanthropy, and show how great a degree of the latter may be compounded with strong religious zeal. He is often happy in the turn of his compliments, and his style is easy and familiar, exactly when he affects a Shandean fabrication of words. But his imagination is wild and extravagant, and escapes incessantly from every restraint of reason and taste, and, in the course of its vagaries, leaves a tract of thought as incoherent and eccentric, as is the course of a meteor through the sky. His subjects should often have led him to a process of sober reasoning; yet we find him always substituting sentiment for demonstration. Upon the whole, though we admit him to first place among those of his own color who have presented themselves to the public judgment, yet when we compare him with the writers of the race among whom he lived and particularly with the epistolary class in which he has taken his own stand, we are compelled to enroll him at the bottom of the column. This criticism supposes the letters published under his name to be genuine, and to have received amendment from no other hand; points which would not be of easy investigation . . ."
    Thomas Jefferson.

At Monticello, on either side of his great clock, Thomas Jefferson mounted the antlers of elk and moose which Lewis and Clark had brought him from their Western expedition which had taken them as far as the mouth of the Columbia River.

The sea,
    it muffles our voices,
it stirs,
    kisses our feet,
reaches our ankles
    and leaves us.

Wolf Creek and Warm Springs Mountains.

A little breeze.

    DAYTON.

DAYTON, TENN., coal state.

Ah, you Northerners, with these Negroes there's no time left to be nice! . . .

Did you remember to buy Kleenex?—Cumberland Caverns,—or the "Solitude" pattern, "touched with beauty, with elegance. Border and decoration in 22-carat gold, dawn gray branch. Remarkably lovely pattern . . . ,"—across the southern state line,

    DAYTON.

The sea,
    thousands of black lips,
thousands of dark tongues,
    countless saliva,
countless sweat,
    inexhaustible bath.

Butterfly orchids,
    green fly orchids,
        pink grass orchids.

They're waiting, these Negroes, they don't even need to talk to each other, all they need to do is see their color, a drop of their color in the milk of a white skin is enough to give them an ally . . .

Guntersville Dam Lake, on the Tennessee.

A pair of warbling vireos on top of a magnolia tree.

FRANKLIN, Monroe County, ALA., the Deep South (. . . only).

The sea,
*   thousands of black pages,*
thousands of dark sheets,
*   thousands of shadowy curls,*
thousands of dim breasts,
*   countless glass in the night.*

Of course they have their traitors, and that should give us hope, you say; of course you help these traitors, and we in the South are wrong not to encourage them in the darkness, you say, but don't trust those traitors . . .

Bearded yellow orchids,
*   water hyacinths,*
*   water lilies.*

Wheeler and Wilson Dam Lakes on the Tennessee.

A cloud has just hidden the moon.

HUNTSVILLE, county seat of Madison County.

It's because they're so profoundly treacherous, these Negroes who play the innocent, these Negroes who act the corrupt, the docile or the scandalized part, depending on the interlocutor they're seducing; it's because they're so sure of their power when they assemble at nightfall on their rickety porches, so sure of the fire of their eyes, so sure of the lure of their black skins . . .

The sea,
> *liquid black glass,*
glacier of black marbles,
> *oven of coolness,*
field of green and black nails,
> *clusters of trembling black velvet.*

Moss verbena,
> *railroad creepers,*
>> *rose gentians.*

Caltex,—a huge orange truck driven by a fat white man sideswipes a green truck parked beside the highway,—Lay, Mitchell and Jordan Dam Lakes on the Alabama.

The wind in the branches.

> JASPER.—Continuing south,

> JASPER.

> *Pink shovelers,*
gannets,
semi-palmated plovers,
> *yellow-crested night herons,*
>> *ruddy ducks.*

> *The sea,*
>> *folded umbrellas,*
> *tanned backs in their hotels,*
>> *rows of chaises longues,*
> *lighted swimming pools,*
>> *overcrowded docks.*

> *Kumquats,*
papayas,
loquats,
> *aloes,*
>> *pandanus,*
>> *flame vines.*

Around 1750, a group of Creek Indians, originally from Georgia, emigrated southward and settled in northern Florida, soon joined by the Muskogees and other Creeks; they formed the Seminoles. They raised maize, hunted, kept cattle, pigs and chickens, made terms with the Spanish and the English . . .

Admit it, you Northerners, you too, at nightfall, you begin to find them beautiful, there are moments when you are less certain of the superiority of your white skin, when your eyes cannot help but follow their walk, lingering before your mind catches itself up in charitable thoughts . . .

Iamonia Lake.

JASPER, county seat of Marion County, mockingbird state.

Northerners, it is your civilization they threaten, they will leave almost nothing of your "American Way of Life"! . . .

Marcella Falls,—Thirsty? Drink Coca-Cola!—Indian Cave,—across the southern state line, but farther east,

    JASPER.

White-tailed kites,
    glossy ibis,
red-headed woodpeckers.

The sea,
    blue-black,
green-black,
    black spatter,
black hollow,
    black foam.

Cycas,
    zamias,
        sago palms.

They won't rise with you, but against you, against what exists now, what America is now, which will not keep them from taking whatever you let them have and, think about it, Northerners, everything you want to keep for yourselves . . .

Blue Ridge Lake.

A pair of phoebes on a cotton plant branch, the calices shedding their cloud of fibers.

CLEVELAND, county seat of White County.

Harris' hawks,
   scarlet ibis,
red-bellied woodpeckers.

The sea,
   thousands of black eyes,
thousands of black irises,
   thousands of black pupils,
thousands of yellow corneas,
   thousands of tears.

You won't be able to imagine their rule, Northerners; all the colored peoples, you suppose, will stay under your white wing . . .

Fern palms,
   fan palms,
     date palms.

Nottely and Chatuge Lakes,—continuing southeast,

   CLEVELAND, FLA., the Deep South (. . . only),
     —the Seminole Indian Reservation.

  Pink flamingos,
 limpkins,
lesser sandpipers,
  water turkeys,
   ruddy egrets.

The sea,
>> *oars shipped,*
waterwings,
>> *robes on hangers,*
empty cabanas,
>> *dripping skirts.*

Avocados,
> *mangos,*

guavas,

> *crotons,*
> *banyans,*

tropical almonds.

While we, in the South, suffer this invincible force every day; we do not despise them, we do not consider them weak, we see them growing, developing, and we shudder when we think what will become of our Washington, our capitol, our monuments . . .

The situation of the Seminoles grew serious when Florida became an American possession in 1821. They sheltered runaway slaves, and the colonists were stealing their lands. In 1835, war broke out. Their villages were burned, and their chief, Osceola, captured by treason. Most of the Seminoles were deported to Oklahoma, then known as Indian Territory. Only a few hundred remained on the Florida reservations. The women weave bright-colored striped fabrics and produce souvenirs for the tourists.

Lakes Talquin and Jackson.

A pair of blue grosbeaks, with a second male, near their nest attached to a leafy dogwood branch.

TRENTON, county seat of Dade County, GA. (. . . only).

Stercoridaes,
> *snowy egrets,*
Louisiana herons.

Because you Northerners suppose that they are good American citizens, ah! how clever they are! They've seen too much, believe us, they won't give you an inch of foothold . . .

The sea,
                thousands of scales,
of black fins,
            of valves,
of gills,
            of black throats.
Queen palms,
            bottle palms,
                      Manila palms.

Caltex,—a black Pontiac, driven by a fat white woman in a tomato-colored dress, passes a huge, overloaded indigo Pontiac driven by a young Negro woman in a vanilla dress, going much faster than the 50-mile night speed limit,—Burton, Rabun and Russell Lakes,—or a "Wet Guard" bedwetting signal, "that often puts an end to the unpleasantness of a wet bed in only two, three or four weeks; invented by a doctor, tested and approved by many doctors; harmless, battery-powered, usable by children from three and a half on; easy to use,—instructions, daily progress chart included; 'Wet Guard' conditions the over-sound sleeper to wake in time, thus counteracting the distressing habit . . . Two aluminum plates, one whole, the other perforated, separated by the sheet, are connected to a six-volt battery. The acids and salts contained in the urine make contact under the weight of the body and set off the buzzer. In a few nights the wet spots shrink. Soon the young sleeper will wake in time . . ."

Is it going to rain?

                    TRENTON.

The black of the sky.

            ARLINGTON, Calhoun County, Cracker State (. . . colored people).

They are among us like another sex, their women tempt our women, their men and their boys disturb us . . .

Wilson's plovers,
   little bitterns,
royal rails.

The sea,
   backs,
bellies,
   sighs,
groans,
   expectorations.

Washington palms,
   fishtail palms,
      golden feather palms.

Sidney Lanier and Allatoona Lakes,—or plastic polyethylene panties for uncontrollable bedwetters, "heat and acid resistant, boilable, bleachable . . . ," page 470.

A drop on the windshield.

FRANKLIN, county seat of Heard County.

If it could all be settled by kindness, don't you Northerners suppose we would have been capable of trying? That we would have made these Negroes our sons-in-law, that we would have enjoyed hearing them sing in the evening, that we would have bounced on our knees our golden grandchildren? But we know them, and the mere notion of that smile they would have, of that arrogance . . .

A flutter of wings,
   a cheeping,
another in reply.

Spanish moss,
   wild pineapples,
      globe moss.

The sea,
      taut skins,
blistered skins,
         oiled skins,
shiny skins,
          varnished skins.

Clark Hill Dam Lake.

Already hundreds of drops.

LEXINGTON.—When it is six P.M. in

LEXINGTON, Central Time, county seat of Henderson County . . .

You have beaten us, Northerners, we who were your ramparts, that's understood; we are waiting, the Negroes have taught us to wait . . .

Ozone Falls,—across the southern state line, but farther west,

LEXINGTON, MISS. (. . . only).

The sea,
      the river,
the ripples of the sea and of the river,
          their torrents and eddies,
whirlpools and rapids,
          all the conspiracy of the black waters.

Long before being conquered by you, we were already beaten by the Negroes; but when you will see the Negroes rise up then we too will have that moment of vengeance they have taught us to expect, and closing our eyes, we will grin . .

Grenada Dam Lake.

In a river landscape with a mountain in the background, a pair of goshawks, one adult and one young, and a Cooper's hawk.

CLEVELAND.— . . . and seven P.M. in

CLEVELAND, Eastern Time,

WELCOME TO TEXAS

                the sun is setting in
CLEVELAND, Central Time.

Not only the Negroes, but the Mexicans.

The sea,
        which will permit me to approach you,
to feel you,
        to touch you,
to caress you,
        to take you.

Glass Mountains.

        CLEVELAND, OKLA., the Middle West (for whites only),
          —the Osage Indian Reservation.

DAYTON, Liberty County.

The sea,
        our car abandoned in the sand,
the wind that sweeps away our footprints,
        the sea that drowns out our voices,
the smells from the ground,
        your fingers that tighten in my hand.

The real Mexico on the other side of the Rio Grande.

Esso,—"he's falling asleep."

DAYTON, N.M., the largest state after Alaska, Texas, California, and Montana, the Far West,—the Apache Indian Reservation.

Approximately nine hundred years ago, hordes of Indians speaking the Athapascan language came down from the North into the Southwest and lived by pillaging the pueblos. They are now called the Navajos. In 1848 the United States Government, which had obtained sovereignty over the Southwest from Mexico, sent Kit Carson to control them. The latter, after having destroyed their herds and reservations, managed to capture some 8,000 of them whom he marched to Fort Sumner in 1864. In 1868, the Navajos signed a peace treaty and returned to the region which is now their reservation. They were given tools and two sheep per person. They work silver and weave wool; their products are prized by tourists. In 1920, important oil and petroleum deposits were found on the Navajo reservation; it was then discovered that high dividends paid to individual Indians for the exploitation of the mineral resources of the territory still acknowledged to be theirs was the best means of corrupting and eliminating them without causing difficulties. Fortunately the Navajos decided to keep this property under collective ownership; the revenues are used by the entire community and assigned to expenditures of general interest. It is this kind of socialism that is permitting them a gradual recovery. Today there are 85,000 Navajos. It goes without saying that the dividends received by the shareholding tribe do not suffice to put an end to the extreme poverty of the majority of its members.

"She's falling asleep,"—Sardine Mountain.

On a butternut, two male sparrowhawks and one female holding a small bird in her talons.

CLEVELAND.

ARLINGTON, Tarrant County, TEX. (. . . whites only),—the Alibamu and Koashati Indian Reservation.

The attraction of that country on the other side of the Rio Grande.

The sea,
>*the flames of the refineries behind us,*
the luminous chessboards of the great hotels,
>*the plane signals in the sky,*
the noise of the wind in the derricks,
>*forget your whiteness in the night.*

An orange Buick driven by a young white woman in a yellow dress with cerise polka dots and a hat with yellow flowers sideswipes an old indigo Buick parked beside the highway, its radio blaring "Texas, Our Texas," "We must have taken the wrong road."

FRANKLIN, Lone Star State (men, women, colored people).

The sea,
>*don't you feel like swimming?*
Haven't you ever gone swimming at night?
>*The sea is warmer at night,*
the sharks are far away,
>*no one can see us.*

The attraction, when you're in El Paso, of the city of Juarez on the other side of the Rio Grande.

The two Cathedral Mountains,—through Sears, Roebuck & Co., you can obtain an Elvis Presley record, "Elvis' Golden Records":
"Hound Dog,
– Loving You,

JASPER, county seat of Jasper County, Tex., oil state ("These premises are restricted").

– Heartbreak Hotel,
– Too Much,

A whole district of Juarez lives exclusively on the tourists from El Paso.

– Jailhouse Rock,
– Love me, etc."

The sea,
   your transistor,
why do you play it so loud?
      Don't bother,
we're too far away now,
         stretch out.

Guadalupe Peak, highest point in the state,—or another Elvis Presley, page 1082, "King Creole":
"King Creole,
– As Long as I Have You,

LEXINGTON. State Flower: bluebonnet.

– Hard-Headed Woman,
– Trouble,

The sea,
      no one will know,
they won't ever find out,
         no one will suspect,
they'll think it was a date,
         like every night.

– Dixieland Rock,
– Lover Doll, etc."

The night clubs and the drinks of Juarez.

Lake Dallas,—or a third Elvis Presley, "For LP Fans Only":
"That's all right,
– Lawdy Miss Clawdy,

HUNTSVILLE, county seat of Walker County, TEX., livestock state

– Mystery Train,
– Playing for Keeps,

The bullfights of Juarez.

– Poor Boy,
– She's Gone, etc."

The sea,
> *you should tell them,*
but you won't,
> *they would make such a fuss,*
that you came out alone with me,
> *so far away along the beach.*

Be sociable! Have a Pepsi!—Or a record by Johnny Cash, "The Fabulous Johnny Cash": "Don't Take Your Guns to Town," "plus many other successes in Johnny's inimitable style."

> HUNTSVILLE, ARK., the South (. . . only).

Two splendid Audubon's caracaras fighting, one clinging to a branch, the other in the air, their open beaks thrusting at each other.

> HUNTSVILLE, MO., the Middle West
> (. . . only).

ALPINE, the mockingbird state.

The sea,
> *your tears are salty like the sea,*
don't be afraid,
> *nothing will happen to you,*
I'm going to give you a little of my blackness,
> *a little sand will be left in your hair.*

For Texas is so big, but Mexico . . .

If you think all dehydrated soups taste the same, it's time you tried Heinz!—or a Johnny Mathis record, "Open Fire, Two Guitars," "mood music as only Johnny Mathis can sing it."

NEWCASTLE, Young County, TEX., a horse-raising state.

The plants of Mexico that it is against the law to bring into the United States.

The sea,
>*cigarette?*
How you're trembling!
>*How close you pressed to me!*
As if you thought I was a . . .
>*The transistor has stopped.*

A package of Salems,—the airports of Dallas, county seat of Dallas County, and of Fort Worth, county seat of Tarrant County.

MILFORD, Ellis County.

The sea,
>*we're so far from the sea,*
we've never seen the sea,
>*except in pictures,*
some day I'll take you to the sea,
>*but I know it'll be too late.*

And the Mexican eyes on the tourists.

The airport at Austin, county seat of Travis County, state capital.—When it is seven P.M. in

WELLINGTON,

Mobile 281

WELCOME TO UTAH

the sun is setting in
WELLINGTON, Mountain Time.

After having walked for months and months through the desert, the Latter-Day Saints came in sight of Great Salt Lake.

Kings Peak, highest point in the state.

WELLINGTON, NEV., the Far West,—the Summit Lake Indian Reservation.

HUNTSVILLE, Weber County.

In July 1847, Brigham Young decided that it was in this place that the city was to be built.

Deadman and Thousand Lake Mountains.

CLEVELAND, Emery County, UTAH,—The Shivwits Indian Reservation.

In 1889, some Oceanians from Hawaii, converted to the Mormon religion, founded the city of Iosepa.

A gray Pontiac driven by an old Negro passes an old black Hudson driven by a young white man going much faster than the daytime speed limit, "go straight ahead."

MILFORD, Mormon state,—the Koosharem Indian Reservation.

In 1893, leprosy broke out among the Hawaiian Mormons of Iosepa.

Through Sears, Roebuck & Co., you can obtain the new "Map of the United States" school bag, "now it is so easy for children to learn something about their country! Bright colored map on the back. Seals of eighteen governmental departments, photographs of the Capitol and the White House on the front . . ."

> MILFORD, WYOMING, the least heavily populated state after Alaska and Nevada,—the Wind River Indian Reservation.

Still a little red sunlight on the mountain tops.

Shoshone National Forest.

On a dead branch, a sharp-shinned hawk, tearing apart a small bird with a purple breast.

> NEWCASTLE.

> NEWCASTLE, Iron County, UTAH, a desert state.—the Ute Indian Reservation.

In 1916, when a Mormon temple was built in Hawaii, the last survivors of the Iosepa colony returned to their country, abandoning the town to its ghosts.

Sand Pass, Thomas Pass.

> NEW CASTLE, COLO.,—Southern Ute Indian Reservation.

ALPINE, UTAH.

In Mountain Meadows, in September 1857, a group of 140 emigrants from Arkansas were stopped by the Federal troops about to invade the Mormon state because the Easterners were scandalized by the practice of polygamy. After a siege lasting several days, the emigrants were massacred. The only survivors, 17 children, were taken back to Arkansas.

Indian Peak.—When it is seven P.M. in

RANDOLPH,

already nine P.M. in
RANDOLPH, Eastern Time.

Are you asleep?

    RANDOLPH.

    The trial of Susanna Martin, Salem, June 29, 1692:
    "11) Jervis Ring testified that about seven or eight years ago he had ben severall times afflicted in the night time by some body or some thing coming up upon him when he was in bed and did sorely afflict by Laying upon him and he could neither move nor speak while it was upon him but sometimes made a kind of noyse; but one time in the night it came upon me as at other times and I did then see the person of Susanna Martin of Amesbury, and she came to this deponent and took him by the hand and bitt him by the finger by force and the print of the bite is yet to be seen on the little finger of his right hand . . ."

CHESTER, Windsor County.

Asleep . . .

    CHESTER, MASS., New England.

    "12) But beyond all these evidences there was a very **marvellous** *testimony of one Joseph Ring produced upon this occasion. This man had been strangely transported by* **demons** *into unknown places where he saw meetings and feastings and*

many strange sights and from August Last he was Dum and could not speake till this last Aprill. He also relates that there was a certain Thos. Hardy which said Hardy demanded of this deponent two shillings and with that dreadfull noyse and hideous shapes of creatures and fireball. About Oct following coming from Hampton in Salsbury pine plane a company of horses with men and women upon them overtook this deponent and the aforesead Hardy being one of them came to this deponent as before and demanded his two shillings of him and threatened to tear him to pieces to whom this deponent made no answer and so he and the rest went away and left this deponent. After this this deponent had divers strange appearances which did force him away with them into unknown places where he saw meetings and he also relates that there did use to come to him a man that did present him a book to which he would have him sett his hand with promise of anything that he would have and there were presented all Delectable things and persons. And places imaginall, but he refusing it would usually and with most dreadful shapes noyses and screeking that almost scared him out of his witts and this was the usuall manner of proceeding with him and one time the book was brought and a pen offered him and to his apprehension there was blod in the Ink horne but he never toucht the pen. He further say that they never told him what he should writt nor he could not speak to ask them what he should writ. He farther say in several their merry meetings he have seen Susanas Martin appear among them. And in that house did also appear the aforesayd Hardy and another female person which the deponent did not know, there they had a good fire and drink it seemed to be sider their continued most part of the night said Martin being then in her natural shape and talking as shee used to do, but toward the morning the said Martine went from the fire made a noyse and turned into the shape of a black hog and went away and so did the other to persons go away and this deponent was strangely caryed away also and the first place he knew was by Salmuel woods house in Amsbury . . ."

CHESTER, CONN., New England.

RICHMOND.

RICHMOND, Chittenden County, VERMONT, New England,—the
 border of the Canadian province of Quebec, one of the least
heavily populated states.

The woods at night.

An old overloaded jeep parked beside the highway; another jeep passes, "turn left."

    RICHMOND.

53,000 Norwegians,
    410,000 Poles,
the Greeks who read the "National Herald,"
    the Hungarians who read the "Amerikai Magyar Nepszava,"
        the Italians who read "Il Progresso."
SATURDAY EVENING POST SATURDAY EVENING POST SATUR

Colombo's, steaks,
    Quo Vadis, French cuisine,
        East of Suez, Indonesian,
White Turkey, American specialties,
    Schine's, Irish,
        Grotta Azzurra, Italian.

The planes leaving for Munich,
    for Léopoldville,
        coming from Beirut,
            from Athens.

WBNX, Ukrainian broadcasts,
    WEVD, Norwegian broadcasts,
        WFUV-FM, Polish broadcasts.

The ships sailing for Boston,
    for Mobile,
        arriving from Philadelphia,
            from Providence.

Even cheaper clothes for women at Macy's, Saks-34th, Gimbels and Ohrbach's.

The Empire State Building: the most powerful searchlights in the world, a city of shops on the street floor.

Loew's Commodore,
    Art Theater,
        Academy of Music.

The subways coming from the far ends of the Bronx, Brooklyn and Queens:
        Northern Boulevard,
    Atlantic Avenue,
Intervale Avenue,
        46 Street,
    De Kalb Avenue,
Prospect Avenue,
        Steinway Street,
    Myrtle Avenue,
Jackson Avenue.
        36 Street,
        (crossing the East River)
        Broadway.
        Queens Plaza.

Museum of Natural History: superb wax reproduction (life size) of a flowering magnolia.

    Alone tonight, baby?
        Thirsty?
  Terribly!
        Do you know them?
That's what he said on television.
    I can't remember their names.
      Great!
  Not bad . . .

Bronx Zoo:
griffon vultures,
    bearded vultures,
        Pondicherry vultures.

Drink Coca-Cola!
       Drink Pepsi-Cola!
              Kleenex!

CHESTER, Orange County.

85,000 Rumanians,
the Hungarians who read "Az Ember,"
Sea Fare, fish,
the planes leaving for Chicago,
       for Istanbul,
WEVD, Spanish broadcasts,
Danny's Hide-a-way, steaks,
the ships leaving for Naples,
       for Tangiers,
Irving Place Theater.

              950,000 Russians,
              the Italians who read the "Corriere degli Italiani,"
              Twenty-One, French cuisine,
              the planes coming from Kansas City,
                     from Teheran,
              WFUV-FM, Russian broadcasts,
              Shanghai, Chinese dishes,
              the ships coming from Genoa,
                     from Madeira,
              Gramercy Theater.

                            The Portuguese who read "A Luta,"
                            San Marino, Italian cuisine,
                            WHOM, Polish broadcasts,
                            Giovanni, Italian specialties,
                            the Empire State Building: 35,000 visitors a day, coming from every country in the world,
                            Murray Hill Theater.

HOLIDAY HOLIDAY HOLIDAY HOLIDAY HOLIDAY HOLIDAY HOL

Cheapest clothes for women, at Klein's.

The subways coming from the Bronx, lower Manhattan, Queens:
Courthouse Square,
Prince Street,
Third Avenue,
Ely Avenue,
Eighth Street,
149 Street,
(crossing the East River)
Lexington Avenue,
Union Square,
(crossing the Harlem River)
135 Street.
Fifth Avenue,
23 Street.
Seventh Avenue.

Museum of Natural History: Audubon Gallery: collection of objects relating to the life and work of John James Audubon; Audubon's original paintings and drawings, and those of his son; some bronze and copper plates used in printing "Birds of America"; portrait of the engraver Robert Havell; plates showing Audubon armed with his rifle.

Bronx Zoo:
white-headed vulture,
white Egyptian vulture,
black East African vulture.

Smoke Chesterfield,
Smoke Lucky Strike,
Smoke Salem!
There must be a mistake.
Not too tired?
I've reserved a room.
Did you hear?
They had to send a bill.
Shut up!
She still hasn't come in.
What can she do?
I've rarely been so bored.

New York Historical Society: sleds and prints of New York winter scenes.

RANDOLPH, Cattaraugus, N.Y.,—the Saint Regis Indian Reservation.

65,000 Scots,
the Japanese who read "Hokubei Shimpo,"
Stouffer's, American specialties,
the planes leaving for Detroit,
  for Karachi,
WEVD, Swedish broadcasts,
Hickory House, steaks,
the ships leaving for the Bahamas,
  for Bermuda,
Cameo Theater,
the subway coming from Harlem:
125 Street,
116 Street,
110 Street,
Bronx Zoo: mountain zebra,
Fly Air France!
THE NEW YORKER THE NEW YORKER THE NEW YORKER THE NEW YO
  25,000 Spaniards,
  the Lithuanians who read "Tevyne,"
  Voisin, French cuisine,
  the planes coming from Montreal,
    from Honolulu,
  WFUV-FM, Spanish broadcasts,
  Miyako, Japanese dishes,
  the ships coming from the Azores,
    from the Windward Islands,
  Loew's Lexington,
  the subway coming from downtown New York:
  28 Street,
  33 Street,
  49 Street,
  57 Street,
  Bronx Zoo: Grant's zebra,
  Fly Pan American!
Fruits and vegetables: Washington, Fulton and Vesey Streets.

*The Norwegians who read the "Nordisk Tidende,"
Café Geiger, German cuisine,
Empire State Building: 16,000 tenants,
WHOM, Russian broadcasts,
Alamo, Mexican specialties,
New York Historical Society: old fire pumps,
R.K.O. 58 Street Theater,
the subway from uptown New York:
50 Street,
42 Street,
Pennsylvania Station,
23 Street,
14 Street,
Bronx Zoo: Grevy's zebra,
Fly TWA!*

Museum of Natural History: hall of human biology: growth and development of the individual, racial classification of man; genetics and mixture of races; population problems; development of a human embryo; life-size figures showing the chief racial types.

New York City Museum: gallery devoted to the history of the fire department of New York.

*Have you been here long?
          Just a minute.
When are you leaving?
          I was late.
A last glass.*
He had to sell his car.
          *Not another.
We're coming.
          I'd never have believed it.
What will you have?*

Shell,—a huge Nash collides with an old one already going much faster than the 50-mile speed limit,—through Mont-

gomery Ward, you can obtain the booklet "Sports Cars of the Future," by Strother MacMinn, "deals with the cars of your dreams planned by European and American builders," as well as the prototypes of the makes:
— Corvette,

WINDSOR, Green Mountain State.

— La Salle II,

The covered bridges at night.

— Oldsmobile F 88,

Through Sears, Roebuck & Co., a "Lady Kenmore" sewing machine, "stitches with inconceivable daintiness. The 20 styles illustrated on the dial can be modified and combined to produce countless intricate decorative variations. You can embroider in two colors thanks to twin needles . . . vary the size of the stitch with the regulator . . ."

— Chrysler Gran Turismo. Also discusses mechanical elements and body design likely to appear in future cars.

WINDSOR, Broome County.

Hep!
Miss!
This isn't for you?
Oh, thank you!
Don't you feel well?
They had to sell their apartment.
Go home.
Go home!
Sleep.
If you think . . .
Did you think . . .

55,000 Swedes,
15,000 Swiss,
32,000 Turks,

>   *the Poles who read the "Nowy Swiat,"*
>   *the Spanish who read "La Prensa,"*
>   *the Swedes who read "Norden,"*
> *Keen's, steaks and chops,*
>   *Côte Basque, French cuisine,*
>   *Berkowitz, Rumanian,*
> *the planes leaving for Lima,*
>   *for Helsinki,*
>   *coming from Bogotá,*
>   *from Oslo,*
>   *Chrysler Building, 77 floors,*
>   *60 Wall Street, 66 floors,*
> *WEVD, Ukrainian broadcasts,*
>   *WHOM, Spanish broadcasts,*
>   *WWRL, Greek broadcasts,*
> *Pen and Pencil, steaks,*
>   *Balalaika, Russian cooking,*
>   *Sevilla, Spanish specialties,*
> *the ships leaving for Bristol,*
>   *for Barcelona,*
>   *coming from Cardiff,*
>   *from Piraeus,*
>   the Seagram Building, like a huge block of solidified whiskey.
>   On top of the Mutual Life Insurance Building, the green star if the weather is going to be fair, orange for cloudy, winking orange for rain, white for snow.
> THE MAGAZINE OF FANTASY AND SCIENCE FICTION THE M
>   EBONY EBONY EBONY EBONY EBONY EBONY EB
>   MAD MAD MAD MAD MAD MAD MAD

> *Flowers, 28 Street and Sixth Avenue,*
>   *linen, Grand Street,*
>   *silver, Lexington Avenue between 56 and 58 Street, and on Nassau Street,*
> *Plaza Theater,*
>   **Baronet Theater,**
>   *Trans-Lux 52 Street Theater,*
> *the subways going to the Bronx, Queens and Brooklyn:*
> *86 Street,*

Fifth Avenue,
West Fourth Street,
96 Street,
Lexington Avenue,
Spring Street,
103 Street.
(crossing the East River)
Queensboro Plaza,
Canal Street,
Beebe Avenue.
Chambers Street,
Broadway, Nassau Street.
Bronx Zoo: cassowaries,
yaks,
ornithorynchus,
New York Historical Society: Audubon Gallery: all the original drawings for "Birds of America,"
New York City Museum: 1920 doll's house, made by Varrie Walter Stettheimer; note the ballroom painting which is a real Marcel Duchamp,
Museum of Natural History:
Planetarium: a new show each month:
Trip to Mercury,
Trip to the Moon,
The End of the World . . .
Fly Sabena,
Fly BOAC,
Fly KLM.

In April 1524, the Florentine navigator Verrazzano piloted the French caravel Dauphine *to the discovery of the port of New York and named the place Angoulême in honor of François I, King of France.*

The drive-in movie is over.

NEWPORT.

NEWPORT, county seat of Orleans County, VT., ski state.

The mountains at night.

NEWPORT.

O night!

NEWPORT.

The sea at night.

BRISTOL, Addison County.

The streams at night.

BRISTOL, Grafton County.

Mother night!

BRISTOL, ME.,—the border of the Canadian provinces of Quebec and New Brunswick,—the Penobscot Indian Reservation.

The rocks at night.

RICHMOND, Cheshire County, N.H.

The highway at night.

Texaco,—a Kaiser passes a shiny Hudson.

The movement of the windshield wipers.

RICHMOND.

The water streaming over the glass.

CHESTER, Rockingham County.

The street lamp at night.

The water streaming over the highway.

DANVILLE.—When it is ten P.M. in DANVILLE,

ten P.M. in
DANVILLE.

"*Notes on the State of Virginia*":
"... *The improvement of the blacks in body and mind, in the first instance of their mixture with the whites, has been observed by every one, and proves that their inferiority is not the effect merely of their condition of life. We know that among the Romans, about the Augustan age especially, the condition of their slaves was much more deplorable than that of the blacks on the continent of America. The two sexes were confined in separate apartments, because to raise a child cost the master more than to buy one. Cato, for a very restricted indulgence to his slaves in this particular, took from them a certain price. But in this country the slaves multiply as fast as the free inhabitants. Their situation and manners place the commerce between the two sexes almost without restraint . . .*"

Thomas Jefferson.

At Monticello, Thomas Jefferson set a light stucco frieze around the ceiling of his hall: griffons, vases, foliage and torches.

    DANVILLE.

      Sleep.

          DANVILLE.

            Sleep.

DANVILLE, KANS.

GLASGOW, Rockbridge County.

At Monticello, Thomas Jefferson installed the first parquet flooring in the United States in his salon.

"... *The same Cato, on a principle of economy, always sold his sick and superannuated slaves. He gives it as a standing precept to a master visiting his farm, to sell his old oxen, old wagons, old tools, old and diseased servants, and everything else become useless* ... *The American slaves cannot enumerate this among the injuries and insults they receive* ..."

Thomas Jefferson.

GLASGOW, KY.

The falls at night.

GLASGOW, MO.

The insomnia.

FRANKLIN.

Green light.

FRANKLIN.

FRANKLIN, Southampton County, VIRGINIA.

"... *It was the common practice to expose in the island Aesculapius in the Tyber, diseased slaves whose cure was like to become tedious The emperor Claudius by an edict, gave freedom to such of them a should recover, and first declared that if any person chose to kill rathe than to expose them, it should not be deemed homicide. The exposin them is a crime of which no instance has existed with us; and were to be followed by death, it would be punished capitally. We are told o a certain Vedius Pollio, who, in the presence of Augustus, would hav given a slave as food to his fish, for having broken a glass. With th Roman, the regular method of taking the evidence of their slaves wc under torture. Here it has been thought better never to resort to their evidence. When a master was murdered, all his slaves, in the same house, or within hearing, were condemned to death. Here punishment falls on the guilty only, and as precise proof is required against him as against a freeman. Yet notwithstanding these and other discouraging circumstances among the Romans, their slaves were often their rarest artists. They excelled too in science, insomuch as to be usually employed as tutors to their masters' children. Epictetus, Terence, and Phaedrus were slaves. But they were of the race of whites . . ."*

Thomas Jefferson.

*Thomas Jefferson,
        at Monticello, above the door from the salon to the dining room, under an elegant pediment, set a light stucco frieze of bucrania, vases, shields, helmets, whose elements were repeated over the mantelpiece.*

FRANKLIN.

The smells of the night.

FRANKLIN, ALA.

BRISTOL, where you can order apple ice cream in the Howard Johnson Restaurant.

At Monticello, Thomas Jefferson had a white stucco eagle set in the entrance hall ceiling, surrounded by eighteen gold stars and holding in its talons the suspension pulleys of a lamp to be raised and lowered which he had purchased in Paris.

Thomas Jefferson.

". . . It is not their condition then, but nature, which has produced the distinction. Whether further observation will or will not verify the conjecture, that nature has been less bountiful to them in the endowments of the head, I believe that in those of the heart she will be found to have done them justice. That disposition to theft with which they have been branded, must be ascribed to their situation, and not to any depravity of the moral sense. The man in whose favor no laws of property exist, probably feels himself less bound to respect those made in favor of others. When arguing for ourselves, we lay it down as a fundamental, that laws, to be just,

must give a reciprocation of right; that, without this, they are mere arbitrary rules of conduct, founded in force, and not in conscience; and it is a problem which I give to the master to solve, whether the religious precepts against the violation of property were not framed for him as well as his slave? And whether the slave may not as justifiably take a little from one who has taken all from him, as he may slay one who would slay him? That a change in the relations in which a man is placed should change his ideas of moral right or wrong, is neither new, nor peculiar to the color of the blacks. Homer tells us it was so two thousand six hundred years ago:

>'Jove fix'd it certain, that whatever day
>Makes man a slave, takes half his worth away.'

But the slaves of which Homer speaks were whites . . ."
Thomas Jefferson.

Through Sears, Roebuck & Co., you can obtain painting equipment that will give hours of pleasure to your whole family: "merely follow the numbers to have fun and relax. Our finest selection: 2 large prepared panels, 30 numbered colors, 3 washable brushes, instructions; choose from:

— bouquet of flowers,
>roses,

— Madonna and Child,

>BRISTOL, TENN.

>the Good Shepherd,

— winter shadows,
>fisherman's luck,

>*If you're not asleep . . .*

— the Last Supper,
>Christ with children,

— decorative owls,

>NEWPORT.

>decorative raccoons,

— the fisherman up in his tree,
>the fisherman on the bank."

NEWPORT, Giles County, VA.

". . . *Notwithstanding these considerations which must weaken their respect for the laws of property, we find among them numerous instances of the most rigid integrity, and as many as among their better instructed masters, of benevolence, gratitude, and unshaken fidelity. The opinion that they are inferior in the faculties of reason and imagination, must be hazarded with great diffidence. To justify a general conclusion, requires many observations, even where the subject may be submitted to the anatomical knife, to optical glasses, to analysis by fire or by solvents. How much more then where it is a faculty, not a substance, we are examining; where it eludes the research of all the senses; where the conditions of its existence are variously combined; where the effects of those which are present or absent bid defiance to calculation; let me add too, as a circumstance of great tenderness, where our conclusion would degrade a whole race of men from the rank in the scale of beings which their Creator may perhaps have given them . . ."*
Thomas Jefferson.

Thomas Jefferson,
     at Monticello, over the mantelpiece of the dining room set exquisite panels of blue-and-white Wedgwood representing Apollo and the Muses.

Or a group of three panels, eighteen jars of paint; choose from "Distant lands:
       – Chinese pagoda,
       – the old mill,
       – lofty mountains,

NEWPORT.

– Biblical subjects:
       – Christ,
       – the Good Shepherd,
       – Jesus in meditation,
       Thieves . . .

– Seascapes:
       – Clipper ship,

    – rocks and beaches,
    – harbor scene,

     NEWPORT, S.C.

– Horses:
    – pride of the stable,
    – out to grass,
    – Derby winner,

     Prowlers . . .

– Far West:
    – majestic canyons,
    – heavenly waterfalls,
    – enchanted valleys,

WINDSOR. State Flower: dogwood.

– Holland:
    – Delft,
    – windmills,
    – canals," page 1037.

At Monticello, in the dining room, on each side of the mantelpiece, Thomas Jefferson ingeniously concealed small bottle elevators connecting with the wine cellar.

". . . To our reproach it must be said, that though for a century and a half we have had under our eyes the races of black and of red men, they have never yet been viewed by us as subjects of natural history. I advance it, therefore, as a suspicion only, that the blacks, whether originally a distinct race, or made distinct by times and circumstances, are inferior to the whites in the endowments both of body and mind. It is not against experience to suppose that different species of the same genus, or varieties of the same species, may possess different qualifications . . ."

                  Thomas Jefferson.

Or a group of four small panels framed in black plastic; choose from: "Birds,

WINDSOR, N.C.

– Dogs,

    Murderers . . .

– Parisian scenes,

WINDSOR.

– Horses."

FRANKLIN.

RICHMOND, where you can order pear ice cream in the Howard Johnson Restaurant, county seat of Henrico County, capital of the state, VA.

"*. . . Will not a lover of natural history then, one who views the gradations in all the races of animals with the eye of philosophy, excuse an effort to keep those in the department of man as distinct as nature has formed them? This unfortunate difference of color, and perhaps of faculty, is a powerful obstacle to the emancipation of these people . . .*"
                                                                 Thomas Jefferson.

Thomas Jefferson,
    at Monticello, situated the slaves' quarters under the southern terrace, so that their comings and goings would not spoil the view.

VIENNA, Fairfax County.

"*. . . Many of their advocates, while they wish to vindicate the liberty of human nature, are anxious also to preserve its dignity and beauty. Some of these, embarrassed by the question, 'What further is to be done with them?' join themselves in opposition with those who are actuated by sordid avarice only. Among the Romans emancipation required but one effort. The slave, when made free, might mix with, without staining the blood of his master. But with us a second is necessary, unknown to history. When freed, he is to be removed beyond the reach of mixture . . .*"
                                                                  Thomas Jefferson.

Thomas Jefferson,
     on January 10, 1806, being then President of the United States, wrote to the chiefs of the Cherokee Nation:
". . . Tell all your chiefs, your men, women and children, that I take them by the hand and hold it fast. That I am their father, wish their happiness and well-being, and am always ready to promote their good. My children, I thank you for your visit and pray to the Great Spirit who made us all and planted us all in this land to live together like brothers that He will conduct you safely to your homes, and grant you to find your families and your friends in good health."

VIENNA, MD.—When it is eleven P.M. in

CHESTER, where you can order pistachio ice cream in the Howard Johnson Restaurant,

eleven o'clock in
CHESTER.

Sleep . . .

        CHESTER.

        Sleep . . .

GLASGOW, Kanawha County.

O night!

VIENNA, Wood County, WEST VIRGINIA.

O cooling shadows!

        VIENNA, OHIO.

        Future America!

        FRANKLIN.

                FRANKLIN, IND.

FRANKLIN, county seat of Pendleton County.

After so many upheavals, convulsions, murders.

      FRANKLIN.

"*Information to Those Who Would Remove to America*":
". . . *Industry and constant Employment are great preservatives of the Morals and Virtue of a Nation. Hence bad examples to Youth are more rare in America, which must be a comfortable Consideration to Parents. To this may be truly added, that serious Religion, under its various Denominations, is not only tolerated, but respected and practised . . .*"
                                             Benjamin Franklin.

      FRANKLIN, N.Y.

25,000 Cubans,
          psst!
uuuiie!
          The Ukrainians who read "Svoboda,"
ssssh!
          baby!
Press Box, steaks,
          coming?
it's late . . .
          Le Bistro, French cuisine,
coming in?
          we're just leaving . . .
The planes leaving for Paris,
          let me alone!
darling!
          for Rome,
let me . . .
          please . . .
WEVD, Yiddish broadcasts,
          it's not late,
going down?
          WWRL, Hungarian,
may I?
          no, thanks . . .

York Playhouse,
   did you see the program?
nothing,
   68 Street Playhouse,
take you home?
   I have my car . . .
The ships leaving for Le Havre,
   be careful,
don't linger,
   for Puerto Rico,
psst!
   cigarette?
Chase Manhattan Bank Building, 71 floors,
   turn the light out, will you?
no, I'm going home,
   RCA Building, 70 floors,
alone?
   yes, please . . .
the subways going downtown:
   86 Street,
shocked?
   no, you don't understand . . .
he's staring at me . . .
   79 Street,
why is he staring at me like that?
   72 Street,
Fly . . .
   Smoke . . .
Look,
   look,
a murder in Central Park,
   why is he chasing me?
The Swedes who read "Nordstjerman,"
   don't leave me alone . . .
alone tonight, baby?
   The Russians, "Novoye Russkoye Slovo,"
thirsty?
   terribly!
Three Crowns, Swedish specialties,
   you know them?

I can't remember their name . . .
        Al Schacht's, steaks,
great!
              not bad . . .
The planes coming from London,
        not too tired?
oh! it's still a long way . . .
        from Stockholm,
I've reserved a room,
        there must be some mistake,
WHOM, Ukrainian broadcasts,
        shut up!
did you hear?
        WWRL, Lithuanian,
she hasn't come in yet,
        what can she do?
Loew's Tower East Theater,
        I've rarely been so bored,
do you think?
        72 Street Playhouse,
we're not going to leave it at that,
        just a minute,
The ships coming from Bremen,
        been here long?
I was late,
        from Rotterdam,
when are you leaving?
        a last glass?
Flatiron Building,
        I can't go on,
we're coming,
        Woolworth Building,
and what do you think of . . .
        I'd never have believed . . .
The subways going uptown:
        Columbus Circle,
really,
        you don't look . . .
and what did your doctor say?
        66 Street,
I think I'm going to fall down right here,

>   *72 Street,*
> *it's not far,*
>   *I like you,*
> *Drink . . .*
>   *Eat . . .*
> *Danger,*
>   *Careful,*
> *I told you,*
>   *I told you so,*
> *I'm scared,*
>   *if only there was a policeman!*
> *he keeps going faster . . .*
>   *hep!*
> *fly . . .*
>   *Miss!*
> *smoke . . .*
>   *yours?*
> *drink . . .*
>   *oh, thanks . . .*
> *eat . . .*
>   *feeling sick?*
> *go home,*
>   *go home,*
> *sleep,*
>   *sleep,*
> *Did you remember to buy Kleenex?*
>   *If you think all concentrated soups . . .*
> *Did you . . .*
>   *If you . . .*
> *uiiie,*
>   *uuiiie,*
> *d'you remember,*
>   *think all,*
> *ly,*
>   *moke,*
> *ca-Cola,*
>   *si-Cola,*
> *clic,*
>   *clac,*
> *what?*
>   *nothing,*

nothing, really,
   nothing,
rink,
   eat,
sick?
   thanks,
here,
   night,
I love you,
   come in,
leep,
   leep,
breathe,
   breathe,
reathe,
   eathe,
the,
   the sounds of the night.

CHESTER, PA.

"... *Atheism is unknown there; Infidelity rare and secret; so that persons may live to a great Age in that Country without having their Piety shocked by meeting with either an Atheist or an Infidel. And the Divine Being seems to have manifested his Approbation of the mutual Forbearance and Kindness with which the different Sects treat each other, by the remarkable Prosperity with which He has been pleased to favor the whole Country.*"

Benjamin Franklin.

The dim rain.

CHESTER.

The headlights through the drops.

  MILTON.—When it is midnight in

MILTON,

still nine P.M. in
MILTON.

The Indian Kolaskin, at the age of twenty, fell seriously ill, his body swelled and was covered with boils, his legs grew stiff and he remained in this state without any remedy bringing him relief or comfort for almost two years. He fell into a trance and remained unconscious for several hours. His parents were preparing for his funeral rites, for they believed him to be dead. Kolaskin recovered consciousness and intoned a new, unheard-of song, declared that he had truly died and that he had received a vision in which he felt restored to life and cured of his long incurable disease. The Creator had entrusted him with the message of a new religion, according to which the Indians must change their ways, abandon alcohol and their thieving, adulterous lives, recite prayers to God morning, evening and at every meal, every hunting expedition and every other important act. Further, every seven days they should address collective prayers and ritual hymns to the Creator . . .

The sea at night.

ARLINGTON, WASHINGTON.

The sea, the sea at night.

After a second vision, the Indian Kolaskin announced an imminent cosmic catastrophe followed by a deluge which ten years hence would destroy humanity. Only those who had listened to the prophet and built a huge ship would survive. They had to construct a sawmill near the cult building and prepare the wood needed for the manufacture of this ark. In 1873, he foretold earthquakes, and indeed several actually occurred.

He became a despotic chief, throwing into prison all those who broke the rules of action he had laid down. Captured by the American Government, he was imprisoned in a Federal penitentiary. When he was released, he renounced his own cult and again became chief of his tribe, but the religion he had founded survived until around 1930.

ARLINGTON, ORE.—When it is ten P.M. in

PLYMOUTH,

          already midnight in
PLYMOUTH.

Sleep . . .

Lac Sault Dore at night.

          PLYMOUTH.

          Dreams . . .

Twelve-Mile Lake at night.

          PLYMOUTH.

          America at night . . .

Sunflower Lake at night.

SUPERIOR, county seat of Douglas County.

O mask!

Lake Beulah and Lake Arbutus at night.

          SUPERIOR, Dickinson County.

Monster . . .

Five Island Lake and Lost Island Lake at night.

SUPERIOR, Nuckolls County, NEBR.

Lies . . .

Duck and Swan Lakes at night.

SUPERIOR, COLO.

ELKHORN, county seat of Walworth County, WISCONSIN.

Earthquake!

Chippewa and Como Lakes at night.

ELKHORN, Shelby County, IOWA.

O land of speed . . .

Eagle, Swan and Lizard Lakes at night.

ELKHORN, Douglas County.

Crossroads . . .

Rat, Pelican and Beaver Lakes at night.

BURLINGTON, Badger State.

Rootless!

Eau Claire and Geneva Lakes at night.

BURLINGTON, Hawkeye State.

O America without the bank . . .

Virgin Lake and Spirit Lake at night.

In a landscape of woods and fields extending to a mountainous horizon, two prairie chickens fighting over a hen, near a tiger lily. The eastern variety, or heath hen, is now completely extinct.

  BUFFALO, Scott County, IOWA.

  O upside-down America!

  Black Hawk Lake at night.

The last drops.

  HUDSON, Black Hawk County.

  O intersection . . .

  Middle River that flows into the Des Moines at night.

The moon is rising.

  ARLINGTON.

It lights up the last clouds.

  ARLINGTON.

ARLINGTON, Columbia County, WIS.

Choir of races . . .

Lake Gordon at night.

  ARLINGTON.

  In years and years . . .

  Brule Lake at night.

  ARLINGTON, S.D.

    ARLINGTON, WYO.

BUFFALO. State Flower: violet.

Will stone be left on stone?

Devils Island in Lake Superior at night.

> BUFFALO, MINN.
>
> *Unrecognizable finally recognizable.*
>
> Buffalo Lake at night.
>
> > BUFFALO, N.D.
> >
> > > BUFFALO, MONT.

A male northern shrike and three females with their plumage for different seasons; the last, winter feathers, beak thrust into the throat of a small bird, on a branch with red berries.

> ALBANY.

ALBANY, Green County, WIS.

Cloth of springs!

Cat Island in Lake Superior at night.

> ALBANY.
>
> *Palpitation under the skin of states . . .*
>
> The airport at Freeport, county seat of Stephenson County at night.
>
> > ALBANY, KY.
> >
> > *Lavish indigence . . .*
> >
> > Uncle Tom's Cabin at night.

BURLINGTON, ILL.

How long we've been waiting for you, America!

The airport at Rockford, county seat of Winnebago County, and at Dixon, county seat of Lee County, at night.

Moonlight on the wet road.

BURLINGTON.

Moonlight on the lake.

PLYMOUTH.

HUDSON, county seat of Saint Croix County.

How long we've been waiting for your return!

Hermit Island in Lake Superior at night.

HUDSON, MICH.

How we spy on you at night!

Marble Lake at night.

PLYMOUTH.—When it is one A.M. in

EDEN,

               midnight in
EDEN, Mountain Time.

O night!

Old Faithful Geyser.

        EDEN, IDA.

SUPERIOR, in huge and almost deserted Sweetwater County.

Mother Night!

Rocket and Grotto Geysers.

        SUPERIOR, MONT.

    Dead of night!

    Glaciers at night.

        EDEN.

ARLINGTON, in huge and almost deserted Carbon County, WYO.

Night of germination!

Great Fountain, White Dome and Waterclock Geysers.

ARLINGTON.

Help us, night!

Roy Lake at night.

ARLINGTON, MINN.

ARLINGTON, WIS.

EDEN, S.D.

O complicity!

Byron and Cavour Lakes at night.

Altair.

HUDSON.

HUDSON, Equality State.

O deaf America at night!

Steamboat and Veteran Geysers.

HUDSON, COLO.

Terra incognita!

The Rocky Mountains at night.

Two ruffed grouse fighting over a black berry near a female on a steep path strewn with pine cones and dead leaves.

BURLINGTON.

ELKHORN, in huge and almost deserted Sublette County, WYO.

Imagination.

Valentine Geyser.

    ELKHORN.

Icy night.

Trout Lake at night.

    ELK HORN.

Aurora borealis at night.

Storm Lake at night.

A pair of passenger pigeons, an extinct bird. Audubon reports having seen a flight of 1,115,136,000 in 1813, near Louisville, Kentucky. They were massacred during the nineteenth century by businessmen who wanted to exploit them commercially. The last known specimen died in the Cincinnati Zoo in 1914.

    ARLINGTON, NEBR.

The brilliant night full of stars.

Twin Lakes at night.

Arcturus.

    ARLINGTON, IOWA.

The clear night.

Blue and Silver Lakes at night.

Aldebaran.

    SUPERIOR.

Algol.

    SUPERIOR.

ALBANY, Albany County.

The night.

Wind River Peak at night.

BUFFALO.

SELECTED DALKEY ARCHIVE PAPERBACKS

PIERRE ALBERT-BIROT, *Grabinoulor*.
YUZ ALESHKOVSKY, *Kangaroo*.
FELIPE ALFAU, *Chromos*.
   Locos.
   Sentimental Songs.
IVAN ÂNGELO, *The Celebration*.
   The Tower of Glass.
ALAN ANSEN, *Contact Highs: Selected Poems 1957-1987*.
DAVID ANTIN, *Talking*.
DJUNA BARNES, *Ladies Almanack*.
   Ryder.
JOHN BARTH, *LETTERS*.
   Sabbatical.
ANDREI BITOV, *Pushkin House*.
LOUIS PAUL BOON, *Chapel Road*.
ROGER BOYLAN, *Killoyle*.
IGNÁCIO DE LOYOLA BRANDÃO, *Zero*.
CHRISTINE BROOKE-ROSE, *Amalgamemnon*.
BRIGID BROPHY, *In Transit*.
MEREDITH BROSNAN, *Mr. Dynamite*.
GERALD L. BRUNS,
   Modern Poetry and the Idea of Language.
GABRIELLE BURTON, *Heartbreak Hotel*.
MICHEL BUTOR, *Mobile*.
   Portrait of the Artist as a Young Ape.
JULIETA CAMPOS, *The Fear of Losing Eurydice*.
ANNE CARSON, *Eros the Bittersweet*.
CAMILO JOSÉ CELA, *The Family of Pascual Duarte*.
   The Hive.
LOUIS-FERDINAND CÉLINE, *Castle to Castle*.
   London Bridge.
   North.
   Rigadoon.
HUGO CHARTERIS, *The Tide Is Right*.
JEROME CHARYN, *The Tar Baby*.
MARC CHOLODENKO, *Mordechai Schamz*.
EMILY HOLMES COLEMAN, *The Shutter of Snow*.
ROBERT COOVER, *A Night at the Movies*.
STANLEY CRAWFORD, *Some Instructions to My Wife*.
ROBERT CREELEY, *Collected Prose*.
RENÉ CREVEL, *Putting My Foot in It*.
RALPH CUSACK, *Cadenza*.
SUSAN DAITCH, *L.C.*
   Storytown.
NIGEL DENNIS, *Cards of Identity*.
PETER DIMOCK,
   A Short Rhetoric for Leaving the Family.
ARIEL DORFMAN, *Konfidenz*.
COLEMAN DOWELL, *The Houses of Children*.
   Island People.
   Too Much Flesh and Jabez.
RIKKI DUCORNET, *The Complete Butcher's Tales*.
   The Fountains of Neptune.
   The Jade Cabinet.
   Phosphor in Dreamland.
   The Stain.
WILLIAM EASTLAKE, *The Bamboo Bed*.
   Castle Keep.
   Lyric of the Circle Heart.
JEAN ECHENOZ, *Chopin's Move*.
STANLEY ELKIN, *A Bad Man*.
   Boswell: A Modern Comedy.
   Criers and Kibitzers, Kibitzers and Criers.
   The Dick Gibson Show.
   The Franchiser.
   George Mills.
   The Living End.
   The MacGuffin.
   The Magic Kingdom.
   Mrs. Ted Bliss.
   The Rabbi of Lud.
   Van Gogh's Room at Arles.
ANNIE ERNAUX, *Cleaned Out*.
LAUREN FAIRBANKS, *Muzzle Thyself*.
   Sister Carrie.
LESLIE A. FIEDLER,
   Love and Death in the American Novel.
FORD MADOX FORD, *The March of Literature*.
CARLOS FUENTES, *Terra Nostra*.
   Where the Air Is Clear.
JANICE GALLOWAY, *Foreign Parts*.
   The Trick Is to Keep Breathing.
WILLIAM H. GASS, *The Tunnel*.
   Willie Masters' Lonesome Wife.
ETIENNE GILSON, *The Arts of the Beautiful*.
   Forms and Substances in the Arts.
C. S. GISCOMBE, *Giscome Road*.
   Here.
DOUGLAS GLOVER, *Bad News of the Heart*.
KAREN ELIZABETH GORDON, *The Red Shoes*.
PATRICK GRAINVILLE, *The Cave of Heaven*.
HENRY GREEN, *Blindness*.
   Concluding.
   Doting.
   Nothing.
JIŘÍ GRUŠA, *The Questionnaire*.
JOHN HAWKES, *Whistlejacket*.
AIDAN HIGGINS, *A Bestiary*.
   Flotsam and Jetsam.
   Langrishe, Go Down.
ALDOUS HUXLEY, *Antic Hay*.
   Crome Yellow.
   Point Counter Point.
   Those Barren Leaves.
   Time Must Have a Stop.
MIKHAIL IOSSEL AND JEFF PARKER, EDS.,
   Amerika: Contemporary Russians View the United States.
GERT JONKE, *Geometric Regional Novel*.
JACQUES JOUET, *Mountain R*.
DANILO KIŠ, *Garden, Ashes*.
   A Tomb for Boris Davidovich.
TADEUSZ KONWICKI, *A Minor Apocalypse*.
   The Polish Complex.
ELAINE KRAF, *The Princess of 72nd Street*.
JIM KRUSOE, *Iceland*.
EWA KURYLUK, *Century 21*.
VIOLETTE LEDUC, *La Bâtarde*.
DEBORAH LEVY, *Billy and Girl*.
   Pillow Talk in Europe and Other Places.
JOSÉ LEZAMA LIMA, *Paradiso*.
OSMAN LINS, *Avalovara*.
   The Queen of the Prisons of Greece.
ALF MAC LOCHLAINN, *The Corpus in the Library*.
   Out of Focus.
RON LOEWINSOHN, *Magnetic Field(s)*.
D. KEITH MANO, *Take Five*.
BEN MARCUS, *The Age of Wire and String*.
WALLACE MARKFIELD, *Teitlebaum's Window*.
   To an Early Grave.

FOR A FULL LIST OF PUBLICATIONS, VISIT:

www.dalkeyarchive.com

SELECTED DALKEY ARCHIVE PAPERBACKS

DAVID MARKSON, *Reader's Block.*
   Springer's Progress.
   Wittgenstein's Mistress.
CAROLE MASO, *AVA.*
LADISLAV MATEJKA AND KRYSTYNA POMORSKA, EDS.,
   Readings in Russian Poetics: Formalist and Structuralist Views.
HARRY MATHEWS,
   The Case of the Persevering Maltese: Collected Essays.
   Cigarettes.
   The Conversions.
   The Human Country: New and Collected Stories.
   The Journalist.
   Singular Pleasures.
   The Sinking of the Odradek Stadium.
   Tlooth.
   20 Lines a Day.
ROBERT L. MCLAUGHLIN, ED.,
   Innovations: An Anthology of Modern & Contemporary Fiction.
STEVEN MILLHAUSER, *The Barnum Museum.*
   In the Penny Arcade.
RALPH J. MILLS, JR., *Essays on Poetry.*
OLIVE MOORE, *Spleen.*
NICHOLAS MOSLEY, *Accident.*
   Assassins.
   Catastrophe Practice.
   Children of Darkness and Light.
   The Hesperides Tree.
   Hopeful Monsters.
   Imago Bird.
   Impossible Object.
   Inventing God.
   Judith.
   Natalie Natalia.
   Serpent.
   The Uses of Slime Mould: Essays of Four Decades.
WARREN F. MOTTE, JR.,
   Fables of the Novel: French Fiction since 1990.
   Oulipo: A Primer of Potential Literature.
YVES NAVARRE, *Our Share of Time.*
WILFRIDO D. NOLLEDO, *But for the Lovers.*
FLANN O'BRIEN, *At Swim-Two-Birds.*
   At War.
   The Best of Myles.
   The Dalkey Archive.
   Further Cuttings.
   The Hard Life.
   The Poor Mouth.
   The Third Policeman.
CLAUDE OLLIER, *The Mise-en-Scène.*
FERNANDO DEL PASO, *Palinuro of Mexico.*
ROBERT PINGET, *The Inquisitory.*
RAYMOND QUENEAU, *The Last Days.*
   Odile.
   Pierrot Mon Ami.
   Saint Glinglin.
ANN QUIN, *Berg.*
   Passages.
   Three.
   Tripticks.
ISHMAEL REED, *The Free-Lance Pallbearers.*
   The Last Days of Louisiana Red.
   Reckless Eyeballing.
   The Terrible Threes.
   The Terrible Twos.
   Yellow Back Radio Broke-Down.
JULIÁN RÍOS, *Poundemonium.*
AUGUSTO ROA BASTOS, *I the Supreme.*
JACQUES ROUBAUD, *The Great Fire of London.*
   Hortense in Exile.
   Hortense Is Abducted.
   The Plurality of Worlds of Lewis.
   The Princess Hoppy.
   Some Thing Black.
LEON S. ROUDIEZ, *French Fiction Revisited.*
LUIS RAFAEL SÁNCHEZ, *Macho Camacho's Beat.*
SEVERO SARDUY, *Cobra & Maitreya.*
NATHALIE SARRAUTE, *Do You Hear Them?*
   Martereau.
ARNO SCHMIDT, *Collected Stories.*
   Nobodaddy's Children.
CHRISTINE SCHUTT, *Nightwork.*
GAIL SCOTT, *My Paris.*
JUNE AKERS SEESE,
   Is This What Other Women Feel Too?
   What Waiting Really Means.
AURELIE SHEEHAN, *Jack Kerouac Is Pregnant.*
VIKTOR SHKLOVSKY,
   A Sentimental Journey: Memoirs 1917-1922.
   Theory of Prose.
   Third Factory.
   Zoo, or Letters Not about Love.
JOSEF ŠKVORECKÝ,
   The Engineer of Human Souls.
CLAUDE SIMON, *The Invitation.*
GILBERT SORRENTINO, *Aberration of Starlight.*
   Blue Pastoral.
   Crystal Vision.
   Imaginative Qualities of Actual Things.
   Mulligan Stew.
   Pack of Lies.
   The Sky Changes.
   Something Said.
   Splendide-Hôtel.
   Steelwork.
   Under the Shadow.
W. M. SPACKMAN, *The Complete Fiction.*
GERTRUDE STEIN, *Lucy Church Amiably.*
   The Making of Americans.
   A Novel of Thank You.
PIOTR SZEWC, *Annihilation.*
ESTHER TUSQUETS, *Stranded.*
DUBRAVKA UGRESIC, *Thank You for Not Reading.*
LUISA VALENZUELA, *He Who Searches.*
BORIS VIAN, *Heartsnatcher.*
PAUL WEST, *Words for a Deaf Daughter & Gala.*
CURTIS WHITE, *Memories of My Father Watching TV.*
   Monstrous Possibility.
   Requiem.
DIANE WILLIAMS, *Excitability: Selected Stories.*
   Romancer Erector.
DOUGLAS WOOLF, *Wall to Wall.*
   Ya! & John-Juan.
PHILIP WYLIE, *Generation of Vipers.*
MARGUERITE YOUNG, *Angel in the Forest.*
   Miss MacIntosh, My Darling.
REYOUNG, *Unbabbling.*
LOUIS ZUKOFSKY, *Collected Fiction.*
SCOTT ZWIREN, *God Head.*

FOR A FULL LIST OF PUBLICATIONS, VISIT:
www.dalkeyarchive.com